"You forget. I said I

"Yes, but you never said anything about being *engaged*!"

Was he being deliberately obtuse? "One follows the other normally, and besides, I will accept nothing less than what my parents have: love. And we—" she gestured between them with a wave of one hand "—do *not* have that!"

"Exactly!" he declared, his knee brushing against hers. He added in a hushed voice, "But we both want independence. Why not have a long engagement with me? My mother will be happy, because I will be settled in her mind, and she will stop finding ways to keep me home. We could then cancel the engagement when I eventually return, or your family might choose to anyway if I'm gone long enough, or—" he paused, scratching the stubble on his chin "—if you change your mind about marriage. I suppose I could marry you on my return, I will need a wife eventually, and it would save you any embarrassment."

Marina shook her head, wondering if this whole thing were a dream—well, a cruel nightmare seemed more appropriate. "Are you mocking me?"

He shook his head vehemently, put aside his brandy glass and reached for her hands. "Never! In fact, the more I think on it, the more perfect I realize you are! We can both live independently and be free to choose our own path in life!"

Author Note

I love museums! Last year, I was invited by Jenni Fletcher, Lotte R. James and Lara Temple to visit Sir John Soane's Museum in London. Sir John Soane was a prominent architect in Georgian/Regency Britain, and his house is an utterly fascinating collection of everything that influenced his work. This book is my first Regency romance, and I was thoroughly inspired by this fun research trip with fellow Harlequin authors. The Fletchers' (my heroine's family) home is almost an exact re-creation of Sir Soane's, except for a couple of tweaks like the addition of a music room. Sadly, Sir Soane was not as understanding with his children as Mr. Fletcher, and he disowned one of his sons for wishing to become a writer rather than an architect (and for marrying without his approval).

Also, I have only just realized my heroine is a Fletcher! A subliminal rather than deliberate choice, and the characters are no reflection on Jenni—although, she is just as lovely as they are. I imagine I used the name without thinking, as she was such a supportive voice when I was worrying about writing in a different era. She reassured me that I could easily do it. So thank you, Jenni, for giving me the courage. I loved writing this Regency and hope to do more!

HOW THE WALLFLOWER WINS A DUKE

LUCY MORRIS

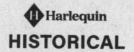

HISTORICAL

**Harlequin®
HISTORICAL**

ISBN-13: 978-1-335-53965-6

How the Wallflower Wins a Duke

Copyright © 2024 by Lucy Morris

Recycling programs for this product may not exist in your area.

Harlequin Enterprises ULC
22 Adelaide St. West, 41st Floor
Toronto, Ontario M5H 4E3, Canada
www.Harlequin.com

Printed in U.S.A.

Lucy Morris lives in Essex, UK, with her husband, two young children and two cats. She has a massive sweet tooth and loves gin, bubbly and Irn-Bru. She's a member of the UK Romantic Novelists' Association. She was delighted to accept a two-book deal with Harlequin after submitting her story to the Warriors Wanted! submission blitz for Viking, medieval and Highlander romances. Writing for Harlequin Historical is a dream come true for her and she hopes you enjoy her books!

Books by Lucy Morris

Harlequin Historical

The Viking She Loves to Hate
Snowed In with the Viking
"Her Bought Viking Husband"
in *Convenient Vows with a Viking*

Shieldmaiden Sisters

The Viking She Would Have Married
Tempted by Her Outcast Viking
Beguiling Her Enemy Warrior

Visit the Author Profile page
at Harlequin.com.

For Jenni Fletcher, Lotte R. James and Lara Temple,
thanks for the inspirational museum trip!

Chapter One

London—June 1816

'Two whole days with those smug Moorcrofts! No, I don't think I can bear it...' grumbled Marina's mother with a heavy sigh, followed shortly by slapping her hands together decisively. 'Colin, I think we should go home—say I am ill or something. I know it is an excellent opportunity. But honestly, it would be better for your practice if we did not go!'

Marina brightened at the prospect. 'I would not mind going home. I have a new melody I wish to practise.' Which was true, but there were other reasons, too—uncomfortable reasons.

Her father shook his head, and both women gave a miserable sigh. Most people would have been thrilled to receive a house party invitation from the Duchess of Framlingham. They would consider it a great honour to stay at the palatial mansion owned by such an illustrious hostess, who was loved and admired by the *ton*, but Marina could not think of anything worse and neither could her mother.

The Moorcrofts spoiled everything!

The rivalry between the two families had been going on for years. Although, until recently it had mainly been one-sided, as Marina's family had always tried their best to ignore it.

It had all begun when her father, the son of a common bricklayer, had dared to not only set up his own architectural practice, but had—more importantly—succeeded at it, winning many contracts that Mr Moorcroft had wrongly presumed were his by right, because, unlike Marina's father, Mr Moorcroft was the son and grandson of celebrated architects.

It wouldn't have been so bad, if it had been confined to their professional lives. But the whole family seemed to take delight in trying to wage a war of their own making.

Herbert and Priscilla Moorcroft were a similar age to Marina and her brother Frederick. They might have been friends, if the Moorcrofts hadn't been so determined to prove they were better than them in every way, sometimes deliberately humiliating or embarrassing them in public to prove their point.

Marina had not cared about it until her most recent humiliation. Still, she should pity poor Frederick more. He had always struggled socially, and was now stuck with *Horrible* Herbert at school.

'Oh, but, Colin, it is not as if they will accept us anyway. Not after the Moorcrofts have got their hooks into them. Which is a pity. But don't you think it is better to cut our losses and run? Rather than face two days of torment for no good reason?'

Her mother's lament was made somehow worse by the sudden jostle of the hackney carriage, which sent her plump mother sprawling into her father's lap. Marina had to grab her own seat and thrust her silk slippers against the opposite bench to stop herself from falling to the floor.

Colin Fletcher, with his usual calm and methodical manner, gently pushed her mother back into her seat, taking a moment to squeeze her hand lightly before releasing it.

'Kitty, my dear, do stop worrying, all will be well!' He gave Marina a sympathetic smile, and she tried her best to return it. 'We will meet with His Grace and the Duchess. *They* will be the ones to decide who will redesign their ancestral home—not I and certainly not the Moorcrofts.' Then he turned to thump the side of the carriage with his large fist and shouted in an authoritative voice that Marina had only ever heard on building sites, 'I will give you an extra shilling if you *slow* down!'

There was no response from their driver, but Marina noticed the carriage gentled to a less terrifying speed. The Duchess's grand home was situated in Twickenham and overlooked the Thames. It was on the north side of the river, so they hadn't had to cross at London Bridge, but it had still taken longer than expected to slip through the swathes of travellers coming in for their evening's entertainment. They must have seemed like a fish fighting against the current as they made their way towards the Duchess's fashionable hideaway on the outskirts of town.

The Duchess's end-of-Season ball was legendary among the *ton*. She was well known for her extravagant house parties, too, and only the most impressive and fashionable of London's high society were ever deemed worthy guests. So, for Marina's family to receive such an honour was incredible and solely due to her father's success.

The two-day event, according to the gold leaf invitation, would consist of a dinner with entertainments upon arrival. The following night there would be a ball, where the entire *ton* would hear of the Duke's exciting plans for his new home.

The Duchess had asked them to stay for two nights so that she could *'better know the families of such incredibly talented architects'*. It was obvious she intended to employ either Marina's father or his rival, Mr Moorcroft, and that this whole event was a competition, with the winner announced on the night of the ball.

All hope of them avoiding such a spectacle had been quickly snuffed out by her father's firm refusal. It was a competition between the two best architects in London and Colin was determined to face it head on—despite the awkward history between the two families.

Marina patted her hair self-consciously to check it was all still in place. It was fashioned in an elegant chignon upon her mother's insistence with curls framing her face. Marina sighed with relief when she realised none of the pins had fallen out after the sudden carriage jolt.

Kitty had not been so lucky. A thick ebony lock had fallen out of place on the side of her head and Marina took a moment to carefully pin it back into place. Her mother gave her a grateful smile when she was done. 'Thank you, darling.'

They both had mountains of thick black hair that was difficult to tame. Marina took after her mother in face and colouring, with her pale complexion, and bright blue eyes. Her mother was a little plumper than she was, but Kitty claimed that was due to having two healthy babies and a husband who could never refuse cake. Neither of them could be described by society as great beauties, but that did not seem to matter to Colin who clearly adored them both.

'It's all a bit tasteless in my opinion. Having you and Mr Moorcroft compete against one another in a social setting! If they want an architect for the remodelling of their ancestral home, then why not request plans like any normal person would? What does it matter if they *like* us or not?' complained Marina, avoiding her mother's eyes—she had spent many days trying to tell Marina the same thing.

'Who are we to question the aristocracy?' said her father pointedly.

Kitty pulled her shawl closer around her shoulders primly. '*We* shouldn't have to waste our time on the eccentric whims of others! Either they want you to work for them or they don't. I agree with Marina. This is *undignified.*'

Marina nodded thoughtfully. 'Still, it is a bit odd that there are so many of us invited to dinner.' She marked off the names of the guests with her fingers. 'The Moorcrofts, Lord Clifton and his sister, Miss Clifton… I suppose I can understand them, I believe they are close friends of the family. But the Redgraves, too? They aren't even architects!'

Her parents exchanged a knowing look, before her father said, 'I think the Duchess is hopeful to find a match for her son as well as an architect. There have already been a lot of engagements this Season—very few debutantes are left.'

'So, *we* are the entertainment.' Marina groaned, then began to speak as if she were reading from one of the scandal sheets. 'Which architect will they choose? Place your bets, ladies and gentlemen! Or, if that doesn't interest you, which young lady will win the hand of the Duke? It is well known that the Duke likes to gamble, but will he gamble with his heart? That is—'

'None of our business,' interrupted her father with a stern expression.

Marina gave a light shrug of acceptance. 'True. Thankfully, it will be the well-bred *ladies* in that race, not I or Miss Moorcroft, as we are not part of the landed gentry.'

'But Mrs Moorcroft is an architect, too—of her own social climbing!' quipped Kitty. 'Don't look at me like that, Colin! She was crowing to Mrs Banks about it at tea last week.' Her mother put on a simpering voice. '*My* Priscilla has already caught the attention of the Duchess of Framlingham and it is barely even the end of her first Season! At this rate, she will be wed before the Princess! After all, she is such a *fine* beauty!' She finished with an insidious laugh that sounded like a cat wheezing.

Marina and her father both chuckled at her oddly accurate impression, although her father quickly tried to appear firm. 'Come now, Kitty. You will get yourself into trouble one of these days!'

But they all knew he would forgive her anything—Kitty had supported and believed in him when no one else had. Part of his great success was due to his constant need to prove her faith in him right.

An outsider might have thought her mother's criticism of the Moorcrofts as harsh, but Marina knew her mother was only trying to make her feel better about facing Priscilla again.

'I promise I will be on my best behaviour, my darling husband,' Kitty replied, before winking at Marina. 'But I suspect she has high expectations for Priscilla and wants someone like Lord Clifton or even, perhaps, the Duke... Which is laughable—I doubt that man will ever settle down, unless it is to avoid bankruptcy!'

Marina squirmed in her seat, uncomfortable with the subject of marriage.

At the beginning of the Season, she had been hopeful, but after that terrible incident at the Haxbys' soirée, she feared marriage was not an option for her. At least not a happy one like her parents' marriage and she wanted nothing less than true love.

Marina had learned in the worst possible way that she wasn't the type to turn heads or make a man fall madly in love with her—no matter what they might say. Especially not when she was sitting next to women like Priscilla.

After much consideration—and tears—she had decided that the prospect of becoming a spinster no longer frightened her. Family would always come first in her mind. Love, or the lack of it, was only a passing disappointment at best.

Music would be the love of her life. There was no *need* for her to marry.

It was as if her father had read her mind, because he said kindly, 'Well, do not feel under pressure to like any man. I would rather keep you at home than hand you over to anyone less deserving of you.'

Marina gave her mother a sharp look, which Kitty pointedly ignored. She had always suspected her mother of telling him about the Haxby incident, even though she'd begged her not to. It certainly explained why he'd never questioned the way in which Mr John Richards had suddenly dropped all interest in courting her.

A cold shiver ran down her spine as she remembered him laughing with Priscilla.

'Oh, she is nothing in comparison to your beauty, Cousin! But a man needs money to live and don't worry—I will put a stop to that awful music once we're wed! Marina the Wallflower Maestro—she is truly ridiculous. If she weren't so wealthy, I would never have considered her!'

Her father's apologetic tone cut through the pain of the memory, as he said, 'I only mean—you have more sense than to set your sights on someone like the Spare Heir Duke.'

Marina flinched at the nickname. She had never met the man, but she thought it very unkind that all of society called him that after his elder brother's sudden death. After all, she knew what it was like to be mocked and ridiculed behind your back.

'Oh, that's so unkind,' said her mother and both women

gave him a reproachful look. 'It must have been hard for the Duke. I hear he lost his father quite young in a riding accident, and then to lose his much older stepbrother in a similar way… He must have felt as if he had lost two fathers! Such a terrible shame.'

'Yes, sorry. I only meant to say that he seems unprepared and unwilling to face the responsibility of his dukedom— and I have heard that he's been quite the cad since returning home from the army. He's always in gaming dens or other places of ill repute. I will be shocked if this new house ever goes ahead—he spends most of his days in White's.'

Marina replied, 'Still, it seems wrong to judge him so harshly on gossip and hearsay…'

Her father nodded thoughtfully. 'I suppose we will discover the truth for ourselves tonight at dinner.'

At that moment, the carriage came to a standstill outside the Duchess's mansion and they carefully stepped out on to the drive. The gas lamps illuminated only half of the imposing building, which was grand in the extreme and built in the Palladian style. The white stucco render gleamed like marble in the lamplight and the ornate columns surrounding its classically styled entrance towered above them on top of a large, stepped entrance. Everything in its design reflected the elegance and wealth of its illustrious owner within.

It was an intimidating sight and Marina glanced at her father to see what his professional eye would make of it. To her surprise, he was staring at Marina pleasantly. 'What do you think? Do you think I could build something better?'

Marina grinned. 'Certainly!'

'That's what I like to hear!' he said and with a grin he turned to help her mother from the carriage. Footmen poured down the steps and began carrying in their luggage silently.

After paying the driver, he nestled each of their arms into his before guiding them up the steps.

They were promptly welcomed and shown into an offensively large drawing room by the butler who was wearing burgundy and gold livery that would have put many of the landed gentry to shame with its elegance. Marina was glad she had worn her best evening gown and she tried to subtly smooth out any creases of her pale blue dress before entering the room.

They were the last of the guests to arrive. The Moorcrofts appeared well settled, as if they'd been there some time—*no doubt blown swiftly here by the winds of their own self-importance*, mused Marina drily.

As the formal introductions were made, Marina couldn't help but stare at the Duke. She had never seen any man quite like him: tall, dark, with pale skin and green eyes that reminded her of a predatory cat. He was handsome in a sharp, cold sort of way, the lines of his body dramatic with narrow hips that flared up to impossibly broad shoulders. She had heard he was at Waterloo and could very well imagine him leading the charge to victory, his imposing figure striking fear into the hearts of the enemy.

Cad did not seem a fitting description for him.

Oh, she could well imagine him ruining many girl's dreams and virtues. But *cad* implied the sort of dandies who lazed around gentlemen's clubs writing bad poetry, in the hopes of becoming another Byron. The type of men who only actually succeeded in indulging in too much brandy, cards and debauchery, their heads too muddled by laudanum and increasing debt to be of any use to anyone.

This man did not look muddled, he looked like a demon, the kind that tempted weaker souls into vice and wickedness.

'What took you so long, Fletcher? Everyone has been

here almost quarter of an hour already,' said Mr Moorcroft, a wide smile that did not reach his eyes spread across his broad face. She had met the others before in passing: the handsome Lord Clifton, his pretty sister Miss Clifton, Lord and Lady Redgrave, Miss Sophia Redgrave and of course the Moorcrofts—minus Horrible Herbert—whom poor Freddie was dealing with even now.

Kenneth Moorcroft was older than Marina's father by at least ten years, his hair fully grey and patchy in areas. He squinted as if his eyes were poor. His body was an average build for a man in his sixties, but he dressed as if he thought himself a fine figure of a man, no doubt trying to hide the fact that he was much older than his wife, who was more around her parents' age. He had children from his first marriage, but little was spoken of them. They had been removed from London to live at one of his estates in the country. Only his current children seemed to matter to him now, as if his dead wife and all that she had left behind had been buried without a trace. All so that he could begin again with a fresh family.

Marina disliked him immensely, even more so when she was in his presence.

Her father looked a little embarrassed, but gestured pointedly at the ornate gold clock on the mantel. 'We are still ten minutes early and I thought it best not to rush our driver.'

'Quite right,' said the Duchess. 'Some of the speeds they drive at are terrifying!' Marina's earlier criticism of the Duchess suddenly felt more than a little mean-spirited as the woman in front of her looked younger than she had expected and was light and friendly in manner. Her gown was elaborately embroidered and as bright as a ruby.

'Did you take a hackney carriage all the way here?' Mr Moorcroft laughed. 'You are an eccentric fellow, Fletcher, walking everywhere! I bought a new carriage last week. A lovely post-chaise, comfortable and convenient. They will even paint your coat of arms on the side and at a good price, too—'

Marina rolled her eyes and deliberately ignored the rest of what Mr Moorcroft had to say. It was heavily laboured with self-indulgent peacocking and she could tell her parents were gritting their teeth through every word.

Green eyes caught hers and she realised the Duke was watching her with interest. Usually no one noticed her, so her little gestures would always go unmarked, but not tonight, it seemed. The smallest tilt at one side of his mouth revealed that he knew what she was thinking and found it amusing. Heat swept up her cheeks and she looked away, praying that he would do the same.

'You can't put a price on comfort! Especially when you travel around the country as much as we do,' said Mrs Moorcroft with a sickly-sweet tone, looping her arm into his and gazing up at him with an adoring smile, as if he wasn't the most odious man on earth. It made Marina's stomach churn just to watch.

'Or health,' added Marina, unable to help herself. 'Father has always been a firm believer in the benefits of walking for one's health and happiness.'

The Duchess smiled warmly at Marina. 'I must agree. I love to walk and ride around our country estate. Anything to get the heart beating! It makes me feel alive!'

Marina nodded— she could well imagine the Moorcrofts boring the Duchess with their talk of connections and travels to all the large country estates, paying less attention to what they had seen and more on the *importance* of where they had been and how much it had cost them to get there.

'I have spent most of my life in London, but sometimes

we travel to the coast and I think there is nothing more beautiful than where the land meets the sea,' said Marina.

'Oh, then you must come to our country estate, Stonecroft Manor. It is the estate we are hoping to modernise,' said the Duchess, 'It is beautiful, but very old. I go to sea bathe there each summer. It is not as entertaining as places like Brighton, but it is just as good for the constitution.'

'What a wonderful idea!' exclaimed Mrs Moorcroft breathlessly, as if she had suddenly realised she was late to the race. 'I also love to sea bathe!'

Glancing back at the Duke, Marina saw his smirk had raised itself another quarter of an inch, but his eyes remained fixed on her and she could not look away, no matter how much she knew she should.

It wasn't so much what the Duchess said next that surprised Marina, but the way in which his mother's words affected him. 'Brook loves it there. The hunting is excellent. I should arrange another house party for this summer! In fact, I should probably have my end-of-Season ball there instead of here! That will make a nice change, won't it, Brook?'

The Duke's amusement dropped like a stone, and his gaze slid to his mother. 'If you wish, but I will not be there. You know my plans. Our business is almost settled and I will be leaving to travel the Continent shortly.'

'Oh, but you have only just left the army and it has been so long since we were at Stonecroft together,' she replied, with a painfully bright smile that seemed a little forced to Marina. 'Surely you can delay a little longer? Besides, I have heard the weather on the Continent has been unseasonably bad this year. Better to stay in England and enjoy the beauty of your own home with friends!'

'I have delayed once already.' There was a firmness to his tone that made his mother flinch and Marina couldn't help but pity her. It was obvious she wanted to spend more time with her son.

How could he be so cruel?

The Duchess's voice was low and quiet. 'Please, Brook…'

'Until the end of the Season,' he snapped, after a moment of hesitation.

When he turned away from his mother, his scowl was thunderous and full of accusation. To Marina's horror it was focused on her, his eyes narrowing as if he blamed *her* for his mother's plans, as if she *alone* had deliberately engineered this invitation—when she'd never intended it in the first place!

Now, she feared she had made an enemy of the Duke and how would that help her father's business? Apart from her music, her family's happiness was the only thing that mattered to her.

Something this Duke could never understand. Look how cruelly he had treated his grieving mother, who wanted nothing more than to spend time with him!

Marina had never met a more offensive or selfish man in her life and for once she was glad she was a wallflower. He would forget her soon enough—all she had to do was suffer a couple of days with him.

Chapter Two

'Ah, the dinner bell! Shall we move into the dining room?' asked his mother and it couldn't have been a timelier break in conversation.

She had done it again!

Extended their time together when she knew full well that he was ready to leave!

This house party to decide on an architect was meant to be the final social commitment, but she'd secured yet another within a few minutes of greeting their guests!

When would it end?

He knew the answer. When he was wed and his bride was settled with him in deepest darkest Suffolk at the new Stonecroft Manor house his mother kept insisting he build.

Why did she want to repeat the past? Suffolk had been miserable for both of them. The past, was a country he had no wish to revisit!

But she seemed obsessed with the need to see him married, constantly requesting that he secure the future line of their family with a wife and heir. Something he was not inclined to grant. For too long he had been the spare heir, forced to make his own way in life, and he wouldn't give up on his plans and dreams to dance to his mother's tune.

Recently, she had become more desperate in her match-making attempts, never passing up on the opportunity to parade him in front of all the young ladies and debutantes of London. It was ironic that she had never cared before, not until his brother, Robert, had died. Then it was as if she had suddenly remembered he existed, dusting him off and reshaping him like an old bonnet she suddenly wished to wear. Perhaps she wanted an excuse for another party? At this point she was becoming so desperate to see him settled, she was even offering him out to her party guests.

Even obnoxious social climbers like the Moorcrofts. They had suffered through nearly half an hour of Mr and Mrs Moorcroft's pointless chatter. The others were nice enough, if quiet, but the Moorcrofts made up for that in bucketloads. Mrs Moorcroft was cheerful and amiable, while Mr Moorcroft was confident and appeared knowledgeable in any manner of subjects—of which he had an opinion on all.

Their daughter, Priscilla, was very pretty, in that innocent debutante sort of way. Accomplished and yet as pure as snow—and definitely *not* the sort of woman he would set his sights on. Although the Moorcrofts appeared to have other ideas, as they kept showing her off like a prize-winning cow to the bachelors present.

In truth, there was nothing offensive in their manners and they seemed incredibly cordial, to the point where Brook almost felt guilty for disliking them. That was, until the Fletchers had arrived and he had seen a darker side to the Moorcrofts' nature.

It was subtle, and he wasn't sure of the reasons behind it, but there was definitely a frostiness between the two families that went beyond professional rivalry. The smiles exchanged were sharp and cool, the pleasantries tinged with disapproval. It intrigued him, and promised for a slightly less dull house party than he'd been expecting—until the second house party invitation, of course!

Good God! How many of these things was his mother going to concoct? Would he ever escape?

At least his friend George Clifton was here. Although he knew his mother wished he would marry George's sister, the truth was he had no interest in any of these young women. Miss Clifton was his friend's sister, and as such, felt like a relation, too. Miss Sophia Redgrave was pretty enough, but had always seemed a little dim and vapid.

In fact, the only woman to intrigue him tonight was the one young woman who was obviously not part of his mother's marriage market plans: the quick-witted Miss Marina Fletcher, who had come to support her father in his potential commission.

It was one thing after another with his mother and he was certain it was all to keep him in England for as long as possible in the hopes to have him married and settled.

First, there'd been the funeral and will arrangements. Sorting out the estate and ensuring the tenants were well settled. Then there'd been his mother's gambling and parties. She had always been extravagant in her social events, but after Robert's death things had got out of hand.

He might have thought she had done it deliberately to keep him close, if he'd thought for one moment she actually *wanted* him by her side, but he doubted it.

Either way, she would end up disappointed—he would finalise his trip first thing tomorrow. If she wanted him to stay until the Stonecroft ball then he would, but he would leave straight afterwards.

His mother's debts were now under control, with a strict allowance set in place that she could no longer break, and he would pick an architect for the new estate in the next couple of days. Already he preferred Mr Fletcher. He seemed like the type of person he could trust to get on with things in his absence.

In contrast, Mr Moorcroft had seemed almost too accommodating, nodding enthusiastically with everything his mother suggested no matter how ridiculous.

Mr Moorcroft was pandering to their egos, he realised. Repeatedly admiring the art and style of the drawing room. Comparing it favourably to all the other great houses they had visited on their countryside tours.

Brook had said nothing in response. The furnishings of this mansion were all done according to his mother's tastes and were a little too extravagant for his liking. After nearly being blown apart on the battlefield more than once, lavishing in such opulence felt almost...vulgar. It was why he lived in a much simpler town house in the heart of the city.

When the Fletchers had swept in, he had expected similar pomposity, but had been pleasantly surprised by Mr Fletcher's no-nonsense honesty. His mother had said he was considered a genius in his field and had worked himself up with grit and determination, as well as the aid of a couple of wealthy benefactors—his wife's family being one of them—who by all accounts still crowed about his *unexpected* success.

Mrs Fletcher and her daughter Marina were both what might be described unkindly as—plain—but to Brook they were deeply charming. There was something compelling about them—a quickness in wit, perhaps? Mother and daughter constantly exchanged glances, as if they were speaking silently to one another with simple raises of their sable brows and twitches of their mouths, quickly hiding their mutual amusement from those around them. He envied such closeness of spirit, to know what another was thinking by a mere silent glance. He had never known such insight and it made a small part of him ache with longing.

Maybe it was the striking darkness of their hair compared to the paleness of their complexion, or the intelligence behind those sapphire eyes, but Brook found himself oddly enthralled by them, especially Marina.

Which was disconcerting and damned inconvenient!

Usually, he would have dismissed her immediately from his mind as he had Priscilla, but then Marina had made that cutting comment about Mr Moorcroft's health in defence of her father and her loyalty had made him smile. She had defended him with a lethal blow that would have put a royal executioner to shame.

He suspected his mother's quick eyes had spotted his mild admiration and had caused her to pounce on the opportunity like a jackal. To be fair, even Marina looked slightly startled by his mother's invitation, while the Moorcrofts looked almost sick with jealousy—at least until they had secured their own invitation.

There was an awkward shuffle around the drawing room, as his mother went through the painful formalities of showing their guests into dinner in order of rank. After the titled guests, the Moorcrofts entered, followed by the Fletchers. As the hosts, he and his mother were the last to take their seats.

Which was just as well, because the exclamations of praise from their guests admiring the sight of the formal dining room made him feel uncomfortable.

The dining room was furnished in an elaborately Gothic style, the walls dripping with gold and rich brocade. The huge chandelier illuminated the painted murals on the ceiling, making it appear as if the angels of heaven were looking down upon them from golden clouds. Vases from the

Orient sat on golden plinths and the furniture shone with gilt and beeswax polish.

He sighed, as he heard Miss Sophia whimsically talking about the baby angels. His mother gave him a sharp tap on the arm with her gloved hand as they entered.

'Behave!' she warned quietly. 'At least try to consider one of them!'

Gritting his teeth, he replied, 'What would be the point? I am leaving, remember.'

His mother's expression stiffened, then she said, 'You are making me sick with worry, Brook. All I want is to see you settled.'

Would she play at being ill next?

It was obvious that she would not give up her schemes without a fight and he was beginning to wonder how he could escape unscathed.

After seating his mother at the head of the long table, he took his place at the foot. Either side of him were Priscilla and Marina, two women who could not be more different in appearance and temperament.

Priscilla with her blonde hair and fashionable dress sat to his right and the dark-haired Marina on his left in a rather drab light blue gown that did nothing for her complexion.

The meal began with a veal soup that was ladled into each person's dish.

'I hear you also have a son at Knights Court, Mr Fletcher,' said his mother, opening the discussion smoothly and deliberately avoiding Mr Moorcroft's eager face. They had all heard *at length* how well Priscilla and Herbert were excelling in their accomplishments and it would make a nice change to hear another person's perspective.

Unfortunately, this did not seem a topic the Fletchers wished to discuss. A furtive look passed between the three of them, before Mr Fletcher eventually spoke. 'Frederick. Yes, he is doing well. At first, it took him a little time to adjust, he missed us. But he is growing in confidence daily.'

Mrs Fletcher gave her husband a bright smile of agreement. 'I am counting down the days until the summer when we can see him again.'

'I am sure you are.' Brook's mother smiled. 'And I hear this is your debut year, Marina. How have you found it so far?'

Marina gave a graceful tilt of her head that showed off her long neck and décolletage. 'I was a little nervous at first. But I have enjoyed it,' she said, not sounding as if she'd enjoyed it at all.

Mrs Fletcher gave an approving nod towards her daughter. 'We are so proud of her. She has handled her coming out with such grace. Honestly, I was so nervous about her first ball I could barely sleep! Not that I doubted our Marina for a moment, but the scrutiny of society can be intimidating for such a young woman. Thankfully, she still triumphed, despite my fears!'

'Young?' Mrs Moorcroft gave a disbelieving laugh. 'You are too cautious, Mrs Fletcher! Priscilla was fine coming out this year and she is only seven and ten! I dread to think how late your Marina's debut was—isn't she twenty now?'

'Yes, she is now twenty. Maybe you are right,' replied Mrs Fletcher, although her face said otherwise, as she cast a subtle glance towards Marina with a knowing smile. 'Perhaps I have been a little over-cautious. I should have known Marina would be perfectly capable and *dignified*, whatever her age.'

Brook tried to smother a grin. This strange duelling of wits was highly entertaining, if bizarre.

Mr Moorcroft gave a malicious chuckle as he drained

the wine in his glass and motioned for a footman to refill it. 'I would be more worried about Frederick, if I were you!'

There was a sharp scrape of cutlery on fine china. It sounded as if it had come from Marina's direction, although by the impassive look on her face he could have been mistaken. Mr and Mrs Fletcher were as still as Grecian statues, as every guest seemed to hold their breath at such a rude comment.

Mrs Fletcher was the first to recover. He could see the pain in her eyes, but her tone was still admirably pleasant. 'How do you mean? Do you know something about my son that I do not?'

Seeming to finally realise the cruelty of his words, Mr Moorcroft blustered and looked down at his bowl as if it were suddenly fascinating. 'Oh, well, you know…how it is with boys.'

Mrs Moorcroft added helpfully, 'They sometimes need an earlier push…'

Mr Moorcroft brightened, as if his wife had handed him the perfect excuse. Unfortunately, he still appeared oblivious to the mood of the room, justifying his rudeness blindly. 'From what Herbert has told us, it sounds as if you should have sent Frederick to school earlier, as we did with Herbert. Herbert hasn't struggled with any of the work and can speak Latin and Greek as if it were his mother's tongue!' Mr Moorcroft chuckled. 'Your Grace, you and your brother were at Knights Court, were you not? Such an excellent school—it has educated the best and the brightest. I believe four prime ministers were once Knights. Now, how old were you when you joined, Your Grace?'

'I was nine.' Brook didn't elaborate, not wanting to upset his mother. He knew she still felt guilty about that time, although they never spoke of it.

He had been sent to Knights Court almost immediately after his father's death. Robert had taken on the dukedom like a duck to water. Older than Brook by ten years, he was already a man and ready for the challenge ahead, insisting that his youngest brother do what all Wyndham men had done previously and start school early.

Brook had never forgiven him for separating them and he had never forgiven his mother for allowing it. Things had been hard, but bearable until then, because they'd at least had each other. Then, it had seemed as if even his mother no longer wanted him.

'The same age as our Herbert!' declared Mr Moorcroft, as if vindicated in his hateful thoughts. 'It certainly did him well to start there early. Now he rules the roost!'

Brook could well imagine what *that* implied. Brook himself had been glad to leave Knights Court at sixteen. His commission in the army had felt like an easy stroll down the promenade, compared to the crippling loneliness and torment he had received during his school days.

The army in contrast had given him purpose. For a time, he had been happy, then death had ruined his life for the second time. He was strangely bitter that his father and brother had died leaving him heir—perhaps he would die soon, too? Was that why his mother was so eager to see him settled? So that the next heir and spare could be set up like little ducks in a row and she wouldn't have had to suffer through years of hell for nothing?

'Mr Moorcroft was saying Herbert is already showing a keen interest in architecture. Do you hope for Frederick to join you in your architectural practice one day, Mr Fletcher?' asked his mother, the brightness of her expression a little forced, although he suspected he would be the only one to notice it.

'If he wishes it,' answered Mr Fletcher tactfully. 'Although I do not wish to push him into following me. A man must choose his own path in life.'

'Well, according to our Herbert,' said Mr Moorcroft after another sip of wine, 'he may *wish* to improve his mathematics first! Or he won't even be able to count your bricks!' Mr Moorcroft gave a snort of laughter and then another awkward silence descended on the meal.

Marina was the first to break the silence, her tone waspish as she announced, 'Frederick is a beautiful painter. He has our father's artistic eye.'

'Yes,' agreed Mrs Moorcroft. 'Your father's designs have such elegant simplicity. Honestly, I do not know how you do it! How would you describe your style, darling?'

Mr Moorcroft, as if waking from a dream, began to babble, spouting words like *renaissance, Gothic* and *baroque,* all while looking deliberately around him at his mother's furnishings. Eventually, to Brook's—and the rest of the table's—relief he fell silent.

The soup course complete, the main dishes were brought in and the tureen replaced with a roasted joint of beef and several side dishes.

'What about you, Mr Fletcher? How would you describe your work?' asked his mother cheerfully. Brook stifled a yawn.

Mr Fletcher smiled. 'I have never been very good with words. I let my buildings and sketches speak for me. Have you seen Lord Thorne's new square, Rosemary Gardens in Mayfair? That was one of my latest commissions.'

That caught Brook's attention. 'You designed it? I have a friend who lives there now. It is a beautiful square.'

'Thank you,' replied Mr Fletcher with an appreciative incline of his head.

'Although Lord Thorne bought the site, he left all the architectural and planning decisions to my father,' said Marina proudly. 'Lord Thorne didn't have the time or inclination to deal with the finer details. Always best to leave it to an expert, especially if you find such things a bore and wish to focus on other pleasurable pursuits...'

Her words tapered off with embarrassment at the end, as if she had realised the implication of her words. To be fair, he'd done nothing to make her think otherwise—he would rather people consider him to be a wasteful cad than look to his mother and realise she was the true devil at the card table.

Marina had probably seen his lack of interest in the project and thought to offer him a practical solution, not realising she was pointing out his supposed flaws. He could not decide whether to applaud or condemn her for her honesty.

'Is that so, Miss Fletcher?' he said, giving her a mildly amused look of warning, while he deliberately avoided looking at his mother. He had managed to hush most of the gossip about her debts, but he didn't wish to fan the flames.

His mother was surprisingly disapproving in her response. 'That is good to know, Miss Fletcher. The Duke is a man of many strengths—he fought at Waterloo and left the army with honours. But he has been somewhat distracted of late and busy with many matters...' She paused, her breath hitching ever so slightly at the silent acknowledgement of the trouble she'd caused. But then she rallied herself with a bright smile '...since he took over his responsibilities.'

Brook turned to the opinionated Miss Fletcher and couldn't help but smile at her discomfort. 'What are *your* interests, Miss Fletcher?'

She stiffened at his words, even though he had spoken mildly, more amused by the turn of conversation than offended.

Her blue eyes focused on him, wide and as bright as sapphires. 'I…enjoy music, Your Grace.'

'Music?' He smiled weakly, trying his best to hide his boredom. 'Listening or playing?'

'Composing,' she said and Marina Fletcher had surprised him once again.

So, there! thought Marina with a large helping of triumph.

It was short lived, however, because he quickly asked, 'Will you play one of your compositions for us after dinner?'

Cold fear washed through her and she stared at the roasted joint of beef in front of her and wondered if she could accidentally choke on a piece of it. Not enough to kill her, but just enough to make her too weak to perform.

'It has been a long time since we heard you play one of your pieces. When was the last time, I wonder…?' asked Mrs Moorcroft thoughtfully, knowing full well that Marina was regretting her impetuous boast.

'At the Haxbys' soirée,' replied Priscilla with a knowing smile that made Marina's stomach twist painfully.

Oh, Lord!

Why hadn't she mumbled something about playing the pianoforte 'tolerably well' and be done with it?

Because you wanted to boast and prove to him that you had more depth and complexity than he could ever imagine! Fool!

Now she would be opening herself up for yet more ridicule and humiliation. All because she couldn't bear for another handsome man to dismiss her and her interests as unimportant.

Why on earth should that matter to her?

But it did. She had not played in public once since the Haxbys' soirée and instead had spent the rest of her debut Season stuck to the wall like a fly, or playing for others' amusement—but never her own work—never again.

'Marina's music is wonderful. Why don't you play something tonight, Marina? Something short and light?' asked her mother and Marina felt the cut of betrayal.

Kitty knew how hard Marina had suffered from Mr Richards's words.

How could she ask her to play again? To offer herself up, like a sacrifice in a den of vipers for a second time.

A small part of her knew her mother wanted the best for her and in Kitty's mind that meant returning to her music. But Marina could not. Mr Richards had known the composition was dedicated to him and the young ladies had all mocked it, and—worst of all—*he* had laughed at it. She had ended things with him immediately and left the soirée with as much dignity as she could muster, but she would never lay out her heart or her music for ridicule ever again. It hurt too much.

'I do not have any with me,' Marina said with a false sigh of regret, 'but I can play "Lavender Lane". Priscilla, I hear you sing that piece beautifully?'

Priscilla's own eyes narrowed, but she nodded. 'I know it well.'

The Duchess smiled. 'That's our evening entertainment sorted!'

Mr and Mrs Moorcroft began to praise the accomplishments of their daughter, while the Duke leaned towards Marina with a lazy expression.

'And when you are not composing, what else do you do, Miss Fletcher?' There was a knowingness in his expression, as if he expected nothing else more interesting from her, but wanted to amuse himself by getting her to admit it.

Irritated, Marina said, 'I sometimes help my father with his correspondence, read and attend social functions—the usual things.'

* * *

Brook was beginning to feel more than a little merry. He'd drunk quite a lot of wine to stomach Mr Moorcroft's boring speech and even the amusing Miss Fletcher seemed a little subdued by the evening. He wanted to spar with her again, wanted to see the light return to those gemstone eyes.

'Ah, yes, the *usual things*. Marriage and ambition go hand in hand for most women,' Brook said drily, his thoughts turning to his mother who had married as a young debutante to a man three times her age and been congratulated by her family for it. Not because she was poor or lacking in title, but for her family's ambition.

He wondered if the talented Miss Fletcher would suffer a similar fate and it made him grateful to be born a boy. Except, now he was the golden fish every ambitious girl in England hoped to catch, when most would have barely known his name up until now.

He made a tiny gesture with his knife towards the other young ladies. 'Look how Priscilla and Sophia are hanging on to George's every word and action—poor man. You would think we were alone at this end of the table! My mother will be disappointed—I think she had hopes that at least one of them would like me. Although I suspect George's sister is her greatest hope for me—sadly, I think of Grace Clifton as more of a sister than a potential match. What about you? Which of us do you want? Lord Clifton, or would you prefer the Spare Heir Duke?' he teased.

'No one!' Marina whispered with a horrified gasp.

He chuckled to himself. 'I am disappointed by your lack of ambition. What a pity, but do not worry, I will explain it to George and I am sure he will recover quickly from the loss. *However*, I am saddened to hear that you have not considered me as a potential match. I rather like your forthright manner and a composing debutante is certainly more interesting than any other woman I have met this Season.'

Her blue eyes suddenly turned hard and cold at his flippancy and with a brittleness that cut straight to the bone, she said, 'There is no need to make fun of me, Your Grace! I am well aware that I am not the brightest diamond in this room and will probably never marry.'

'That's not—'

But before he had a chance to explain himself, she went on briskly, 'And I hope you *also* never marry. You do not deserve a woman by your side with that attitude, even a dull one.'

An unexpected wave of shame washed over him and the worst thing was that he deserved it entirely. She was right to reprimand him, not only for being so dismissive of women in general, but for making her feel less than deserving of respect.

How many times had he been dismissed by his father and brother as unimportant, as the *stupid brat*, repeatedly informed that his sole purpose in life was to be their backup plan and nothing more.

After his father's death, his brother had turned to him with a sardonic smile and said, *'You're one step closer, little brat. But be careful this wolf doesn't turn around and eat you!'*

He knew what it was like to be bullied. He should know better than to make another person feel small with his own thoughtless words. 'Forgive me, my behaviour has been far from gentlemanly. Please know that I had no intention of making fun of you, I was mocking my own situation. I meant no disrespect and you—' He was about to compliment her, but she cut him off at the knees.

'And I suppose I should be grateful for your respect, when, by your own words, no other woman deserves it?'

He stared back at her, unsure of what to say, especially when she was so rightly justified in calling him out on his behaviour.

Marina blinked, as if waking from a dream. He could see the exact moment when her stomach must have dropped and she realised she had broken the rules of society by berating a *duke* on his behaviour.

'Forgive me, Your Grace. I should not have said that, it was disrespectful.' She looked down at her plate and began to cut up her meat with surprising force. Her cheeks flushed pink with anger and embarrassment.

'You are right to rebuke me,' he said and her cutlery paused mid-slice. 'I am sorry for being such a rude and arrogant brute. I should not have said any of that and I am the one who should be on my knees begging forgiveness— I will do so if you wish it.'

Her eyes were wide when they flicked up to meet his, as if she had never expected him to apologise for his foolish words. She glanced around the table, but no one was listening to them. 'I think doing *that* would only make the situation worse...'

'Then please accept my words. *Truly, I am sorry.*'

Their eyes locked and he was once again intrigued by the clarity and brightness of her eyes. She was utterly fascinating, a strange whirlpool of characteristics that he could not define: innocent, shy and nervous in nature, but also candid, intelligent and outspoken in action.

He spoke quietly, enjoying this strange intimacy between them. 'I should not have been so dismissive of all women and you are wrong to think you do not shine in this room. I honestly consider you the brightest gem here.' He gave her what he hoped was a charming smile and she managed a slightly stiff nod, although he could tell she didn't believe a word of it.

There was a long moment of silence between them. The rest of the dinner guests were talking excitedly about the upcoming ball and Lord Clifton was laughing good-naturedly with everyone about how he adored the waltz, a new scandalous dance from Vienna.

Marina focused her attention on the conversation for a short time, before realising that no one was interested in even looking her way, and she turned back to him to ask politely, 'What do you like to do in your free time, Your Grace?'

'Oh, you know, the three Cs,' he replied casually, unable to resist teasing her once more—she was a keg of gunpowder wrapped up in pale silk.

She frowned. 'What are the three Cs?'

And, just because he wanted to see her blush for a second time, he leaned in and whispered, 'Cards, claret and… carnal pleasures.'

Chapter Three

Marina was still rattled from her strange conversation with the Duke at dinner. Thankfully, the conversations had turned to a more open one involving everyone and she had retreated into herself, choosing silence over further embarrassment. What had possessed her to speak so directly and rudely to him? It had been as if she were arguing with her brother or her mother, without a single care to social convention.

Something about him brought out the worst in her.

Was it his arrogance?

Surely not—she had faced plenty of pompous and odious men like Mr Moorcroft without losing her composure.

Was it because he was handsome?

Possibly. Most aristocrats were arrogant, but the Duke had even more reason to be so: he was young, good looking and powerful. She had fallen for Mr Richards and he wasn't even half as impressive!

With a heartfelt sigh, she realised the Duke had every right to look down on her—because, quite frankly, she *was* beneath him, in every way. But rather than being humbled by such knowledge, it only seemed to enrage her further until her blood was almost boiling with fury and she'd unwittingly released it on him like a vengeful Hera.

She took a sip of her wine and realised her hand was trembling. Quickly she placed it in her lap, catching the Duke's emerald gaze and then deliberately avoiding it. She tried to pay attention to what Lord and Lady Redgrave were talking about—something to do with the pleasure gardens they'd recently visited. She pretended to find their conversation fascinating.

No doubt the Duke thought her pitiful. A plain wallflower who had had the gumption to rebuke him on his condescending cruelty. For once, she took no pleasure in being morally right, because in the end she was still a nobody—and he would still laugh at her.

'Ladies, let us leave the men to their port,' said the Duchess, after the final course was complete, and a short time later all the women were gathered in the drawing room, sipping tea.

Marina tried her best to forget about him. She performed with Priscilla, who as always hit every note impeccably, but with about as much passion as if she were reading the obituaries. Then she played for the two young ladies, Miss Sophia Redgrave and Miss Grace Clifton, who seemed eager to show off their accomplishments to the Duchess.

It was no hardship, as they were all songs that she could play with her eyes closed, and, in fact, she suspected if the pianoforte could play itself, no one would miss her presence or her skill.

Usually, Marina did not mind, as it allowed her to avoid long and boring conversations, but tonight she found her eyes constantly flitting back to the doors and wondering when the men would return.

When they did, she breathed a sigh of relief, because Lord Clifton and the Duke were absent.

'They had some private matter to discuss,' declared Mr

Moorcroft, who could always be relied on to know everybody's business.

The Duchess gave a delighted smile and raised her brow in Miss Clifton's direction. The young lady blushed, but said nothing.

Poor Miss Grace Clifton, thought Marina with a sigh, *she will never know how little he really thinks of her.*

'You must be tired after all that playing,' said her mother, patting the silk cushion beside her.

'Oh, but surely there is something of your own work you could play for us? If you wrote it, you must remember it.' Mrs Moorcroft laughed, and several others chuckled in response.

Kitty stared at Marina for a moment, trying to judge her mood, then took pity on her and said, 'Next time, she can bring her compositions.'

'What else do you like?' asked Miss Clifton gently. 'You play so beautifully, I would love to hear one more piece. Something of your own choosing.'

Marina gave Miss Clifton a weak smile. She'd come to like the young woman, she was sweet and kind, but she wasn't sure they would like anything she liked.

'Surely you can play one more. It's hardly taxing, sitting down all this time,' joked Mr Moorcroft and she saw her father's jaw twitch.

'One more, then,' she said, flexing her fingers over the keys, as she tried to forget the audience watching.

Performing as an accompaniment to a singer was easy, she faded into the background when other people sang, but now all eyes and ears were focused on her, waiting to see what she would play.

She should pick something easy and gentle, unoffensive to the ear. But for some reason, the Duke's green eyes and mocking smile came into her mind and, when her fingers dropped to the keys, she began to play one of her favourites. Not a gentle lullaby, or sweet dancing song, but something dramatic and wild.

Beethoven's Piano Sonata No. 14, something brooding and powerful that suited *him*.

Unable to help herself, she lost herself in the music, her fingers sweeping across the keys and her body jerking with the emotion of the piece. Her elegant chignon slipped free of its pins to drop two locks down her back, but she ignored them. She played with her heart, and when the final notes faded away, she realised how silent the room had become.

Her parents, who had heard her play daily, were as equally shocked as the rest of her audience. She felt as odd and as awkward as when the ladies had sniggered at her performance at the Haxbys' soirée. She had hoped by playing another man's music it would absolve her of ridicule, but she was wrong.

Mrs Moorcroft and Priscilla looked as if they were trying to smother their laughter, while her mother scowled at them.

Marina dropped her head as a familiar heat rushed up her face and neck.

A loud clap vibrated across the room and the rest of the audience seemed to wake from their shock and joined it. Curious as to who had been kind enough to support her, Marina looked up and saw the Duke grinning at her from the doorway, as if she had surprised and delighted him especially for his own amusement.

She wanted to climb inside the pianoforte and never return.

Brook watched the rain pouring down his bedroom windows with uninterest, a book forgotten in his hands. The wind rattled the glass like an angry debt collector. It had been a miserable spring and the current weather did not bode well for the summer ahead.

Another summer at his mother's side was something he refused to do. Tonight, she had taken him aside and begged him once more to stay in England.

'I have much to apologise for, I know that. But please consider starting a family. I am desperate to see you happy and settled. That will bring you true happiness...not running away from your responsibilities,' she had said, her gaze imploring and filled with a heavy measure of guilt.

It had taken all of his willpower to not bite back some sarcastic remark. To remind her that she had lost him more than once already. That the only reason she now cared for him was to ensure her own security in the world.

Happy and settled!

He knew what that meant—marriage and heirs.

Although he had no problem with the creation of heirs, he did have a problem with choosing a woman to live the rest of his life with. A family would restrict him and force him to stay home when there was so much more he wanted to do.

He wanted to live! Why couldn't he leave? Why couldn't he have fun and experience the world for one, or two, or even ten years before accepting his fate? He had spent his entire life doing what was expected of him and he had been miserable because of it. Now *he* was the one in charge and he could finally do what *he* wanted!

His brother's unexpected death had shocked him, reminding him of the fragility of his life. But his mother's debts had been astounding...

It had taken months to drag out all the names of her debtors and when he settled one account another quickly popped up, like the one George Clifton had informed him of tonight. It was an old debt, to be fair, one she swore she had merely forgotten, but it made him wonder if there were other similar debts hidden away. He hoped she realised the seriousness of her gambling habit and how close to disaster she had brought them.

He'd even considered selling this house—perhaps he still should. It would certainly take her away from temptation and the bad influence of her so-called friends.

Currently, she still dismissed her gambling as *'a little fun that got out of hand'.*

It had taken months of hard work, some wise investments and a few visits to some of the more debauched areas of the city to clear it. A little more hard work and he had finally managed to secure the family estate enough that it was profitable again.

But now his mother expected him to revamp the old estate on top of everything else—he suspected it was just another distraction for her. She could not bear to sit in idleness and sought out fun and entertainment wherever she went, like a reckless youth.

Honestly, he sometimes felt more like the parent in their relationship.

Well, he would not spend any more time dealing with her. Tonight, after dinner, he had sent instruction to purchase passage for him on the next ship that left after his mother's blasted end-of-Season ball. Nothing would stop him this time—his mind was firmly set.

Finally, he could enjoy life, after years of marching through war-torn bloody fields. He had seen enough young men die to know that he was lucky to be alive and, as his life was short, he wished to enjoy all that it had to offer.

No more pain and loss—he wanted to see beauty and wonder instead.

Sighing, he put down the book he'd been trying to read and picked up the oil lamp beside his bed. Usually when he couldn't sleep, he went for a walk in the gardens, but there was no chance of that in this weather. So, instead, he would take a walk through the house. It was large and familiar enough to give him some exercise, then maybe he would be able to finally sleep. If nothing else, he could go to the library and try to find something more interesting to read.

He padded out of his room barefoot, in only his white dress shirt that he had loosened for comfort and his breeches. No one would be up and about at this time. Everyone had gone to bed early, wanting to prepare themselves for the ball tomorrow night.

Mr Fletcher and Mr Moorcroft had talked over some potential designs while they drank port and he was more inclined towards Mr Fletcher out of the two architects, especially now that he knew his friend's beautiful town house had been designed by the man.

His designs were classically elegant and he had suggested a couple of options, while Mr Moorcroft had insisted the entirety of the old house needed to be demolished.

To his credit, Mr Fletcher had also said he would prefer to build an entirely new building. Although he had suggested the Duke find an alternative location and leave the old Tudor building as it would, in his words, *'be a shame to destroy something that has survived reformation and a civil war'*.

Brook was more inclined to agree with Mr Fletcher, realising that part of his duty was to protect his ancestral home or at the very least improve it. Just because he hated his memories of Stonecroft did not mean he should destroy it entirely.

He wondered what the prim and disapproving Miss Marina Fletcher would think of his epiphany on duty and legacy. At dinner she had reprimanded him firmly for speaking out of turn and then stunned him with her passionate playing later that evening.

He hadn't recognised the composition, but then he'd not spent much time at concerts or music halls. Before he'd even entered the room, he had known instinctively that it was Marina at the pianoforte. The notes were struck hard and quick, reflecting the clever and decisive nature of the woman who played it. The music had grown louder and more dramatic with each note and, by the time he had entered the room, he had been thoroughly enthralled by the passionate and carefree manner of her playing.

She had been lost in her music, the shocked audience staring at her with a mixture of awe and uncertainty, because the woman who played was not a blushing debutante, but an artist, wild and dramatic, and filled with heart. It was only when she stopped playing, and awoke as if from a spell, that she witnessed the reaction of her audience and he saw the wallflower return. It had pained him to see her confidence falter.

Of course, that wasn't the only reason he had clapped so loudly. But he suspected that she had seen it as a kindness, possibly a better apology for his earlier behaviour. He had wanted so much for her to stay, but she had quickly claimed tiredness and fled for bed. The first to leave that night and he had ground his teeth to stop from shouting at Mrs Moorcroft when she had made some unsubtle teasing about the 'passions of youth'.

Why couldn't a young woman be passionate?

He would certainly prefer Marina's company than the insipid wheeze laughing of Mrs Moorcroft.

He strode down the hall, towards the library, but stilled at the door when he saw a light swinging lightly from side to side. He set down his own lamp on a nearby desk and then walked over to the open door.

Marina, wearing only a night rail and frothy pink dressing gown, was balanced on one of the library ladders, trying to reach precariously for a book. The lamp was hanging from one wrist, while the other arm was loaded with a pile of large tomes. Her hair fell in a black waterfall down her back. He smiled when he realised she was reaching for a song book, one of the many volumes in the library that consisted entirely of bound music sheets. Even her choice of reading material was led by her passion.

The fact that they were both alone and in a state of undress was not lost on him—if he were a gentleman, he would leave without even alerting her to his presence.

But he was not a gentleman.

Creeping forward, he stared greedily at her bare feet and milky white skin. She was showing an indecent amount of shapely calf as she stretched towards the shelf.

'Can I help you?' he asked mildly and winced when she let out a sharp scream and dropped the books she was holding on top of his head. They thudded around his feet, as she turned her lamp towards him.

'Your Grace!' She scrambled down the ladder, her face flushed as she tried to do a curtsy. It looked more like a strange squat as she tilted awkwardly to the side, stumbling on the fallen books. He reached out a hand to steady her and she stumbled back into the ladder with another thud.

'What are you doing here?' she snapped angrily, as if he had stridden into her bedroom unannounced.

'This is my mother's home,' he reminded her with a lazy smile. 'But if you are asking why I am *here,* at this hour, then I suppose I have the same reason as you. I could not sleep and wished for a distraction.'

'Forgive me, Your Grace!' she gasped, staring in horror at the leatherbound books that lay scattered around him, before dipping to retrieve them. 'I...I didn't think anyone would be here at this time of night. Otherwise, I wouldn't have—'

He crouched to help her and, if anything, that seemed to only panic her more because she jumped up suddenly, causing the lamp to swing precariously on her wrist.

He picked up the last of the books, placed them on a nearby table and then took the lamp. 'Please be careful. I wouldn't want my mother's library to go up in flames and—' he paused, admiring how her loose hair softened her features '—we are friends now, Marina. Call me Brook, there is no need for titles.'

'I do not think that is appropriate!' gasped Marina.

He smiled. 'And this is?' He gestured at the dark and empty library. 'If we are found together, it would be considered quite *scandalous*!'

He shouldn't have teased her. She looked around in horror as if the *ton* might be watching from the shadows and wrapped her arms around her chest. 'No one need ever know, Your Grace.' She spoke politely but there was censure in her tone.

'True, as long as no one heard your scream.'

'Oh, Lord!' she gasped and tried to hurry around him.

For some reason he didn't want her to leave. 'I am teasing you! No one would hear you from this side of the house, besides you weren't that loud. You'll make more noise if you run back to your room in too much haste.'

Her eyes widened a little at his words, but she gave a

little uncertain nod of acceptance. 'Then I shall be quiet.'
She reached for the lamp.

'I am seriously considering employing your father for
Stonecroft Manor,' he said and her hand dropped away as
she turned to face him.

'Good, you will find no better architect than him. You
didn't need to bring both families here to compete against
one another. If you had asked for some designs in the *usual*
way, you would have quickly realised he was the best man
for the job.'

'Really?' Brook replied, taking note of her censure regarding the competition his mother had concocted. Unable
to stop himself from teasing her, Marina's unwavering love
and loyalty towards her family was deeply charming, probably because he had experienced very little in his own. 'Mr
Moorcroft has worked for some fine families and is highly
recommended by them…'

Her expression turned to granite. 'Mr Moorcroft has the
good fortune to be related to some of his patrons, while my
father's recommendations are for his work alone and are
not due to any familial connection.'

'Indeed, I heard as much. Your mother's family were
his early benefactors, I believe—sent him on a grand tour
of Europe and helped set up his business? His success is
admirable.'

Marina's face flushed with anger, and his chest tightened with anticipation.

Would she rail at him again?

Strangely, he hoped she would.

'My father was the son of a bricklayer and, yes, his talent was nurtured by my mother's family. But his success
is his own. He has never had to *ask* for work!'

'I meant no offence.'

'And I took none!' she snapped, her tone so sharp he could have shaved with it. She must have seen the mischief in his eyes, because she tutted and looked away, a rosy blush filling her cheeks. 'I am proud of my father's humble beginnings. It only means he is the greater man for it. His achievements were not handed to him on a plate like some…'

She must have realised what she had implied with such a statement, because the colour quickly drained from her face. He liked to see her vexed by him, but not afraid, and so he quickly nodded.

'I agree with you. Your father has done very well for himself and you are right to be proud of him. I had a very privileged start in life and I sometimes forget that.'

Quietly, she replied, 'Thank you.'

'I suspect I am jealous,' he added, 'The only places I have seen in Europe are battlefields. One blood-soaked field looks much the same as another.'

Her eyes met his again and there was sympathy in them this time. 'You should visit our house some time; my father has a large collection of antiquities from his travels you might like to see.'

'Are you inviting me to call on you, Miss Marina?' he asked, enjoying the way she stiffened primly at his teasing.

'I only thought—' She bristled and he took her by the elbow and guided her to one of the silk couches.

'Sit, tell me about your home. I would like to know more about it and about your family, too. Perhaps, it will give me a greater insight into your father's artistic eye, allowing me to know him better.'

She bit her lip, her eyes darting to the door which was slightly ajar. 'Tomorrow—it would not be appropriate now.' But she sat down and that gave him hope.

'But we both cannot sleep. Let's share a small brandy together and then we can both go to bed afterwards.'

He moved away giving her the space she needed to make her decision while he poured them both a glass of brandy from the cabinet. Insomnia was always at its worst when he was around his mother, so he kept a supply of it in the library.

When he returned, he held out the glass towards her and, after a moment of hesitation, she took it. He sat down in the armchair beside her couch, her knees lightly brushing against his long legs as he sat down. She turned them a little away, rearranging the pink silk dressing gown to better cover her frothy night rail, which seemed oddly coquettish on such a prim woman. The truth was, she was as covered as much as she would have been during the day and more than she would have been at a ball, but there was something strangely arousing about seeing her in her night clothes that he couldn't quite place.

Was it because no other man would have seen her like this?

'Now let's take a tour of your home…lead the way,' he said, waving his hand as he gestured for her to begin their imaginary walk through her home. 'I can't wait to see your father's treasures!'

She sipped on the brandy thoughtfully. Then, when he feared she would refuse him, she gave a little shrug and said, 'Very well.'

Starting from the outside, she described the classical sculptures that guarded her home from above, the pillars and iron railings of their three-storey town house, then guided him up the steps and through the front door into the hallway where a bust of Shakespeare awaited him. Briskly she walked him through the drawing room and dining room.

'My father loves light—he uses round mirrors in each corner to bounce light around the room. We have a lot of books, not as many as you have here, but a lot in comparison, so there are books on every shelf and lining most corridors.'

'Your father certainly is impressive. Talented artist, well travelled and well read.'

'Most of them are my mother's, but he likes to read, too,' Marina replied curtly.

He smiled at her tone. Marina was a lioness when it came to defending her family. 'I doubt my mother has read a single one of these,' he said mildly, gesturing to the hundreds of books surrounding them. 'What room follows your dining room, then?'

'There's my music room and after that—'

Interrupting her before she could move on, he remembered to give her the compliment she deserved. 'You play beautifully, by the way. I was most impressed.'

Her face flushed. 'I sometimes get a little…overzealous.'

'You play with passion, just like all the other great composers and musicians. You must have practised for many hours to play the pianoforte so well.'

A spark of pride filled her eyes. 'I play the harp, violin, cello and flute just as well. What instruments do you play?'

He laughed. 'None.'

Her mouth parted with a sigh of disappointment and he wished he could tell her he was a master of at least one of them, but that would be a lie and he never lied. 'I never had the skill or patience for playing anything, although I am an enthusiastic audience. Would you play some of your own compositions for me one day? No need for the others if you are shy.'

Marina's eyes widened and she seemed to realise how intimately alone they currently were. 'I should go to bed.'

His heart began to race. 'But you haven't even reached the antiquities yet. I heard he has a sarcophagus from the tombs in Egypt.'

'He does.' There was a momentary hesitation in her eyes and he could tell she was enjoying this just as much as he was. 'It lies under the glass dome at the back of the house. Light pours over the marble sarcophagus from above, making it shimmer in the morning light. It is empty, of course. But Father placed copies of Greek and Roman statues beside it. He loves history and has collected many coins, shells, sculptures and weapons over the years and displays them on stone plinths or under glass cloches. We also have a huge blue and white vase from the Orient, two rugs from the Middle East hung up like paintings against the wall and several models of ancient buildings meticulously recreating the ancient world in miniature.

'We have the Colosseum, the Parthenon, Great Pyramid of Giza and some more fun pieces, like the Tower of Babel—or at least what my father imagines the Tower of Babel might have looked like. That is my favourite. I helped him glue on the top section when I was five—which is why it's a little askew—but my father said that only adds to the story.' She smiled warmly as she spoke and he found himself admiring the lines of her face and neck instead of trying to imagine the alabaster tower.

'Because we all know Babel eventually falls,' he said and her blue eyes looked up at him and sparkled with amusement.

'Exactly.'

Brook felt as if he were falling. His heart was pounding in his chest and he wanted nothing more than to sweep aside the tumbling dark locks that had somehow worked their way back over her shoulders.

What would she do if he laid her down against the silk and kissed her thoroughly?

Be sensible! he reproached himself.

She represented everything he was hoping to avoid, at least for a few more years. A debutante ready for the marriage market, sweet and devoted to her family. She might have been surrounded by the exotic treasures of the world growing up, but somehow there was something deeply sad about that, perhaps because it was unlikely she would ever get to see them in person.

'I want to travel—more than anything,' he said firmly, as if his mother were in the room with them, demanding he stay for *just one more party.*

Marina nodded. 'So would I. I would like to go to Vienna one day…for the music.'

Brook blinked back his surprise. Wealthy young men such as himself went on grand tours. Even some aristocratic ladies travelled the Continent with their families. But someone like Marina never would, with her respectable, yet untitled family. The best she could hope for was a marriage to a wealthy man in trade or someone from the landed gentry.

'When you marry, perhaps your husband will take you there on honeymoon,' he said, not wanting to spoil her dreams.

She laughed. 'I meant what I said earlier. I will probably never marry—in fact, I *know* I won't!'

'And I promise you I meant no disrespect. You are an attractive, clever and wealthy woman. A man would be lucky to have you.' Brook felt bad for thinking of her as plain before—the more time he spent in her company, the more unique and interesting he realised she was. Marina was like a piece of artwork or one of her father's treasures—they weren't meant to be pretty—they were meant to provoke thoughts and feelings. And Marina did; she made him think and feel all sort of things…

She raised a dark brow at his words, but the smile on her face never wavered. 'Thank you for the *kind* words. But I think you misunderstand me. I really *don't* want to marry— ever. You see, my parents have spoiled marriage for me.'

'But they seem so…' He struggled for the word, never having experienced it in his own family. 'Happy?'

'Oh, they are!' she declared cheerfully. 'Terribly happy, so much so that I have come to realise how *unusual* such a loving marriage is. I will accept nothing less and so I will probably never marry, which does not bother me. I am quite content at home with my family and my music. I will leave the finding of a husband to the other girls. And, when I eventually decline into my spinster years—hopefully, not that long away—then I will be free to use my dowry to go to Vienna, or wherever I choose, and travel the world as an eccentric old maid. I have no fears for the future. As you say, I am rich and my family love me. I will always have a home.'

She smiled and it was breathtaking.

It was the certainty of her words that shocked him the most. There were no shadows or doubts in her mind: her family loved her and always would. No matter what she did, or what conventions she broke, they would care for her regardless.

He could not say the same.

But he wished he could and emotions buried deep in the heart of him twisted like roots around a stone. It was hunger, in its most raw and primal form, and he realised he had never wanted a woman more.

Chapter Four

Brook was staring at her, but not with horror as she might have expected from her bold confession, but something else, something that made her chest painfully tight and her body ache.

'What?' she asked, beginning to doubt herself.

Did he not believe her?

The shadows of the room closed in on her and with a shiver she remembered where she was. In a library, in the middle of the night, with a half-dressed man—it was—what was the word he had used?—*scandalous!*

She had never been scandalous in her life. Naive and ridiculous, but never…*wicked.*

Brook looked scandalous and wicked. Without his cravat, his white shirt billowed around him loosely, showing a triangle of flesh at his open collar. She stared at his Adam's apple, watching it bob ever so slightly as he breathed, a vein pulsing along the side of his neck, and she swallowed down the sudden lump in her own throat.

Brook stared at her for another long moment before answering, 'You constantly surprise me, Marina. Frankly, I am in awe of you.' It was the first time he had used her name without 'Miss' in front of it and her name sounded strangely beautiful and intimate on his lips.

There was a sultry heat in his gaze and he was staring

into her eyes so deeply, she thought he might see everything beneath her bravado. The nerves, the longing and, worst of all, the suffocating weight of fear.

'I can understand your dreams for independence and freedom. But will you deny yourself pleasure?' he asked, his voice smoky and deep like the bottom of a whisky barrel.

'Pleasure?' She tried to give a dismissive snort, but it sounded a little choked. Clearing her throat, she explained, 'I believe *that* is also rare in a marriage. It is why so many stray, is it not? Or avoid marriage completely. Like you...'

He leaned forward and she was startled by how close he was, the edge of his shirt within easy reach of her fingers. A shocking thought entered her head.

What if she reached out and gripped his shirt and pulled him close? What if she pressed a kiss to his lips?

She bit her bottom lip, to remind herself that this wasn't a dream.

His eyes slid down to her lips following her movement like a cat.

He is a predator! she warned herself, leaning back into her seat to gain some distance between them.

He had told her so himself at dinner, and she had blushed like a simpleton over it. What if he were only teasing her? It wouldn't be the first time she had fallen for a man's lies.

Well, she would prove to him now that she wasn't a fool!

'That is what you said, wasn't it? That you preferred to fill your time with cards, claret and...' But she couldn't bring herself to say it, not with him watching her like a hawk.

What did she know of carnal pleasures? She hadn't even kissed Mr Richards—or anyone for that matter.

A slow smile spread across his face, showing off sharp, pearly white canines. 'Carnal pleasures?' The words stroked over her like velvet, soft and luxurious. Then he sighed, leaning away from her with feigned disappointment, although there was still something bright and wickedly devious in his eyes that made her hot and nervous. 'Perhaps you are right. I hope you manage to avoid the shackles of marriage. I fear I will be unable to.'

She rolled her eyes. 'You are a duke—you can do whatever you wish!'

'Not in my mother's eyes. She wants me to marry and soon, to provide her with an heir. But I wish to travel and see the world—like your father did.' For once the mask of bored entitlement slipped and she realised he longed to be free just as much as she did—although in different ways.

'And you couldn't do that *with* a wife?' she asked drily, reminding herself that she had no reason to pity him.

'I would prefer to travel alone.'

She gave a huff of disgust. 'I see. To enjoy the three Cs. How *inspiring*!'

He smiled wickedly, but then surprised her by shrugging. 'I have always done as my father and brother expected of me. But now I am my own man. I am in control of my estate and my future. But I am not sure what to do with it—or myself. I hope by travelling I will learn what I want and who I am now that they are gone.'

The honesty of his words surprised her. 'I understand,' she said quietly and she truly did, because she knew what it was like to have the foundations of yourself shaken until you no longer recognised yourself.

He smiled at her and tilted his head thoughtfully. 'Do you not fear the ridicule of being an old maid? I can't imagine people like the Moorcrofts will be very kind about it.'

She stiffened, but tried her best to shrug it off. 'I will just have to bear the comparison, I suppose, as Freddie has at school. They will forget about me eventually, once

Priscilla marries—someone very rich and titled, I imagine. You might wish to warn your friend George, I believe they have eyes on him, as well as you—you would be the best catch of all—as a duke.'

The Duke chuckled. 'I am sure they do.' He paused, steepling his fingers before asking casually, 'Speaking of your brother... I know the new headmaster of the school. I will send him a letter asking him to keep an eye on him if you wish.'

Surprised at his kindness, she nodded eagerly. 'That would be very kind of you, thank you.'

'Perhaps we can help each other in other ways?'

Suddenly, Marina felt as if she had just stepped out on to a tightrope. 'What do you mean?'

'My mother is determined to find me a bride. Ideally, she would like Miss Clifton for me, but I believe she is willing to overlook a noble bloodline for someone rich, like Priscilla Moorcroft, for example...'

Marina scoffed, 'My father is wealthier! Honestly, I do not want to speak ill of your mother, but I think she has begun to believe Mr Moorcroft's ridiculous boasting. Just because he has a carriage and we do not does not mean he has any more money than we do—he is just more vulgar with it.'

'I am glad you agree.'

What exactly had she agreed to?

But before she could question it, he continued, 'I, on the other hand, wish only to travel. If I did accept someone such as Miss Moorcroft, then I am sure they would insist on a short engagement.'

She nodded. 'True.'

'But you would not mind a long engagement. One, two, *ten* years—it would not matter to you, would it?' he asked mildly, a predatory knowingness in his smile, as if he were a cat toying with a mouse.

'You forget. I said I would never marry.'

'Yes, but you never said anything about being *engaged*!'

Was he being deliberately obtuse?

'One follows the other normally. Besides, I will accept nothing less than what my parents have: love. And we—' she gestured between them with a wave of one hand '—do *not* have that!'

'Exactly!' he declared, his knee brushing against hers, as he added in a hushed voice, 'But we both want independence. Why not have a long engagement with me? My mother will be happy, because I will be settled in her mind, and she will stop finding ways to keep me home. We could then cancel the engagement when I eventually return, or your family might choose to anyway if I am gone long enough, or—' he paused, scratching the stubble on his chin '—if you changed your mind about marriage. I suppose I could marry you on my return. I will need a wife eventually and it would save you any embarrassment.'

Marina shook her head, wondering if this whole thing were a dream—well, a cruel nightmare seemed more appropriate. 'Are you mocking me?'

He shook his head vehemently, put aside his brandy glass and reached for her hands. 'Never! In fact, the more I think about it, the more perfect I realise you are! We can both live independently and be free to choose our own path in life!'

'Absolutely not!'

The eagerness in his expression was quickly dashed as if she had thrown cold water on him. But he didn't let go of her—instead he stared down at her hands, her fingers wrapped protectively around the brandy glass and his hands cupping hers. 'Then...perhaps—it doesn't have to be too long an engagement? After I go travelling you could reject me. Claim you have heard some scandal of mine. I am sure there will be one or two, then we can part ways almost immediately.'

She tugged her hands away and set her glass on the table next to his. She noticed they were both empty. 'You have had too much to drink. And I have let this—whatever *this* is—go on for far too long!' She gestured to the empty library and her night attire, before turning away to leave.

A hand snapped out grabbing her wrist, the hold not painful, but firm as if he were pleading with her to stay. But when she looked down, he was not looking at her, as if the grab of her hand were a concession to his pride he could not acknowledge.

'It would annoy *them*—the Moorcrofts,' he said softly, his eyes fixed firmly ahead.

'That is not a good enough reason,' she whispered, although the warmth of his hand held her back and that was even more of a ridiculous reason to agree to his scheme.

'But it will make your triumph sweeter. To have me as your suitor…a duke.'

Her heart hammered in her chest as his fingers flexed ever so lightly around her pulse, as if he knew how much the idea excited her.

She shouldn't even be considering such a thing! It was ridiculous and petty! And yet excitement fluttered in her chest, when she imagined standing beside the Duke, her arm in his.

His gaze slid up to meet hers, trailing sensually up her arm, neck and face to finally meet her eyes. 'Not only that, but I can help you in other ways—with your father's business—'

'Use my father for your house because you like his work and not for any other reason. It is an insult to suggest otherwise!' she snapped angrily, but he was like a dog with a bone.

'Fine, with your music then. Connections, gravitas— whatever you want—no one says no to a duke.' He grinned, his handsome face glowing with confidence.

In a moment of madness, she thought, *I don't actually want to say no to him.*

He must have sensed it, because he rose slowly from his seat and took her other hand in his so that she was trapped within. He reached up and touched her cheek. The touch should have felt shocking, but when the heat of his palm kissed her cheek, she realised how much she had anticipated and longed for it. A delicious dizziness overwhelmed her and she closed her eyes, basking in the sensation, the smell of brandy, leather-bound books and warm linen filling her nose.

'Think how it would feel to be in control of your own fate. To have your music succeed, and played in concert halls, theatres, wherever you wish. As the fiancée of a duke, doors once closed would open for you. Not only that, but you could go and do as you pleased, you wouldn't be a young debutante any more, dismissed and sheltered like a child. That's what rankles you, isn't it? That you can't be free to live as you wish...' he whispered and when she opened her eyes, his face was close and his eyes were locked on her lips. He brushed his thumb over her bottom lip and it sent shivers down her spine.

He smiled, pleased with her response. 'I could pretend to be in love with you, if you like? That would make Priscilla sick with jealousy.'

He had almost tempted her, this devil incarnate. But she quickly came to her senses when she heard the word *pretend* and *Priscilla* in the same sentence. She tugged her wrist from his grip.

'How *generous,* that you would lower yourself so! But, no thank you, Your Grace! I would never accept such a disgusting arrangement! Just because you are a duke does not mean that you are a fine catch for *me!*'

She began to stride away, only to hear his angry voice behind her.

'Believe me, I will not make such an offer again!'

'Good!' she snapped, throwing it over her shoulder and wishing it were something more tangible like a rock or a knife. She hated him at this moment, not for his offer, but because she had almost accepted it.

Chapter Five

Marina was late down to breakfast the following day. She'd
spent what was left of the night and early hours of this morning tossing and turning, until she'd finally managed to get
some sleep.

'Are you ill?' asked her mother quietly, as she sat down
at the breakfast table. Everyone had finished eating, and
were now drinking tea or coffee while they talked over the
morning papers.

'I couldn't sleep,' Marina explained, and her parents'
frowns of concern eased a little. They were used to her occasional bouts of insomnia, although usually they were due
to bursts of creativity.

Mr Moorcroft chuckled as he sipped from his dainty cup
that looked almost comical in his big hands. 'You did seem
a little out of character last night, Miss Fletcher.'

There were a couple of stifled giggles around the room
and she felt her mother's hand pat her leg lightly beneath
the table, a silent gesture of support.

Miss Clifton gave her a warm smile. 'I loved your playing, Miss Fletcher. I hope you will do so again soon.'

Priscilla nodded with a sly smile. 'There is a beautiful
music room in the east wing—I saw it on our tour yesterday, before you arrived. That would be ideal for tonight,

far enough away from the dancing so that you're not disturbed by clashing music.'

Miss Clifton looked startled by the suggestion. 'Oh, I only meant for another time. I wouldn't want to take you away from tonight's amusements.'

'Marina rarely dances!' Priscilla laughed.

Marina buttered some bread, keeping her eyes firmly away from the rest of the group. 'I would not like to distract from the other musicians.'

'Quite right, best to leave it to the professionals,' declared Mr Moorcroft.

The Duchess quickly interrupted before Mr Moorcroft said anything more offensive. 'What if we go to the pleasure gardens today? Followed by an early dinner, then we will have plenty of time to prepare for the ball.'

'Will the Duke be joining us?' asked Priscilla hopefully.

'Possibly—he had business in town this morning, but I told him that he could find us at the pleasure gardens.'

'Perhaps, you should stay home and rest, Marina?' suggested her father, 'To ensure you are fit for the ball tonight.'

'Yes, I think I will do just that,' replied Marina, grateful for some excuse to avoid the Duke for as long as possible. The ball would be a grand affair and, God willing, she would only have to see him at dinner, then she could avoid him for the rest of the night, too.

Brook returned to his mother's house at the perfect moment.

No one was there.

He had finally tracked down the last of his mother's debtors, he had closed the account swiftly, and paid for the man's silence. As usual it had cost him more than he had expected and he was in no mood to behave pleasantly to his mother.

After washing the grime of the London backstreets off his face and hands, he went to take a walk in the gardens overlooking the river.

There were carefully landscaped low hedges and paths that wound in geometric patterns towards a central fountain. Beyond that was a much larger wall of greenery that separated the garden from the riverbank. As he walked among the pathways, he could almost believe he was back at Stonecroft Manor, as there were so many flowers in abundance. He walked past the fountain with its leaping dolphins and wondered if he should go for a swim in the river. It was much cleaner this far from the city, but he decided that cooling off his feet might be the safest choice.

What he did not expect to see, as he came out of the hedge's archway and on to the riverbank, was Miss Marina Fletcher asleep on a blanket, laid on her back with her eyes closed, her mouth slightly parted as she deeply breathed in and out.

'Isn't it damp lying there?' he asked, testing the spongy rain-soaked earth with his boot.

Her eyes flew open and she sat up with a jerk, spluttering and gasping for air at being suddenly awoken. 'What are you doing here?'

'Why are you always so surprised to see me?' Brook asked casually as he dropped down on the blanket beside her. He pushed his hand against the cloth and was unsurprised when cold moisture hit his palm. 'You will get ill sleeping out here.'

'I am perfectly fine!' she snapped, although he could tell by the uncomfortable wince as she shuffled her bottom that the wet earth had managed to permeate through to her dress.

She looked around her wildly and then up at the cloudy sky. 'What time is it?'

Taking out his fob watch, he said, 'One o'clock.'

'Oh,' she said, her shoulders sinking, although whether with relief or disappointment he wasn't sure. 'I wasn't asleep for long then.' Another thought seemed to occur to her as she wiped absently at her face. 'Surely you haven't returned from the pleasure gardens already?'

'I never went to the pleasure gardens.' He had given some vague comment to his mother about *possibly* going there after sorting out *her* debt. But he'd had no intention of going, partly because he wanted to avoid seeing Marina again. Which immediately begged the question, why had he disturbed her in the first place? 'Why didn't you go with them?'

A blush crept up her cheeks. 'I…I didn't feel like it.'

'You were tired, I suppose. I did keep you up late last night,' he said, unable to hide his amusement at her indignant bristle.

'Do *not* say such things! I would much rather pretend it never happened.' She rose up on to her feet slightly unsteadily and tried to yank the blanket up from beneath him. It remained solidly in place.

He took the corner of the fabric from her and stood, cracking the cloth to remove the moisture before folding it into a neat pile and handing it to her. She took it with a bad-tempered 'thank you' before heading back towards the house.

He would have left it at that if he hadn't spotted a movement from behind the hedge out of the corner of his eye.

'Who goes there?' he shouted and at the snap of authority in his voice Marina stopped walking and turned back to him in surprise. Her gaze immediately following his to the topiary hedge at the side of them.

She stepped forward, as if to try to peer through at whoever was hiding there, and he strode forward, ready to shield her if necessary.

To his surprise she called out, '*Freddie?* Is that you?'

A young man who looked no older than thirteen or fourteen stepped out from the hedgerow. He was thin, shorter than his sister by a foot, with pale skin and a mop of dark curly hair. His eyes matched the brilliant blue of his sister's eyes, and it gave his face a haunted quality to it, as if he were much older than he seemed, while also being far more fragile than a boy his age should be.

Sheepishly the boy said, 'Hello, Sis.'

'What are *you* doing here?' Marina snapped, followed by a quickly muttered, 'Good Lord, why do I keep saying that?'

'I heard you were staying here and I wanted to see you.'

Marina gave her brother an angry glare. 'Does the school even know you are here?' Her brother's eyes dropped to the ground guiltily. 'Oh, Freddie! What were you *thinking*?'

Her brother's bottom lip began to tremble at her harsh words and she stepped forward.

'How did you even get here from Knights Court? It's nearly ten miles away!'

Tears began to fill his eyes and her little brother suddenly looked a lot younger than his thirteen years.

'Are you all right, Freddie?' she asked more gently this time and her brother's head dropped as he walked forward. Immediately she opened her arms to receive him and he fell into her embrace. She gathered her brother into a comforting hug, his thin wide shoulders folding forward like bird's wings.

Brook stared at them—the easy affection and genuine concern Marina felt for her brother was obvious. It made him wish he'd had a better relationship with his own brother growing up, someone to lean on in times of hardship. But his brother had always seemed as remote as his father, especially after he'd become the Duke.

The boy began to weep, slowly at first and with more painful misery with each breath he took. He began to mumble, 'I can't go back there. I hate it. I want to come home.'

Brook could well imagine the torment young Frederick had suffered at school—he himself had taken his fair share of bullying from both pupils and teachers. Being pushed around in the corridors, beatings back at the boarding house, punishments for every tiny mistake... He had hated it, too, but he at least had already been used to such treatment, it wasn't so different from life under his father's rule.

No wonder Frederick had run away. Brook might have done the same, except he'd known *his* brother wouldn't have cared and would have sent him straight back. Robert had learned how to manage a household from their father and would have probably taken a switch to him just as their father would have. His mother would have tried to stop him and then he would have had to watch her being punished as well. No, he'd had no option but to stay and silently bear it.

Marina glanced over her brother's shoulder at him helplessly, obviously unsure of what to do with either of them at this moment. Not wanting to add to her troubles, he quickly said, 'Let's go inside and have some tea.'

She nodded quickly as if relieved by his suggestion. 'Tea...yes, what a good idea! We had an excellent sponge this morning, I'm sure you'd love a piece, Freddie.'

They made their way swiftly to his mother's parlour,

where Brook called for the servants to bring tea with a healthy side of cake.

Marina settled her brother into an armchair and used her blanket to wrap around his shoulders. 'You're frozen to the bone!' she said, rubbing his arms furiously to get his blood pumping. 'Did you really walk all the way here?'

Brook shovelled some coal on to the fire and lit it, hoping to help in any way that he could—especially as Marina was busy settling her distraught brother and he had no idea how to help in that regard. He then reached for a blanket from one of his mother's chests and Marina gratefully took it, replacing the damp one.

Frederick shook his head. 'I rode in the back of a farmer's cart for some of the way. But I think that was just as slow as walking. Only less tiring.'

'Oh, Freddie!' Marina sighed as she took a seat beside him. The maid entered then with a tray, swiftly performing a curtsy before leaving. If the servants were surprised by the turn of events, they were wise enough not to show it. It made him wonder what else they'd turned a blind eye to during his mother's many parties and balls.

As if remembering he was still there, Marina hastily introduced him to her brother. 'Umm... Frederick, this is the Duke of Framlingham—'

Freddie stared up at him with wide horrified eyes. After pouring the tea, she passed a cup and saucer to her brother and the china rattled in an alarming way.

'Call me Brook,' Brook said immediately with what he hoped was a friendly smile. 'I also went to Knights Court. It can be tough at first...' he said, feeling awful that he couldn't offer any more comfort than that, but the truth was some boys excelled at school, and some, like himself, struggled. 'Ironically, I found army life easier.' He laughed, his amusement dying when he realised they didn't return it. Bad-temperedly, he added, 'At least, in the army you don't have to learn a dead language.'

That seemed to brighten Frederick's expression, as he hissed in agreement, 'Exactly, I *detest* Latin and Greek!' He sipped his tea from a now steady cup.

Brook smiled and took a seat on the other side of the table. 'Totally pointless!' he agreed and Marina gave him a disapproving scowl.

'Latin and Greek are not pointless. They are the foundation of language, and the myths are—'

'I know!' grumbled Frederick with a weary sigh. 'Please don't reprimand me. I've had enough of it to last me a lifetime...'

Marina's gaze softened with sympathy and she cut the cake, placing an extra-large slice of sponge on a plate for her brother, before handing it to him. He took it gratefully and began to greedily demolish it. She then glanced at Brook, her knife hesitating over the cake like the sword of Damocles. 'If you wish to leave, we will understand.'

Amused, he reached over and covered her hand with his own, pressing it down to slice through the fluffy texture. 'I will stay for cake. I can never resist a dessert.' Her hand felt warm and silky smooth beneath his fingers and he forgot for a moment they were in her brother's company.

'That's what Father says...' said Frederick and then fresh tears threatened to fall with the increasing wobble of his chin. 'I'm going to have to go back, aren't I? Otherwise, Father will be ridiculed by everyone for having such a weak and stupid son! It's just—I heard you were staying here and you seemed so near—I wanted to see you all, just for a bit. But that was a mistake, wasn't it?'

With a clatter Marina plopped Brook's cake slice on a

plate and shoved it towards him. He took it quickly before it ended up in his lap.

'You are neither weak nor stupid, Freddie! So, how can Father *ever* be ashamed of you?' Despite the fierceness of her words, Brook was impressed by her loyalty and compassion.

The truth was quite the opposite—running away from Knights Court would bring shame and ridicule on Mr Fletcher, especially as the Fletchers were not part of the aristocracy. Knights Court was an elite school—even the wealthiest men had to prove themselves worthy of securing a place for their sons. He imagined Mr Fletcher's son had had to be recommended by someone like Lord Thorne just to gain admittance. If Frederick proved himself unworthy of the place, he embarrassed both his father and the gentleman who had recommended him. Not to mention the fact that young Frederick had arrived at the Duchess's house uninvited.

'Why did you leave?' Brook asked quietly, hoping that by getting to the bottom of the issue he might be able to help resolve it. *Why* he wanted to help was still beyond him—maybe he was bored?

'I couldn't stand it…' said Frederick with a miserable expression. 'Herbert and his stupid friends! They kept calling me brick—and it's—infuriating.'

'Brick?' asked Marina, a flush of indignation on her face. 'Because our grandfather was a bricklayer? That's nothing to be ashamed of. Father worked hard to get where he is now and there are at least a couple of other boys at that school who come originally from trade. Even Herbert! Yes, he has titled relations—but he's no better than you—!'

'It's more than that…' interrupted Frederick miserably, his gaze dropping to stare into his tea as if he were reading his fortune and finding it lacking. 'They say I have a brick for brains…'

'You don't!' snapped Marina, dropping her cup into the saucer with a sharp clatter. 'You are just as good as any of those boys! Better even. They are nasty, entitled, small-minded—' She took a deep breath as if trying to steady herself, and Brook sipped his tea to hide his smile. How he wished he'd had such a lioness in his corner of the ring when he was a child.

'It wasn't a boy that first said it…'

'What do you mean? Surely it wasn't one of your teachers? That would be outrageous!'

Brook could tell Marina was about to explode like a barrel of gunpowder so he quickly interrupted, 'Was it Master Thornton, perhaps? *Good Lord!* That man haunted the halls even in my day! I shouldn't give a fig what he says. The man's never left Knights, let alone England!'

Frederick nodded. 'It was him and then the other boys thought they could say whatever they liked after that. Still… I shouldn't have run away. I've just made it all so much worse.'

'You haven't been gone long,' said Marina thoughtfully. 'They might not even realise you are missing at the boarding house yet. If we put you in a hackney carriage now—'

'I will take him back,' Brook interrupted, taking a sip of his tea, while he waited for their astonishment to subside. 'I can have a word with the new headmaster on your behalf, Reverend Peasbody. I actually went to school with him and he's a reasonable chap. I am sure we can sort something out.'

'We couldn't ask that of you,' gasped Marina.

'It might help, though…' said Frederick, giving his sister a hard look that said *Don't interfere. This man could be my saving grace!*

Brook sat back and watched the two siblings battle it out silently, while he enjoyed the cook's delicious sponge.

'Let's wait until our parents are home before we make any decisions!'

'You want the Moorcrofts to know about this?' asked Brook casually, knowing full well she would wish nothing of the sort.

'Oh, Lord! Don't tell me the Moorcrofts are here, too! Mother's letter only mentioned you staying with the Duchess this week.' He looked a little ill as he glanced at the Duke and then back to Marina. 'I've made things difficult for you and Father, haven't I?'

'All will be well,' Marina said dismissively and Brook wondered at her brother's words. Difficult for her father he could understand—but why was it difficult for Marina?

'Then I must go immediately! If I try to leave school now, it will only make matters *worse*!' cried Frederick, looking fearfully at the door as if the Moorcrofts would burst in at any moment. Then, looking at Brook, he pleaded, 'Will you really take me back, Your Grace?'

'Of course, and don't worry, they won't be back from the pleasure gardens yet.'

'I will have to come, too, and make sure you don't get into trouble for leaving. Mother will never forgive me otherwise.' Marina glanced at Brook and he tried his best to look suddenly enthralled by his tea and cake. 'If the Duke doesn't mind?'

'More the merrier, but you will need a chaperon,' he reminded softly, before adding, 'For the journey back.'

'Oh.' Marina blushed, as if she'd not considered she would have to return in a carriage alone with him. She thought for a moment and then brightened. 'I will bring

my maid Betsy with us, then. No one can claim impropri-
ety then!'

Brook wasn't so sure of that. They'd already spent an
indecent amount of time alone together, but for some reason he didn't care to argue it.

Chapter Six

The Duke's barouche certainly caused a stir as it rolled into the school grounds of Knights Court. Boys ran to peer out of windows and the cricket game was abruptly halted. One poor boy was hit on the head by a rogue ball as Marina stepped out of the carriage.

Normally Marina would have been concerned about the child hit by a rogue ball, except she couldn't help but wonder if any of these boys were the same ones who had tormented Freddie. If that was the case, she wouldn't have minded if they were hit by half a dozen balls. It might have knocked some good sense into their narrow little minds!

'Betsy, why don't you stay here with the driver? We won't be long,' said Marina turning back to her maid. Betsy wasn't the best traveller and she looked pale and sickly after an hour of being bounced around in a carriage.

'Yes, Miss.' She nodded quickly, looking as if she might cry with relief.

The headmaster, Reverend Peasbody, must have seen their carriage coming up the long drive because he rushed out to greet them. His small round cheeks flushed with colour as he rushed out of the building. He seemed a nice enough man, if a little young to be a headmaster. He was short and only came up to Marina's cleavage, which was a little disconcerting, but he had a friendly smile and gentle brown eyes behind the spectacles balanced on his nose.

'Is that you, Brook—I mean—Your Grace…?' said the headmaster, who looked almost sick with fear at his mistake.

'Edward! Good to see you again!' called out Brook with a loud and commanding voice. 'And call me Brook. We are old friends, after all!'

Reverend Peasbody looked a bit startled by Brook's words, but then his face softened like a blushing bride. 'How kind of you to say.'

The cricketers on the field continued to watch in oddly sombre fascination, like spectres at the feast. Frederick kept glancing towards them and she was sure the bowler was Herbert, although she couldn't be certain from this distance.

Brook slapped an arm around Frederick's shoulders and gave him a playful shake that almost toppled her brother over. 'I've brought back one of your knights! I am sorry if he worried you, he missed his family. You know how it is…'

The last was said with a long and meaningful look that made the Reverend nod slowly with understanding, a ghost of sadness crossing his own face.

'I understand. Perhaps we should speak privately? Would you like to come to my office? Frederick, Miss Fletcher, Your Grace—I mean—Brook, follow me, please.'

Marina felt the tension in her shoulders drain from her, as Brook quickly commanded the situation with a persuasive kindness she found admirable. It was clear that he had been close with the Reverend *Edward* Peasbody as a child and that both men remembered the friendship with affection.

But there were also secrets, too, the burdens of a difficult childhood. She remembered Brook had started school at a young age from the conversation at dinner. He'd been nine years old when he'd been sent away to school. She had no idea how difficult that must have been for him, but she could well imagine.

However, such hardships had not hardened him, as it might have done to another person. Brook spoke to the much smaller man with a great deal of respect, and everything he had done so far had been to help Frederick out of this difficult situation. The Duke was not the same arrogant man she had met that first night. The man in front of her now, was gentle, charming and, most of all…kind.

It wasn't long until they were settled in Edward's office, a large room overlooking a pretty coppice of oak and ash trees that Brook remembered sitting in as a child. He had climbed them to avoid the bigger boys and had found Edward there already, perched like an owl, his head in one of his books, his spectacles cracked in one lens.

Brook hated this place, but Edward had more reason to hate it than he did.

What had possessed Edward to return here? And why had Brook?

The last time he'd left through those wrought-iron gates, he had vowed to never return, yet here he was—sitting in a damask chair in a room where he'd received some of the worst beatings of his life.

'The Duke mentioned this was your first year as headmaster and that you took over the position in January—is that true?' asked Marina, smoothing out the wrinkles of her mint-green dress. Despite her gentle tone, Brook could tell she was preparing for battle by the sharpness of her gaze as it surveyed the room and the headmaster without missing a speck of dust.

Her eyes lingered over the apple crates scattered around the room, overflowing with books and papers, then fixed on Edward with a raised eyebrow, as if to say *Are you not ready for this position?*

'It's my first term—the last headmaster only stayed for a year. They hoped I would be more suited to the position, as I am familiar with the school,' said Edward, pouring tea for them.

'I am surprised you came back. I could not imagine anything worse,' said Brook with a dry chuckle and he avoided the startled and curious look Marina gave him. It was not his story to tell, which is why he had avoided talking about his old friend on the journey here. It might have done more harm than good to have Marina or her brother hear about it.

Edward smiled, a soft knowing smile that reminded him of the gentle-hearted boy he'd once known. 'As am I, but sometimes we must face the past to overcome it. I want to improve this school—for the children. Tell me, Frederick, why did you return home? Was it *just* because you missed your family?'

Frederick had become quiet and withdrawn since entering the grounds of Knights Court and even though Brook was a man now—who had seen war in all its blood and pointless misery— he also knew how it felt to be a boy, miserable and alone.

He would not wish that on any child, and wished he could reassure him that it would get easier with time. That it was only a few years and then Frederick would walk out of those gates, just as Brook had done, and never look back. But he also knew those words would be like a cruel slap in the face, because how could someone who had only lived thirteen years know that this was only a passing phase of his life? Each day must feel like an eternity—school were the longest days and shortest years of your life.

'Frederick has been having a difficult time since starting this school. Not only from ill-mannered boys who should know better, but also from one of your teachers, a Master Thornton. And I would have thought—considering how much my father pays for him to attend this school—you would treat *all* your students with kindness and respect!' Marina demanded, her chin high and her tone imposing.

'Marina, please, I—' Frederick looked sick with embarrassment and despair. 'It was only a little name calling. I should have ignored it.'

Edward frowned, but nodded with understanding. 'I see. Let me reassure you, Miss Fletcher, that I do not tolerate any form of disrespect either to or from my students. Let us forget today's absence. I shall say your family needed to speak with Frederick urgently and that is the reason for his lateness. I will also remind all students and teachers about the appropriate behaviour I expect from them all.'

'Thank you,' Marina said curtly, although Brook could tell she wasn't entirely reassured by Edward's words.

'Yes, thank you, Edward. I would consider it a personal favour if you looked after Frederick well. He reminds me of myself.'

Edward smiled, another blush staining his collar, and he cleared his throat. 'Come, Frederick, let us take a walk before luncheon. You can tell me what has been troubling you. Perhaps you would suit moving to another boarding house?'

Frederick's eyes lit up. 'Could I do that? So late in the term?'

'I am sure we can sort something for you.'

They said their goodbyes, Marina and Frederick hugging each other so fiercely that it made his chest ache as if he'd been kicked in the chest by a bull.

'We should probably get going. I know you left them a note, but your parents will begin to worry if we are not back soon.'

Marina nodded, then gave her brother one last squeeze before letting go. 'We all have our own gifts,' she said firmly, 'Don't let them make you feel small just because they are too blind to see them. If you do decide to leave, let us know and we can arrange something quietly, I promise.'

Frederick gave a little nod, his face scrunched up as if he were trying to stop himself from crying.

'We should go,' said Brook, firmly taking Marina's arm.

'I will get a hamper made for you, for the journey back,' offered Edward.

Brook placed a hand on Edward's shoulder. 'I may not be glad to see this place again, but I am glad to see you, old friend. Thank you, for everything.'

Edward smiled. 'Come back whenever you like, you might find it helps.'

It wasn't long until they were settled back in the barouche on their way back to his mother's house.

Marina deliberately sat opposite the Duke, so that Betsy would be facing towards their direction of travel. She hoped that it would help with her maid's nausea. They'd been facing away from it previously and she was certain that hadn't helped.

The wind had picked up since this morning and the fresh air seemed to have brought some colour back into her cheeks. Betsy even nibbled on some of the bread and cheese, before the rocking of the carriage sent her nodding off to sleep.

Unable to stifle her curiosity a moment longer, Marina asked, 'Why did you hate coming here?'

Brook raised a raven brow and smiled. 'I did not hate coming here. I wanted to help.'

Marina rolled her eyes. 'You are being deliberately obtuse! I meant, why did you hate coming here as a boy?'

'Many reasons,' he replied with an insolent shrug that suggested he would not expand on the subject. He slapped his leather gloves lightly on his breeches and she was suddenly aware of how big he was in the carriage, his legs spread lazily in front of her, taking up most of the space between them.

You should not be looking!

She snapped her eyes back to his face. Thankfully he was gazing out at the passing countryside. The roads were getting better, signalling they weren't far from the grand estates of Twickenham and would soon be arriving at his mother's house.

Marina leaned forward a little, capturing his attention. 'Please,' she said softly, 'I need to know what it's like there—for Frederick. Should my parents take him out? We didn't before because so many people said it took a while for boys to settle in. But we don't want him to be miserable.'

That seemed to crumble some of Brook's resolve because, with a resigned sigh, he said, 'It can be hard for certain boys—I was one of them.'

Chapter Seven

'I don't believe that!' she scoffed. 'You're so—*confident.*'

Heat warmed her face and Brook wasn't the only one to suddenly become fascinated by the fleeting countryside.

He chuckled. 'I wasn't when I was nine.'

'That is too young to be away from your family,' Marina said, then she realised how that must have sounded like a criticism and she stumbled to correct herself. 'I mean—it seems young to *me*, but I am sure your parents had their reasons.'

'My brother insisted I come here after my father died,' Brook said simply, as if he were commenting on the weather.

'Oh,' she said and guilt washed through her. 'I am sorry...truly.'

Brook shrugged, giving her a light smile that seemed utterly forced. 'We have been an unlucky family. My father fell when riding and broke his neck, and my brother died in a carriage accident. Perhaps I should steer clear of horses in the future? I might live longer.'

The joke was dipped in poor taste and was probably intended to stop all further talk on the subject. For some reason, Marina didn't want to ignore his pain, instead she wanted to understand him better. 'Being so young—it must have felt like you had lost both of your parents, when you were sent to Knights Court,' she said, her heart breaking for the little boy he had been.

He watched her closely, his green eyes almost serpent-like as they searched her for any sign of weakness. She wondered if he would pretend bravado as he had done before.

But he surprised her by eventually nodding in agreement. 'It did. But things got better with time.' His brow creased as if he were struggling to find the words. 'I was small when I first arrived, because I was so much younger than the other boys. Some of them took pity on me, like Edward. They made it easier for me.'

'*Edward* protected you?'

Her surprise must have been obvious, because Brook laughed, a rich and throaty sound that made her blush for some unknown reason. Probably because it sounded wickedly sinful.

'Is Edward not the gallant knight in shining armour that you imagined?'

Marina squirmed in her seat. 'Well, I am sure he is a decent man and he seemed keen to help Frederick. Only, I can't imagine him standing up to bullies as a child. He's rather—*petite* in comparison to—well, you know what I mean.' Her eyes travelled meaningfully up the Duke's long legs and impossibly wide shoulders. She couldn't help but compare the two men. If she were to imagine one of them as the hero of a tale, it would not have been the Reverend Peasbody. 'But I suppose at nine years old you must have been much smaller than him and the other boys.'

'Edward has always been small in stature, but never in spirit. Although, come to think of it, he wasn't much taller than me even then and he was tormented by them just as much, if not worse than I ever was. But he used to help me hide and he used to comfort me when I was sad. As we grew older, I became bigger and stronger. I even managed to hold my own against the older boys so I was able to return his kindness, in my own way.'

He smiled roguishly and she could well imagine him giving back some hard punches of his own. 'But I will never forget how good Edward was to me those first couple of years. I tried to protect him when I could—in return he helped me with my Latin and Greek.' He paused, that kind gentleness returning to his face, as he tried to reassure her, 'Frederick will be in a much better position now that Edward is aware of his troubles. Believe me, what Edward lacks in stature, he makes up for in cunning.'

He chuckled to himself, as if remembering some amusing story from long ago, but then his smile became bittersweet. 'When he finished school, I couldn't bear it a moment longer...so I begged my brother to let me leave. Second sons usually go into the church or the army anyway, so it wasn't too much trouble to get me a commission.'

When Brook spoke of his brother, there was no affection in his tone, not in the same way he had spoken about Reverend Peasbody. It was as if he were talking about an employer or a landlord, not family.

She asked the question, already suspecting the answer, but wanting to know more anyway, 'I was sorry to hear about your brother's death. Were you close?'

'No,' he said, shaking his head. 'We never grew up together like normal brothers. You see, he was the son of my father's first wife. When my parents married, Robert was already a grown man.'

'Why...?' She stopped speaking, realising how rude her question might seem. Yes, she was curious, but she was worried she was becoming almost impertinent in her questions.

Brook did not seem to care—in fact, he laughed. 'Why didn't my mother marry the heir rather than my father? A couple of reasons. Firstly, my brother was not inclined to marry yet, and secondly...' He paused, glancing at her as if to check she were listening carefully. Curious, she leaned closer, and he said, 'My mother was very young, innocent and rich. Apparently, such qualities appealed to my father at the time, but the novelty of a young wife soon grew tiresome.'

Marina gasped, horrified at the implied cruelty. 'Was he unkind to her?'

Brook's face twisted into a bitter grimace. 'My father ruled his house with an iron fist. None of us could do anything without his approval. Even what we ate and wore was all dictated by my father and we were both punished for any misbehaviour. We were trapped at Stonecroft, never allowed to leave unless it was with my father. Most of the day my mother and I would hide from him on the estate—it was too much of a risk to stay inside. As long as we weren't seen or heard by him, we were free to do as we pleased and because my mother was so young she was happy to keep me company. We climbed trees, built dens and campfires, fenced with sticks. I would rescue her from the imaginary kraken—that sort of thing...'

He smiled warmly at the memory and she suspected he had greatly enjoyed those days playing with his mother, but then the smile dropped. 'When my father died, I thought we would both be free. But in the end, it was worse—at least for me—Robert didn't even allow us to stay together after Father died. A spare heir was no good to him and neither was his father's widow. We had to prove our worth...'

'How so?' she asked softly, feeling as if she were pulling on a tangled embroidery thread. She feared that if she pulled too hard this connection between them might suddenly break.

Brook sighed. 'My brother believed my mother was immature and weak, that she needed to live up to her responsibilities. He wanted her to become an impressive duchess, to arrange grand balls and parties, to be the feminine presence of our family in high society—while he continued to live the life of a bachelor. She did as he asked and, to his surprise, she excelled at it. Perhaps, now that she was finally free of our father's tyranny, she could live the life she had always wanted. She might have even been glad of it—to no longer be restricted by the presence of her son.

'I hated him for separating us, but I hated her more for agreeing to it. At least, for a while I did, until I grew up and realised I didn't want to become the monster that took away her freedom. To be honest, when Robert died, I didn't care. I remember only thinking what an unfortunate mess he had made of my plans. I never wanted to be the Duke, or become like either of them. But here I am—the damned Duke of Framlingham!' He stared down at his signet ring as if it were a shackle.

'You won't become like them,' Marina said firmly, struggling to think of something more comforting to add. 'Life is full of twists and turns. At least your mother is now free of them both.'

'A little too free sometimes...' He said the last words with a sourness that surprised her.

'What do you mean?'

'My brother has been proven right on at least one thing. She is childish. She still has a habit of throwing extravagant parties for no reason and for excessive gambling. I have spent some time paying off her debts.'

Understanding dawned and she realised she had misjudged the Duke harshly in the past. 'Is that why you have been in so many gambling dens? Since returning home from war and becoming the Duke?'

'Possibly…' He laughed.

'So, you are not a rake and a scoundrel?'

His laugh grew louder, and she shushed him, for fear that he would wake Betsy. 'I wish I was. But if anything, I am a heartbroken man.'

'Heartbroken?'

'Is that so hard to believe?'

'What happened?'

'I was disappointed by love—most people are at some point in their lives. Let us leave it at that.' A confused look followed by a frown of disapproval swept over his handsome features and he leaned forward, his head tilting slightly to the side as he asked, 'Why am I telling you all of this, Marina? Why can I not hide anything from you? You ask me questions and I answer them, without a thought to the consequences. Why is that? What hold do you have over me?'

Shocked, she sank back into her luxuriously padded seat and tried to regain her composure. His words had struck her hard, because she knew all too well how it felt to be disappointed in love. 'I apologise, I let my curiosity get the better of me, Your Grace. But let me assure you, I would not share anything you have told me with anyone. Not even my family.'

'Don't call me that,' he said softly, leaning forward to invade her space once more and remind her that—with the exception of a snoring maid—they were alone. 'Call me Brook.'

'But… I can't!' she said weakly, although he had already changed in her mind from the Duke to a man—to Brook. It was only the rules of society that held her tongue in check.

'If I say you can, then you can. It really is a pity you did not agree to be my fiancée, it really could have helped you today—'

'I said no for several very good reasons!' she snapped.

'I remember—' he laughed '—I was quite put out by it! But a trip together to visit your brother would have made so much more sense if we were engaged. Don't you think? I could say that I wanted to meet him as part of our courtship. Always good to know every member of your future relatives, especially the heirs.'

Marina couldn't help it; she pulled a very undignified expression of disgust. 'What nonsense!'

'Well, we shall have to think of something else then.'

'Better to stick as close to the truth as possible. Freddie came to visit us as we were so close—'

'Close? It's nearly ten miles!'

She glared at him, but continued, 'He didn't realise how long it would take, which is why we gave him a ride back in your carriage *and* because you were keen to converse with an old friend!'

'Hmm, I suppose it could work.'

'Of course it will!'

Again, a slow smile spread across his face, making her imagine him as a very large cat—or wolf—or some kind of predatory beast. 'Now, that I have shared so much personal information with you I wish to know something about you, Marina. Something that I am most curious about.'

Why did his smile make her nervous?

Her fingers crushed the skirt of her dress between her gloved fingertips. 'What do you wish to know?'

'Explain the history of this bad blood between your family and the Moorcrofts.'

Marina's fingers relaxed.

What question had she expected him to ask?

'Oh, they have always disliked us. Professional rivalry which has become more personal over the years. Silly, really. If you decide against using my father for your house, then that is your prerogative. My family would not hold it against you. Although I believe you would be a fool to not use my father, he is excellent and allows his work to speak for itself.'

Unlike Mr Moorcroft! she added silently.

'No. There is something else. I can't quite put my finger on it, but I can sense it…' he said with a sly narrowing of his eyes. 'Your brother seemed upset about putting your father in a difficult position, which I can understand, but then he mentioned you, too.'

Her stomach lurched and her gloved fingers dug into her leg until she felt the pinch of her nails through the muslin.

His expression gentled as he leaned forward. 'I told you some of my secrets—give me just a taste of yours.'

Why did everything he say sound like a seduction?

But strangely she wanted to tell him anyway, to remove the chains of Mr Richards and the Haxbys' soirée from around her throat. Speaking of it to another person might help her gain perspective. And he *had* told her about his own misfortunes. It seemed churlish to not do the same. She forced each finger to relax and took a deep breath.

'I…'

How could she even explain it?

His words were soft and coaxing, without condemnation or even teasing now. 'Just tell me.'

She took a deep breath and then the words poured out of her. 'I liked Priscilla's cousin and I thought he liked me back, but he never did. He thought I was ridiculous.' She winced at her clumsy explanation, but it was as if a dam had broken inside of her and she quickly rushed to explain herself, unable to meet his eyes. 'His name was Mr Richards, I met him at a dance at one of the assembly rooms. I didn't even realise he was related to the Moorcrofts until later on.' *At the soirée.* 'You don't want to hear the details!' she cried with a wave of her hand, suddenly losing confidence. She hadn't realised she had raised her voice until Betsy started to grumble in her sleep beside her.

'Go on,' Brook urged patiently.

Marina lowered her voice, and gently nudged Betsy back into a more comfortable position. 'It was nothing really,' she said with a shrug, but she still could not meet his eyes. 'We weren't even officially courting. A few empty compliments, one dance… Hardly a grand love affair. I wasn't entirely sure if I wanted him to court me, but—I was flattered. He asked me to come and play for a friend of his at a soirée.

'They were having an informal night of entertainments with performances from all the young ladies. That's when I realised Priscilla was related to him, because she and her mother were there, too. I played for him and his friends, I thought they liked me. As we were leaving, my mother remembered she'd left her reticule in the drawing room. I went back to retrieve it. I wasn't eavesdropping. They just didn't notice me come in until it was too late…' Her voice dried up. The moment when everyone realised and turned to stare at her would haunt her for the rest of her life. She had felt…worthless.

'They were talking about you…' Brook said, finishing her sentence for her. Their eyes met and the sympathy in his gave her the strength to continue.

'They were laughing about me. It seems Mr Richards was only interested in my fortune and that he found my music—not to his taste.' She took a deep cleansing breath.

'I am glad, in a way. I might have made a terrible mistake otherwise.'

'I agree,' he said kindly, 'but I can see why coming to stay with them at my mother's would have made you feel uncomfortable. I am sorry about that.'

Marina shrugged. 'It makes no difference really, they move in the same social circles as us. We could not avoid them forever, we just have to get on with it, I suppose.' A flash of irritation sparked within her and she immediately contradicted her words of peace and harmony, unable to help herself. 'But how they spoke about Freddie during dinner? That was uncalled for and *cruel*—and it's also not the first time they have said such things! Freddie may not be a genius or a sportsman like Herbert, but he is just as good as any Moorcroft. Better, even, because he is kind and good, and a wonderful painter. It was why we picked Knights Court in the first place—we were told they cared about the arts.'

Brook seemed to wince at her statement. 'In my experience Knights Court have only cared about the money in their coffers. But I am sure that will change under Edward's guardianship.'

'Perhaps I should encourage my parents to remove him?'

Again, Brook looked a little surprised by her words and he leaned forward. 'That would bring ridicule upon your father. To have a son publicly fail at such an elite school—your brother wasn't lying when he said that.'

Marina dismissed his words with an irritated wave of her hand. 'My parents would not care about that! Besides, we could think up an acceptable excuse. Maybe send him to be an apprentice with a famous painter...'

Brook leaned back as if considering her words with careful thought. 'I would still recommend waiting. The first year is the hardest and, for all its faults, Knights Court does help you decide one thing at least—what you want in life. I realised I could not be a scholar—I am a man of action…' He frowned, his words trailing off. She could well imagine what he was thinking.

'Is that why you are so adamant about going travelling alone—because you're no longer sure what you want in life?'

He laughed dismissively, the mask of humour trying to hide his uncertainty. 'I know what I want—the three Cs, of course!'

Marina stared at him, and then realised something that made her smile. Brook was as fearful and unsure as she was, which seemed so strange considering how handsome and privileged he was. She had far more in common with him than she might have thought. 'I don't believe you.'

His salacious smile dropped, but he didn't reply, and as their carriage rolled up to his mother's house he answered, 'I have heard travel changes a man, focuses him—perhaps it will do the same for me. At the moment, I feel as if I am lost at sea.'

Her heart ached for him, and she opened her mouth to try to offer some words of comfort, but it was too late. He got out of the carriage and offered her his hand to help her down. 'Don't feel too bad for me, Marina. I have faced things much worse and time alone has always helped me in the end…' She took his hand, the warmth of it permeating through her gloves.

She gently nudged Betsy with her foot as she got out, waking the maid, who with a start grabbed the picnic and Marina's discarded shawl. As she stepped out on to the gravel drive, another three more barouches pulled up behind them, the open tops allowing for everyone to see their untimely arrival.

'Where have you two been?' called Mr Moorcroft from his seat before the carriage had even stilled.

The Duke smiled good-naturedly. 'We had an unexpected, but very welcome visitor. Come inside and Marina can tell you all about it.'

Marina flinched at the overly familiar use of her name and her parents gave her an alarmed look of concern. She gave them a weak smile, hoping to reassure them, but she feared it only made them worry more. Brook turned to help Betsy out of the carriage, a kind gesture that caused the maid to blush furiously and give an awkward curtsy in thanks.

The others began to get out of their carriages and she'd not realised he was so close until he bent down to whisper in her ear, 'See, it could be worse— I could be Mr Moorcroft for a start.'

At that moment, Mr Moorcroft was clambering out of his carriage in an ungainly manner and refusing all help from her father.

'No,' she said under her breath. 'You could never be him.'

Mr Moorcroft slipped on the carriage step and was only saved by the quick reaction of his wife who yanked him upright by the arm. Without missing a heartbeat he began to grumble that the servant hadn't dropped the steps properly.

Marina caught the glint of amusement in Brook's eyes and they both had to sharply look away to stop from laughing.

Chapter Eight

Brook tried not to tap his foot with impatience as his mother poured the tea. Why she had chosen this moment to speak with him privately he had no idea. But she had been very firm with her offer.

Everyone else was busy preparing for the ball. He could hear the servants hurrying from room to room, doors clapping shut and then reopening moments later, hushed voices as creaky furniture was moved around. The activity wasn't limited to inside the house—carts were arriving constantly with food from his country estate. All manner of exotic and delicious fruits were delivered from the hothouses, as well as huge blocks of ice which would be cut up and shaved for the drinks or to make flavoured ices with. He cringed when he thought of the cost.

'I hope you have remained within your allowance,' he said mildly, accepting the cup she offered him.

Her hand paused for a moment and then stirred her tea gently. 'I am well aware of my *allowance*—there is no need to remind me of it.'

Brook said nothing—there was more than enough reason to remind her of it, but he was not so unfeeling as to point it out for a second time.

'Did you enjoy your little jaunt to Knights? It must have

been lovely to reacquaint yourself with an old friend,' she said cheerfully, a tender smile on her face as if she were the one reminiscing at that moment.

Did she really believe he had been happy there?

The idea seemed so strange to him, but then his letters had always been brief and he had never mentioned the hardships, knowing that his brother would have seen it as a weakness and would have reprimanded him for it. His mother had never written to him. Robert had said it was because she was too busy with her social engagements, of which there were many.

Brook had also suspected it was because she was happy, finally free from her husband and the burden of motherhood. What would have been the point in telling her the truth? There was nothing she could have done about it anyway and it was a case of out of sight, out of mind.

The first year he'd only been allowed back to Stonecroft Manor once, for Christmas, and that had been so miserable he'd wished he'd stayed at the boarding house. His mother had spent most of it locked away in her rooms, while his brother made awkward small talk and explained his mother was a little tired from her parties and needed to rest.

The following years, he had stayed every holiday at the boarding house, only occasionally visiting his mother when his brother agreed it well in advance, so that she could *make time* for him. Over the years those invitations had become less and less frequent, until he had felt almost like a stranger in her presence.

Maybe it was his recent visit to Knights Court, but he couldn't shake the memories of those painful years. When he looked at his mother now, a heavy resentment sat like a cannon ball in the pit of his stomach. It was unfair, he knew it was, but as a child he had always wondered why she hadn't once insisted he stay home. Why she suddenly no longer wished to play with him as she had before. Why she no longer cared...

'It was good to see my friend Edward. I have high hopes he will be a good headmaster there,' he replied, sipping from his cup and grimacing.

'Is the tea not to your liking?' she asked, a ghost of worry crossing her face.

'I don't take sugar any more.'

He hadn't since he was a child.

'Oh, I will make you another!' A servant hurried forward, but Brook waved him away.

'No need. I am not thirsty.' He set down the cup and saucer and his mother looked at it with a disappointed expression. 'What did you want to ask me?' He was beginning to suspect this whole farce was to needle something more from him.

She looked up at him, her jaw tightening slightly, before she said, 'It was rather reckless of you to take Miss Fletcher with you.' His mother did not seem concerned, he could practically see her salivating over the possibility of a scandal. Not because she particularly enjoyed gossip or the fall of her son's reputation—if such a thing were possible—but that such a connection with a young debutante might force him into wedded bliss.

'She was chaperoned.'

'True, but only by her brother—a child—and a young maid. It could still lead to gossip.'

Strange how his mother considered a thirteen-year-old boy to be a child only when it suited her, when she had considered him old enough at nine to live alone.

Again, the resentment was quickly followed by a large

gulp of guilt that soured his tongue. 'It was perfectly respectable as you well know! I have much to do—'

She sighed dramatically, as if she'd not even heard him.
'*Really*, Brook, I thought you better than to tease a young
woman like that! It sounds like something your brother
might have done! Trifle with widows all you like, but leave
the debutantes for men who are interested in making wives
out of them. Especially the poor plain ones who have little
choice as it is.'

Brook was sure that if he'd still been holding his teacup,
he would have cracked it, so fiercely did his fists clench at
his mother's words. 'Miss Fletcher is not plain.'

His anger quickly flipped to discomfort when he saw his
mother's mouth twist ever so slightly into a smirk—quickly
hidden by the raising of her cup. 'Is she not?' she asked in-
nocently before she took a sip.

Brook paused, unsure of whether he should admit the
truth. It could make things awkward for both himself and
Marina. Still, it irritated him to hear her described in such
a way. 'No, she is not as pretty as some of the other young
ladies here, perhaps. But I would not describe her as a *poor
plain one*.'

His mother smiled. 'True. She is *definitely* not poor and,
if you like her, then you have my approval, but you must
court her properly, take your time to get to know one another first. I want no scandal with such a wealthy family.
Already some of our guests are muttering about how odd
your little excursion was...'

'I am sure they are,' he said drily. 'But I am surprised
you are so open to me courting an untitled lady.'

'I mean, Miss Grace Clifton would have been the perfect match for you. But I will accept any woman as long as
you like her and she is decent. I must insist that you find

yourself a bride while you are young, I know from experience—a significant age difference between a couple only leads to a life full of difficulty. Forget this idea of gallivanting around the world, or at least delay it until you have secured a match. If you like Marina, then you should court her quickly and do not think you can delay until your return to England. No woman will wait forever, especially one that is decent *and* rich.'

'You forget, I am also rich and a duke as well.'

His mother glared at him petulantly. 'Yes, you are. Perhaps, if you marry into even more money, you will stop pestering me about mine!'

He raised a brow at his mother, who set down her cup with a clatter and then primly placed her hands in her lap.

'Forgive me, it has been difficult to change my habits, but I am trying.'

Brook nodded. 'I know.'

She had not gambled once since she'd confessed to her debts. The latest debt did indeed appear to be an old one and he had to concede she might genuinely have forgotten about it. It was a little harsh of him to still condemn her for it.

Her head lowered, her words so quiet, he had to lean forward to hear them. 'It was never a problem before. But then Robert died and I—' she stopped speaking, as if unable to find the right words to explain her complicated emotions '—couldn't control myself.'

He paused, considering her words. She had had zero freedom under his father's reign, then she had done as she was told under Robert's. Freedom, but still confined by another man's rules. Brook had been so busy sorting out the estate and arrangements he'd not realised how quickly and violently she had spiralled.

'I understand.' He did not wish to suffocate or control

her like the rest of the men in his family had. 'But you need to be responsible for yourself now. Which means you are in charge of your own finances, but you must exercise personal restraint. You may spend your money however you wish, but stick to the allowance—not for me, but for the good of the estate and the people who rely on us—and—no more lies.'

'Yes, darling. Of course,' she said demurely.

When she next raised her head, he could tell she had pushed the darkness of the past deep down inside of her. It had always been her way of coping. When things were difficult, she would wear a mask of forced joviality and push aside her problems quickly as if she were sweeping away dust with a new broom. Usually, she would declare she had invented a new game or story for them to act out, while covering her bruised face with a handmade mask.

Today I will be a sleepy cat. Meow! Come, let us curl up in blankets together!

Brook was awoken from his daydream by his mother's pondering voice, 'Why did her little brother come here anyway? It seems a little impulsive. Is he in his right mind? Mr Moorcroft mentioned something about him being a difficult child.'

Again, he had to bite back his anger. 'He ran away. It seems some of the boys—including Mr Moorcroft's son— have been very unkind to him,' answered Brook, adding firmly, 'Although I would rather that was not common knowledge—it could cause problems for his father and Freddie regretted his rashness immediately. We used the excuse of his family being close by as too much of a temptation for him not to try to see them.'

'Oh! How awful! School should be the best years of your life. That's what your father and brother always used to say.' His mother looked horrified and for the first time he wondered if his mother truly did not realise the effect sending him away had had on him.

'Not always,' he replied softly.

She opened her mouth, as if to ask him something, and he tensed, waiting for the moment when they would finally be open about the past. But instead, she smiled cheerfully and said, 'Then, if anyone asks me, I shall say the same. In fact, I will tell them all what a delightful boy you found him to be. You did find him delightful, didn't you?'

'I did.' He smiled, painfully reminded that he did love his mother, despite her flaws.

The shadows of his father and brother still silencing them even now.

'Don't you think it's a little…revealing?' asked Marina, her hands absently touching the very low décolletage of her ruby gown.

Her parents answered at the same time, her mother saying, 'No!' and her father mumbling, 'A little…'

Her father was overruled by her mother's slap to his arm. 'It is all the rage!' she declared, then gave Marina an encouraging nod. 'You'll be certain to turn a few heads.'

Marina ran her hand down the silk—she wasn't so sure, but for once she hoped she would. Brook's green eyes came to mind and she wondered if he had even once thought of her as a woman. Of course, he had teased and flirted with her, but they were the actions of a man who thought to gain something by flattering her. It was also, she suspected, his way, as much of a habit as biting your nails might be.

It was as if her mother had read her mind, because she approached her and gently started to check the pins of her hair. 'It was kind of the Duke to intervene on our behalf with Freddie's situation.'

'Yes, I am sure he will be better supported now that Reverend Peasbody is in charge of the situation.' Marina had had to reassure her parents several times that Freddie was well—her father had been all set to leave immediately to collect his son when he'd heard about him running away.

'Well, it's not long until the end of term, then we can speak with Freddie about whether he returns there in the autumn,' said her father thoughtfully, before he returned to his sketchpad. Drawings of random ideas lay sprawled across the bed linen; it seemed he'd been inspired by the visit to the pleasure gardens.

'You should put that away,' said Kitty. 'We will be going downstairs shortly.'

Nodding, Colin got off the bed and began to tidy up his papers. It was a habit of his to work wherever the mood took him and both mother and daughter were used to his ways. He'd designed Blacksmith's Bank while sitting in his wife's bedchamber waiting for her to give birth to Marina and that building had received outstanding praise from the Prince Regent.

'I have a couple of ideas, but I'm unsure if the current structure will allow it. I really must ask the Duke if I can visit Stonecroft Manor before giving him my ideas. I will have a much better idea then which route to go.'

Kitty smiled indulgently. 'I am sure he will allow it, if you ask. It is a shame he still hasn't decided who to use. But I'm relieved we won't have to suffer the announcement at tonight's ball. It would be awkward regardless of whom he chose in the end.'

Marina nodded in enthusiastic agreement and she wondered if Brook had realised how humiliating such a public reveal would be for both architects. She had lightly reprimanded him about it in the library, but hadn't realised he would take her criticism about the nature of the competition on board.

Her father nodded. 'Yes, that is a relief. The aristocracy have always danced to the beat of their own drum. But I wouldn't be surprised if he'd just moved it to the next house party the Duchess mentioned—we shall have to wait and see.'

'Your past work speaks for you. I am sure he will pick you in the end,' reassured Marina.

Kitty's eyes met hers in the dressing table mirror. 'Did he mention anything about it on your journey back from Knights Court?'

'No, he did not speak of it,' said Marina.

'Then what did you speak about?' asked Kitty in a curious tone.

Usually, Marina enjoyed sitting with her parents as they got ready for a ball—her mother was never ready on time. But now she regretted her habit, as rather than easing her nerves like it usually did, she was beginning to feel as if she had been put in the dock for questioning.

'Nothing much,' she lied and then, because the guilt was already gnawing on her bones, she sprinkled it with some truth. 'He told me about his childhood, how he'd found Knights Court. He said he struggled at first, too, like Freddie, but that he'd found his way in the end.'

'I see,' sighed her mother, looking a little disappointed. Picking up her rouge blush, she painted a light veil over Marina's lips. 'There, that's better, it brings out your complexion.'

'Thank you.' Marina smiled at her reflection. A secret part of her hoped the Duke would notice her tonight, not because she would make the perfect shield to protect his freedom, but because she was a woman, deserving of affection and love like any other.

Chapter Nine

Dinner was only a simple meal, as the men and women were already dressed in their finery for the ball later and there would be plenty of refreshments available throughout the night.

All hopes that the Duke would be impressed by her appearance were quickly dashed when she entered the drawing room. His back had been towards her when her family walked in and he'd barely looked at her since, giving her the curtest of greetings and barely even looking at her throughout the meal.

Perhaps he found her presence tiresome after spending so much time with her?

She tried not to take offence and instead found herself talking with Lord Clifton, an incredibly likeable man with dark blond curls, soft brown eyes and a quick broad smile that made him easily the friendliest face out of the entire company. He enjoyed music and had been to several of the same concerts she had been to, so they had a lot in common.

She missed Lord Clifton's easy conversation when the ladies all retired to the drawing room and left the men to drink their port. Possibly she had spent too much time avoiding Brook, because it had obviously been noticed by some of the ladies.

Mrs Moorcroft was the first to mention it. 'You seem as if you have a lot to say to Lord Clifton, Marina. What were you talking about for so long?'

'We spoke of music and the concerts we have been to.'

'Really...you seemed to be in quite the discussion!' Priscilla laughed, but there was a sharp jealousy in her eyes that made Marina tense.

'I wonder—has my home inspired you to write, Miss Fletcher? I heard you were writing music in the gardens this morning,' asked the Duchess with a bright and inquisitive smile.

There was a cry of delight in the corner from Sophia who was playing backgammon with her mother, Lady Redgrave. 'Oh! Would you play again for us, Miss Fletcher? I would love to hear your own compositions.'

'I am afraid I didn't write anything in the end,' explained Marina, shaking her head and praying they would not force the issue. She would have to explain falling asleep in the gardens, perhaps mention Brook finding her there. She grimaced at the thought.

'But we are relying on you for our entertainment!' cried Mrs Moorcroft with a smirk.

'Why don't you play some country dances, Marina? It will get us in the mood for the ball,' said her mother with a reassuring smile.

'Do you know any good ones?' asked Priscilla with a cool granite expression. 'Your repertoire so far has been only the big dramatic pieces. I dare say you fancy yourself to be the next Haydn or Beethoven. And you seem to have channelled their passion in your gown tonight. What a delightfully brave choice of colour.'

'I know plenty of folk songs,' replied Marina, trying not to let her irritation show and ignoring the barb thrown at her choice of dress. She tried to remind herself it was because Priscilla had made the mistake of wearing a similar pastel pink to Miss Redgrave and Miss Clifton and was probably jealous that she would not stand out as Marina did.

Still, was it perhaps a little too bright?

Was that the reason why the Duke refused to look at her? Was she gaudy in comparison to the prettier women?

Priscilla gave her a simpering smile of cruel pleasure before turning another page of her book thoughtfully. 'Although, be a little careful with your fingers. Last time I sang for you, you missed several beats.'

No, I did not. You missed your cue! she thought belligerently, but she wouldn't stoop to Priscilla's level by pointing it out. She went to the pianoforte and spent what felt like hours playing every folk song she could think of.

Eventually she stopped playing and returned to her seat, explaining as she did so, 'I should probably stop now. It won't be long until your guests start arriving.'

'Indeed!' The Duchess clapped cheerfully and took a large sip from her champagne flute before catching the eye of her servant so that she could refill it. 'It feels like an age since I threw a ball! I cannot wait for everyone to arrive.'

'How about a quick game of quadrille to pass the time?' asked Mrs Moorcroft.

A moment of hesitation passed across the Duchess's face, and Marina remembered that Brook had mentioned his mother having a gambling habit. But the Duchess's uncertainty was gone in the blink of an eye as she said, 'Yes, let's do that. But let's not take any real bets, as we may need to stop the game at any moment. I have many guests to welcome tonight. Who else will play with me and Mrs Moorcroft?'

'I'll play,' declared Marina's mother.

'One more, to complete our table?' asked the Duchess.

Miss Clifton rose from her seat. 'I'm a little rusty, but I will join you.'

The women quickly gathered at the card table, which meant that everyone was engaged in activity except for Marina and Priscilla who remained where they were seated on a *chaise* by the window, both pretending to read, while secretly cursing the Redgraves for claiming the only remaining card table.

Priscilla spoke so quietly that Marina doubted anyone not sitting as close as she was would be able to hear a word. 'Do you have hopes for Lord Clifton?'

'Hopes? What do you mean by hopes?' asked Marina, genuinely confused by such a question. Brook's face flashed across her mind.

He could have been mine.

She shook away the wicked thought as soon as it came to her.

Priscilla seemed to relax a little at her shocked expression, although her relief did not lessen the venom in her tone. 'Good, because you would not be a suitable match for him. The only reason you are here is because the Duke may decide to employ your father and I would not wish for you to embarrass yourself. He will have no *real* interest in you, after all.'

Marina stiffened—it was a brutal reminder of Mr Richards and the lack of genuine feelings he'd had towards her. Bitter anger poured through her and she snapped, 'Really? And you would know what interests Lord Clifton—or any other man for that matter?'

Oh, Lord! Why had she said that?

There was only one other bachelor in residence and it did not take a genius to make the connection.

Priscilla's head tilted towards her. Anyone looking at them from the other side of the room would imagine they were two young women gossiping cheerfully with one another. They would not see the vicious rage in Priscilla's expression unless they were, like Marina, facing her.

Marina could hardly believe Priscilla's change of tone, or the cruelty of the smile that swept across her face.

Priscilla whispered harshly, 'Do you honestly believe your little *trip* with the Duke this morning meant anything? You really are a simpleton, but then again, it wouldn't be the first time!'

Marina flinched. Priscilla's nasty laugh sounded like a badly tuned violin, piercing and offensive to her ears. Not wishing to dwell on the return of her brother in case that caused more problems for Frederick later, she instead rolled her eyes as if she were completely unbothered. 'I believe no such thing. What I *do* believe is that you have no reason to make any assumptions about anyone's feelings. Especially mine!'

Priscilla gave her a disgusted look. 'You do think highly of yourself! The Duke would never consider a little wallflower like you, no matter how much scarlet silk you wrap yourself in, or how much cheap rouge you plaster on to that plain face of yours! He will marry someone like Sophia or Grace!'

Just to deliberately infuriate Priscilla further, Marina smiled. 'Ah, I see, you have it all arranged in your head and you want Lord Clifton for yourself, I presume? That's why you are getting such a bee in your bonnet about me speaking with him. Have you asked the men for their opinion on the matter? I wonder what they would say about such plans?'

Priscilla scowled. 'I am sure they are well aware of the purpose of this visit.'

'Then why am *I* here? I know that I am an unlikely match for either gentleman, but I was also invited. So perhaps this isn't the matchmaking party you hoped for after all?' Marina chuckled, thinking of how Brook had spoken of travelling Europe and Lord Clifton had spoken to her about a new business venture with the theatres in town. Neither man seemed on the precipice of matrimonial bliss—no matter what their families hoped.

Priscilla's gaze sharpened, her canines flashing in the candlelight. 'I don't understand why you or your family are here either. Perhaps they took pity on you, like Mr Richards did?'

'Oh, look!' cried the Duchess loudly. 'The gentlemen are back. Let's put an end to this silly little game. We weren't betting anyway, so nothing's lost.'

The men entered the drawing room and Priscilla's cruel face was immediately masked with a sweet smile. She shone in the candlelight like a golden angel and Marina wanted nothing more than to tear out every strand of her golden hair.

Marina had never hated Priscilla until now. Actually, she had always felt a little sorry for her, what with her mother's constant comparison of them both and the way she scolded her, if Marina bettered her in anyway—which, to be fair, wasn't often.

Now, she felt no compassion. If they had been men, she would have demanded a duel to the death to win back her honour after so many insults. As it was, all she could do was remain politely silent as the men entered. For the first time since their journey back from Knights Court, she searched for Brook's eyes and was relieved to finally meet them.

'Once the ladies are done, would you care for a game of cards, *Brook*?' she asked sweetly, not caring at the silence that descended upon the entire room at her impertinence. She wanted to silence them, silence everybody who thought less of her and her family.

Brook was as shocked as the rest of the room by what he had heard. Even his mother and George, who were used to his unconventional ways, like insisting friends called him by his first name.

Did Marina think of him as a friend?

Why did that thought please him so much?

He had asked her more than once to call him by his Christian name, more to tease her than from any expectation that she would. But when she'd finally said his name, it had been in a deliberately provocative tone, her eyes filled with defiance and challenge. It had warmed Brook in a way no amount of port or cigars ever could.

Had something happened since dinner?

Marina had been all but ignoring him before, but now she seemed to have changed her attitude towards him—as if she now *welcomed* him, when they had tactfully ignored each other throughout dinner.

Although that was his fault. When she'd arrived downstairs for dinner, he'd been checking the clock on the mantelpiece, impatiently waiting for her arrival. He had hoped to try to flirt with her that evening, to subtly convince her that it would be worth her agreeing to his plans. But then he had seen her in the mirror's reflection and his plans had been shattered.

Marina looked breathtaking tonight. The bright scarlet of her gown had brought out the paleness of her complexion and the glossy shine of her ebony hair. What a fool might have called plain now seemed exotic and unusual, especially when surrounded by pale pastel flowers. She was an oil painting among a sea of water colours. Vibrant and rich.

And it had reminded him what an arrogant ass he had been in proposing such an offensive plan to her in the first place.

She was a young woman, in the prime of her life, and what did he want to do? Use her by offering her an engagement that would never bear fruit. That would, in fact, leave her alone for the rest of her life. She had said that was what she wanted, but was it? Surely another man would see what he saw in her, the beauty and strength of will that made her a formidable match for any man. She had been let down in the past, but that was only one idiot and someone else was bound to follow and sweep her off her feet as she deserved.

His stomach twisted as he remembered his mother's words of warning. *No woman will wait forever.* But he did not want her to wait for him! he reminded himself firmly.

He had no right to take the possibility of a happy marriage from her. Not only that, but he could no longer pretend to admire her, because he realised now that he did find her attractive in every way and it somehow seemed doubly ridiculous for him to pretend otherwise.

But now he had a dilemma. If she were keen to go ahead with his plan, should he put a stop to it now? In front of the very people who had embarrassed her in the past? It would humiliate her if he showed no interest now. Even worse, if he rebuked her for the informality—not that he ever would—it would be a social embarrassment that would haunt her for many years to come. She had trusted him, however blindly, to have her back in this situation and he could not fail her.

He smiled as if she had offered him the whole world on a golden platter. 'I would be delighted, Marina!'

His mother was casting him enquiring looks, but after seeing her at a card table he wasn't in the mood to grant her any explanation. Yes, she had quickly denied betting, but he wondered how different things would have been if he weren't here.

Well, if he truly were determined to leave, then he would have to trust her to behave.

Priscilla stood and elegantly brushed imaginary dust off her skirts. 'I would like to play and why don't you also join us, Sophia?'

Sophia looked a little helpless, but her mother quickly pushed aside the backgammon board with a smile and moved to sit in one of the armchairs. 'Go ahead, my dear.'

'I…I am not very good at card games.'

'I will help you,' reassured Lord Clifton.

They gathered around the table, the men helping the ladies to their seats, then Marina deftly shuffled the pack. 'What game shall we play? I know you are a bit of an expert when it comes to cards.' She looked pointedly at Brook.

Considering the levels of expertise around the table, he said, 'A game of chance, perhaps?'

'I know hazard…' offered Sophia with a blush.

'Hazard it is!' declared Marina. 'Do we have any dice?'

'Of course!' Brook stood and got a pair of dice from the games cupboard, before returning to his seat.

Lord Clifton gave Marina and Sophia a mischievous wink. 'We should still place wagers, though? Don't you think? Keep it exciting.'

Brook half expected Marina to argue it, but to his surprise she was the first to agree.

'Keep it within reason, though,' warned Brook and George gave him a quick nod of agreement—and a slight wince at his thoughtlessness. George knew of his struggles with his mother, but Brook was sure he had only meant to tease Sophia with his words.

* * *

Some time later, only he and Marina remained playing. Lord Clifton and Sophia had given up on the game and had gone to watch the others.

Brook didn't care. he was fixed to the table, unable to leave because Marina sat in front of him, and he could tell something had changed. Not only on the outside with her vibrant gown, but something within had shifted, too. When she looked at him, there was a hint of anticipation in her gaze as if she were waiting for him to do something important. Unfortunately, he had no idea what, as she had repeatedly told him that she was not interested in his devious schemes.

He focused on the game. They were evenly matched, the notes of their current winnings sitting beside them. They'd only played in shillings, so it was less than a few guineas between them.

'We will be playing all night, if one of us does not forfeit soon,' said Brook and, although everyone had left to pursue other entertainments, he could not bear to concede defeat. It was not in his nature and neither was it in Marina's by the determined look in her eye.

'Then you should forfeit,' she declared, picking up the dice.

A cheer rang out from the other card table and everyone gathered around it to laugh and see what was happening.

Brook took the opportunity while everyone was distracted to lean forward towards her. 'What if we go all in on the next roll of the dice? Even and you win, odd and I win.'

'That's not the game,' she said, but her eyes caught the candlelight and there was a flicker of interest within. It seemed the prim and sensible Marina, was a risk taker at heart. Although he knew that already, every interaction he'd had with her had proven it. In the library, in the garden, in the carriage and even when she played her music. She was a woman not averse to excitement or conflict, but rather than seeking it for her own pleasure, she sought it to help others.

'But I will need to leave to start welcoming guests soon and will have to forfeit the game, unless we end it quickly.' He paused, before whispering, 'What do you want?' She flinched at his directness, and he added, 'Do not deny it, you called me by name, you flirted with me throughout this game. Surely you haven't changed your mind about my disagreeable offer? Remember, I swore I would not make such an offer again.'

Had he sworn it?

He wasn't entirely sure what he had done and for some reason his heart beat furiously at the idea that she might accept him.

Which was ridiculous!

Why should he care if a self-proclaimed wallflower had changed her mind about him? But it did matter, because he wanted nothing more than for her to be his. It was a strangely possessive thought and he found himself imagining how their previous interactions might have been different if they were already engaged. She would walk beside him, her arm tucked into his elbow, they could have lain on the wet grass side by side, she could have pressed against him and kissed him back in the darkened library.

Marina picked up the dice and rolled them in the palm of her hand thoughtfully, her eyes straying to Priscilla who was commanding the conversation of a large group of young women by the doorway to the garden. Their eyes occasionally strayed to where he and Marina sat, curiosity, disbelief and disgust written all over the faces.

Marina's voice brought his attention back to her. 'Maybe I have decided it is not so disagreeable after all…'

The air felt tight in his lungs and he stared at her nimble fingers with expectation. 'If you win, I shall make you my offer for a second time…'

He had never wanted to lose anything in his life, but he did now.

She rolled the dice and it landed on a two. Her eyes met his, as bright as a starlit sky, and his fist clenched beneath the table, unwilling to show her how much he wanted her to win.

A hesitant smile teased the corner of her lips. 'I accept your offer. A long engagement it is.'

Chapter Ten

'The guests have started to arrive! Brook, we need to go and greet them!' called his mother, hurrying from the room. But Brook didn't move. He continued staring at her, his green eyes sharp as emeralds, as if he were trying to cut through and see into the heart of her.

The room began to buzz with activity, Priscilla with her flock of chattering hens only a few feet away, but they all fell away as Brook's smile widened. She had taken a huge step into the unknown and he was there waiting for her, the risk and fears forgotten as exhilaration flooded her veins like the finest and most intoxicating champagne.

He picked up the dice, playing with them lightly as he tossed them from hand to hand. 'Are there any rules?'

'Rules?' she asked, confused by the question.

'Anything you do or don't want to happen?' The question was asked mildly, but his long fingers had captured her attention and she swallowed deeply as she saw the dice fall helplessly, only to be caught moments later by Brook's quick hands.

Why did she feel as helpless as those dice, when he had been the one to capitulate to her demands? He had said he would not ask her again, but he had, and he had lost his word on the fall of fate. In contrast she had won—*him*.

'I don't know what you mean,' she answered, her voice surprisingly husky and faint.

His head tilted. 'What do you want? Ultimately.'

'To be free to be myself, with no judgement or ridicule. To *live*, for myself and for my music,' she said immediately and he reached across. Heat slid over her gloved hand and she wondered what it would feel like to touch his bare skin. They stood and he led her from the room. Priscilla and the women gathered around her stopped speaking, their eyes following them so closely she could feel their piercing gaze like a hundred needles pricked into her back.

Marina knew it was petty, she knew her triumph and pleasure were unfounded, but it felt glorious. To be the centre of attention, to be envied and special for once. She knew she was talented with her music, but she also knew how strange people found her interests and passions. No one could call her odd or dull now, she had the finest bachelor on her arm, and when she glanced up at him, she saw that he was walking proudly with her, as if she really were a diamond of the Season.

The entrance was filling with guests, carriages rolling up outside, as more and more people poured in from the dark.

Marina yelped as Brook turned abruptly and guided her towards the champagne stand.

He spoke quietly to her as he handed her a glass, the painted eyes of his ancestors and important figures peering down at them from above and all sides. 'To our engagement,' he said quietly, clinking her glass with one he'd picked up.

Then, without waiting for her, he knocked it back and set it down on the table, a servant whisking it away immediately. 'I have some rules.'

She took a step back startled, and almost tripped on her dress. 'Oh…go ahead.'

Cringing at her awkwardness. Would he ask her not to call him by his Christian name? She was still slightly mortified she'd done that. It could have completely ruined her if he'd been openly offended by it. But maybe there was a side of her that liked to gamble? Tonight, certainly proved as much.

Reaching out he gently cupped her elbow drawing her close. 'Always call me Brook, and never—even when this is over—*never* sell yourself so cheaply ever again. You deserve better.'

She stared up at him, feeling as if she were floating on a cloud.

'I need to go welcome guests. Wait for me here.'

She nodded dumbly and he swung away from her, his broad shoulders making their way through the incoming crowd, which greeted him with delighted smiles.

The greetings of guests seemed to take forever, as more and more fashionable people poured into the house. Music began to play and, when Marina had finished her third glass of champagne, she felt a little dizzy and decided it should probably be her last.

She said hello to a couple of acquaintances, but the majority of the high society guests washed past her without a glance.

Marina yelped again when Brook returned to her side, from a completely different direction to the one she had expected.

'I am sorry that took so long. I hadn't realised my mother had invited quite so many people!' he said with a momentary frown, before his expression brightened and he offered her his arm. 'Shall we?'

They entered the ballroom and Marina gasped with wonder at the grand scale of the room. Golden chandeliers glittered overhead, a celestial scene was painted on the ceiling with cherubs and angels looking down on them from above as if they were in heaven itself. It reminded her of the one in the dining room, but on a more ambitious scale.

A rush of silence rippled through the room as everyone turned to stare at their entrance. Then, whispers began to flurry around them like a snowstorm.

'Who is she?'

'Fletcher?'

'The architect's daughter?'

'What is she doing with the Duke?'

Brook walked her into the room and people stared at them as they passed.

'Do you know how to waltz?' he asked and her throat tightened considerably.

'Yes… I mean… Well, I've played it, but I've never danced it. I know how to do it in theory.' She was babbling now, but she wasn't sure how to stop herself. 'It's a little scandalous though, isn't it?'

He leaned in towards her. 'Is there a better way to announce our courtship? And do not worry about the steps, they are easy—with your musician's ear you will pick it up in no time.'

As the previous song came to an end, Brook quickly left her to make his request. People were staring at her, she noticed with a tremor of fear, they were staring at her as if she were a drop of blood on a bed sheet—shocking and unwelcome.

Marina had no title, was not beautiful, yet the Duke was paying attention to *her*, while other aristocratic ladies stood alone and without a dancing partner. She could feel their animosity cut through her like a knife.

But when Brook returned to her with a beaming smile,

all awkwardness vanished from her mind and she was swept up into his strong embrace.

Brook was right, she picked up the beat and movement quickly, and being twirled and spun around the room by Brook felt as natural as playing one of her favourite pieces. Allowing herself to be swept up into the music, she forgot everything around her.

It was easy, because Brook was an exceptional dancer. Despite his size, he led her around the polished floor with such comfortable elegance that she felt as if she were being twirled around the room on a cloud. If she threw back her arms, she would feel as if she were flying.

Thankfully, she was too busy following his steps to embarrass herself so openly. But she indulged herself by closing her eyes, sighing with pleasure as she was spun around the room and imagined that they were alone together. No eyes watching and judging them, only themselves moving freely, the only anchor the weight of each other's arms.

'You should smile,' he teased, 'otherwise you don't look as if you are enjoying it.'

Her eyes flicked open to stare up into his handsome face, committing him to memory as if he were a score of notes.

'I can't…' she whispered.

'Why not?'

'Because I want this to last forever and I know it won't.'

His fingers flexed against the silk of her dress, tightening on her waist, and crushing the silk beneath. He leaned close, his breath making the curls beside her ear tremble. 'This won't be the last time. I swear it.'

She giggled, she couldn't help herself. 'You always make your promises with such conviction. You swore you would not offer yourself again, yet you did. How can I ever trust you?' she teased, gasping and then sighing with pleasure as he made a sharp turn and then dipped her low with confident ease.

'You can't,' he murmured huskily with a sinful smile. 'But I promise, if you do, you'll never regret it.'

Delicious joy rose up like a golden bubble and she could feel a broad smile bloom across her face. Brook's eyes lowered, focusing hungrily on her mouth as he whispered, 'I love your smile.'

The music came to an end, the final notes vibrating through Marina and leaving her breathless. She clung to his thick biceps for a little longer than was probably decent and stepped away from him with what she imagined was a deep blush staining her cheeks.

'Let's get you something to drink,' he said and walked over to the champagnes and punch bowl.

Despite her earlier resolution, she gladly drank the flute of champagne he offered, mumbling to herself, 'Well, in for a penny, in for a pound, as they say.' As she knocked back the flute, Brook smiled curiously at her comment, but then raised his own in toast.

'Indeed, no more half-measures! From now on, we are in this—together.'

She choked a little on her champagne, but nodded in agreement.

A man came over and Brook introduced them, although he didn't seem happy about it, and she forgot his name as soon as it was spoken, because she was so overwhelmed by the occasion and by Brook's lingering gaze.

Why did he not stop looking at her?

Was it all part of his performance, was this what men did when they were falling in love? Marina couldn't decide, but she knew she liked it. It made her feel as if she were the centre of his world and it felt wonderful—even if it were a lie.

Enjoy it. Maybe he does want you and maybe you'll let him have you, whispered an inner voice seductively, and she tried to hide the delicious shiver that ran down her spine at the thought.

The man must have asked her something, because he was staring at her expectantly. In a panic she tried to remember what they had been talking about, but found herself stumbling over her words like a village idiot.

Thankfully, Brook interjected on her behalf, 'She has already agreed to dance the next one with me.'

Good God! Had this man asked her to dance?

The man looked a little shocked and the significance slowly dawned on her. If the waltz wasn't scandalous enough, dancing twice within quick succession with the same partner was unheard of. Social etiquette dictated that only engaged—or as good as engaged—couples danced more than one song together, at least without having a break between partners.

To be fair, it wasn't something that had ever been a problem for her in the past. She had gone to the assembly halls regularly enough, but she'd never had a full dance card like some of the prettier girls, so it had never been an issue.

Should she dance with someone else? Maybe she should ask her father—except, she didn't want to dance with anyone other than Brook. He had spoiled her for all other men.

'Perhaps later then?' asked the man persistently.

Again, she gasped for words as if she were a fish out of water and found Brook replying frostily for her.

'I doubt it, but you can always try your luck.'

The man gave a dignified bow despite his rude rejection and stiffly walked away.

'Sorry…who was that?' she asked. 'I wasn't paying attention.'

'Baron Hampstead. I knew him from school,' he said coldly.

Suddenly his rude behaviour made sense. 'I presume he wasn't one of the nice ones—like Edward?'

'No,' Brook said with a disgusted snort. 'If my brother hadn't died, I doubt that man would even acknowledge me in the street.'

Marina sighed, realising that as a second son, the young Brook would not have had the same respect as he held now. Especially as his brother was already a fully grown man when Brook had been born. A spare heir was only important through the difficult years of the firstborn's childhood when sadly the likelihood of an untimely death was high. Once the heir was an adult, the spare had no choice but to find a profession in the military or church to occupy him for the rest of his life.

Brook took the glass from her and put it on a passing servant's empty tray. 'Come, let's dance.'

They danced a cotillion this time and Marina could clearly see the curious faces now that she wasn't twirling around the room. It made her feel a strange mixture of pride and fear. Pride because her mother and father were now being spoken to by every aristocrat there and fear because she worried that it might all come crashing down around her head if their deceit were ever discovered.

Afterwards they joined her parents and Brook spoke pleasantly with them for some time before he left to join Lord Clifton in the billiards room. Brook did not ask any other woman to dance that night and it was noted by everyone there.

As she drank champagne and tried to temper her racing

heart, her mother pulled her aside and whispered, 'What is happening between you and the Duke?'

Marina didn't want to lie to her mother, so she skirted the question as best she could. 'I honestly don't know. It appears that His Grace wishes…to court me.'

'That's wonderful!' declared Kitty brightly, never a moment of doubt on her face when it came to her children. It only made Marina feel worse for lying.

Her father, who had been listening to their conversation, nodded gravely before warning, 'Be careful, my dear. Men with that much power rarely follow their hearts.'

Kitty scowled up at her father as if he had done something unforgivable from a great height. 'Really? Well, thank you for that great pearl of wisdom, Husband. We shall be sure to make a note of that incredibly unhelpful opinion. Perhaps you should clarify the Duke's intentions yourself and save us from having to guess?'

Colin sighed, looking worried. He took a deep sip of his drink before answering, 'There is no *harm* in being cautious.'

'I'll do you some *harm*, if you keep talking like that!' mumbled her mother ungraciously, and after a moment the three of them caught each other's eyes and laughed at the absurdity of it all.

Marina didn't see the Duke again after their dancing. She ended up dancing with quite a few gentlemen that night, far more than she would have normally. It was fun, but after a couple of hours she felt a little light-headed from the constant small talk and champagne-fuelled dancing. She was exhausted, but the rest of the revellers appeared to show no sign of winding down.

Her mother and father were somewhere, but she had lost

them at some point during the many dances. She wasn't overly worried, though, and checked for them in the drawing room before deciding to retire for the night. Lord and Lady Redgrave were there, so she said, 'If you see my parents, will you be kind enough to inform them that I have gone to bed?' and Lady Redgrave gave her an amiable smile and agreed to do just that.

She went out into the hallway and spotted Priscilla blocking the stairway with a group of her friends. She couldn't face them, they would only spoil what so far had been a wonderful evening. So, she slipped into the library instead. From her tour of the house and walk in the gardens, she knew she could go through the library to reach the side veranda and sneak up the servants' stairs to the second floor where her bedroom was situated. Last time she'd done it during the day the key had been left in the lock. She hoped it would be again.

The library was dark and empty, but she knew it well enough to get to the veranda doors. She slipped behind the heavy brocade curtain and out of the doors and as she had hoped the key was in the lock, but she didn't even need to use it as the door was slightly ajar. Maybe someone had used it earlier? It made for an easy shortcut.

Rain was pouring down, which was no surprise as the summer this year had been uncommonly poor. But the covered walkway allowed people to enjoy the fragrant garden and fresh night air without getting wet. She could see the glow of the ballroom from the back of the house, hear the music and chatter, but thankfully no one was on this side of the house or walking down the veranda.

Some of the windows in the rooms above were brightly lit with oil lamps, illuminating the landscaped gardens below, but she doubted anyone could see her here unless they leaned precariously out of their windows.

Beautiful fragrance permeated the air from the damp climbing roses that trailed along the iron railings. She took a deep and steadying breath, enjoying the fresh clean air before slipping off her silk gloves, laying them over the railings and reaching out a hand to touch the rain. The cool water dripping down her fingers like ribbons of moonlight.

'Hello, Marina,' said a familiarly deep voice from behind her and she spun on her heel, the gloves falling to the ground.

Brook was sitting on a bench just behind the open door of the library. He had a glass of whisky in his hand and was casually swirling the amber liquid thoughtfully.

'Oh! Sorry!' she cried, her heart still racing, but this time due to the sight of him languidly sprawled on his bench. How on earth had she missed him?

With an amused chuckle as warm and as rich as the whisky he knocked back with one gulp, he put down the glass on the bench and stood. A slow, languid unfolding that seemed to make him seem impossibly large in this narrow window of space.

'Would you like a drink?'

She shook her head. 'No, I think I have had too much already. I was going to bed.'

'A wise choice,' replied Brook, coming to stand beside her. He leaned against the stone column, his hand sliding absently along the black railing as he watched her. For some reason she did not move, it was as if they were both waiting for something. 'It's another beautiful night,' he said drily, his gaze eventually moving out towards the garden and the heavy downpour still falling.

She should say goodnight and leave as quickly and as

quietly as she had arrived. It was indecent to be alone with a bachelor, but even though she knew this, she could not order her feet to walk away. Brook seemed sad and she did not want to leave him alone.

'Are you well?' she asked softly, gripping the cold railing behind her to help steady her nerves.

He smiled, but it did not reach his eyes. 'A little drunk, but otherwise I am perfectly fine.' He reached out to touch the rain as she had done, letting it fall and drip down his hand to wet his sleeve. He had taken off his jacket, waistcoat and cravat, as if he did not plan to return to the ball—it amused her, that at every opportunity Brook seemed to strip off his clothes like a child who could not stand the itch of starched fabric.

'Both our names mean water,' Brook said thoughtfully, dropping his hand to rest it on the railing next to hers. She could have sworn she felt the heat of it, despite the inch of space between them.

'Yes, I never thought of that. Except, a marina is always still, a port in a storm, while a brook is always moving...'

What an idiotic thing to say!

To her surprise, he suddenly dipped down to kneel in front of her. She gasped at the unexpected movement, but quickly realised he was only picking up her fallen gloves from the floor, before rising once again.

'Thank you,' she said, but he had made no move to hand them back to her. Instead, he stroked them softly as if he were smoothing away invisible dust and grime. Butterflies began to flip and twirl in her stomach, as she watched his long fingers caress them.

'I happened to speak with your father earlier.'

'Oh, you did?' She waited for him to say something more, but he didn't, and she found herself filling the void between them. 'Oh, do ignore him, he's just a little worried about your intentions towards me and being overly cautious—'

'Yes,' replied Brook, his eyes rising from the silk to look at her face. 'He said something similar. I have to say, I felt like a bastard afterwards.'

Marina flinched. 'Why? I hope my father wasn't rude. If he was, it is only because he worries about me.'

Brook nodded. 'Your father is a good man. He offered to step away from the competition—for redesigning Stonecroft. He didn't want to cause any conflict of interest between us.'

'What?' cried Marina, outraged that her father would make such a stupid business decision. 'Please tell me you didn't let him!'

Brook laughed. 'Don't worry, I convinced him that whatever intentions I have towards you are separate to any business arrangements.'

'For goodness' sake!' hissed Marina, causing another chuckle from Brook.

'Don't be angry at your father. He was quite…sweet. He wants only the best for you and he was worried after seeing us dance together.'

'Why? How would courting me—?'

'He thought I might want his designs at a reduced cost.'

Pain lanced through Marina like a knife, stealing the breath from her lungs. She managed only a rough 'oh' before she had to fight back her tears. Even her own father thought it impossible that Brook would be interested in her. She could understand the likes of Priscilla and Mr Richards, but her father?

Brook reached out to grip her arm. 'I wouldn't do that to you and it made me realise that we should take it more slowly, if it is to be—believable.' He ran a hand roughly through his hair, a guilty expression on his face, although whether it was for her father or for her she couldn't be sure.

'What did you tell him?' she asked, finally beginning to win back some control over her emotions and think more clearly.

'I told him I admired how witty you were at dinner, was touched by how gentle and kind you were with your brother. How impressed I am by your intelligence and artistic talent. I told him that I thought you looked radiant tonight—which you do—and I told him that *none* of my behaviour towards you has anything to do with the redesign of my house, which is also true. You believe me, don't you?'

When he was finished, he appeared breathless, his chest rising and falling with each laboured breath as if the admission had wrung something from him.

'Yes, our pretend engagement is to benefit us and only us. You want to leave without worrying your mother and I want to focus on my music without the distraction and humiliation of the marriage market.' Marina gave him a weak smile. 'Thank you for what you said to my father—that was very kind of you.'

Her eyes burned and she tried to turn away, but his grip tightened and he pulled her close, his chest pressing against hers.

'But…it's all true!' he declared huskily, his breathing heavy with repressed emotion. He reached out to cup her face before his mouth crushed against hers in a searing kiss.

She had never been kissed before and gasped at the unexpected touch of his lips against hers. He pressed closer, his grip tightening and gathering around her to pull her even deeper into his embrace. His tongue licked forward, ever so gently, to taste between her lips, his body pressing forward a little harder, pushing her backwards until her back lightly thumped against the opposite pillar behind her.

'You deserve to be loved,' he murmured, trailing kisses down her burning cheek and neck. 'Thoroughly and without apology.'

Somehow her hands found their way to press against his chest, but it wasn't to push him away. Instead, they clung to his shirt, her fingers grasping the fabric and bunching it between her fingers, wanting more of him.

He cupped her face, tilting her up to look him in the eyes. The rain still poured beside them, coating the world in liquid silver and the heavy perfume of roses. 'You should know pleasure, even if you never wish to marry.'

His mouth descended and this time she opened for him willingly, wanting nothing more than to feel his warmth. He tasted of oak-aged whisky and delightful sin and she wanted nothing more than to drown in his essence.

His hands roamed down past her waist. Gripping her hips, he pushed against her until she felt the hard ridge of his desire. Marina might never have been kissed, but she had seen plenty of classical art to know what lay between a man's legs and guess its purpose.

But experiencing something first hand was completely different and Marina wasn't sure whether to be frightened or aroused by it. Either way, she didn't have time to consider it for long. His tongue stroked hers as his kiss deepened, then he was lifting one of her legs and pushing her scarlet skirt up to grip her ribbon-tied garters and bare thigh, angling himself against her pelvis so that she rubbed intimately against the front of his breeches.

It felt wonderful, soothing an ache inside her she hadn't realised was there. She moaned against his tongue as he rocked against her, his palm smoothing up the back of her thigh to cup her bare bottom, angling her body even closer to his. Her fingers were gripping the back of his shirt, the nails digging into the linen, as her hips rode him with increasing desperation. Their breath mingled, as their mouths remained in a locked embrace their bodies were desperate to mimic.

She stumbled, trying to balance on one leg, and he gathered them both around his waist, pressing her hard against the stone column. She broke from the kiss and whimpered into his neck as her body tightened. He only had to rub against her a little longer, a few more strokes and—

There was a loud bang from inside the library, followed by giggling and whispering. They both froze, their heads snapping to the open door only a few feet away. Marina let out a choked sigh of relief when she realised no one was there—yet.

Brook slowly set her down on the patio and stepped away from her, shielding her body in case someone came through the veranda doors. Thankfully, no one did and Marina hastily dropped her skirts, brushing down the fabric as quietly as she could and looking for her silk slipper that had fallen from one of her feet during their passionate kiss.

It was more than a kiss, Marina thought with a pinch of embarrassment, *they'd practically been fornicating!*

Brook moved towards the doorway, and gently closed the door, but not before she heard more thuds, grunts and movement beyond. It sounded as if someone were casting aside books and hastily tugging off clothing. There was hushed urgent whispering, followed by a feminine giggle. It seemed they were not the only couple to become intimately acquainted with one another tonight.

What would have happened if they hadn't been interrupted?

Her body still ached with longing and she suspected she would have allowed Brook to do anything to ease it—including ruin her! She glanced around at the shadows of the garden. Anyone could be watching them from the darkness...

Horrified by her own wanton behaviour, she ran as quickly as her feet could carry her down the stone veranda to the servants' entrance and then up the stairs. She did not look back or say anything to Brook for fear of being discovered by the two lovers in the library.

When she finally reached the safety of her room she sank against the door with a sigh of relief. Breathless, her body still ached with unfulfilled pleasure and she wondered if she would ever come down from the tightly wound tension that held her body captive.

Hitching up her skirts, she reached between her legs to feel the dampness there. She moaned as her fingers brushed against the spot that Brook's hips had rocked against, He had wrung such unexpected and passionate responses from her body that she could still feel the needy ache from moments before.

Closing her eyes, she remembered the feel of his hardness rubbing against her, the muscles of his shoulders flexing beneath her nails. She stroked herself for a second time and then, as if burned, she flipped her skirts back over her knees, mortified by her wicked thoughts, and dropped her head into her hands.

What had she done?

There were some mysteries in life she really shouldn't explore. Especially not with Brook Wyndham, the Duke of Framlingham.

Chapter Eleven

Marina's mother came into her room as she was getting ready for breakfast. Her mother was fully dressed, but looked a little pale and had dark smudges beneath her eyes.

'Good morning, darling,' she said weakly, flopping down on the bedspread with a dull thud. It was actually well past noon, but nobody cared after a ball—especially one that had gone on as late as last night's.

Marina was being laced up by Betsy, so the best she could do was to look at her mother through the mirror. 'Did you not sleep well?'

Her mother fanned herself with her hand. 'Good God, no! Did you? Honestly, the Duchess and His Grace certainly know how to throw a party, but I think I am a little out of practice! I think there were still people playing cards and dancing well after dawn. You were wise to go to bed when you did! I am exhausted, and more than a little…*jaded*.' Kitty looked a little green as she said the last word and Marina tried her best not to laugh at her mother's expense.

'Did you get a little merry, Mother?' she asked with a knowing smile.

'*Merry?* I marched right past *merry* and ended up truly *sozzled*!' exclaimed her mother grimly, covering her eyes with a damp cloth. Marina giggled and her mother raised the corner of her compress just enough to give her a mischievous wink.

'Oh, dear. Poor you, Mama!'

'Save your pity for your father, he is faring much worse—too much *water of life*, I believe—wicked stuff!'

'It's not like Father to drink whisky,' Marina mused thoughtfully, then remembered how Brook had been drinking it when they'd met last night on the veranda. She winced.

'Blame His Grace—apparently they were drinking it as they chatted over business. We just can't keep up with the young ones like we used to,' said her mother with a resigned sigh, the cloth firmly back over her eyes.

Marina said nothing. She could well imagine the difficult conversation that had caused her father to drink more than he would normally. Brook had told her as much. Her father had feared she was being used by him and, because her father loved her, he had offered to step away from the competition rather than have his daughter disappointed in the long run.

'I told him that I thought you looked radiant tonight—which you do—and I told him that none *of my behaviour towards you has anything to do with the redesign of my house, which is also true. You believe me, don't you?'*

Did she believe him?

Marina had been surprised and flattered by Brook's words and, although her father's reaction had hurt her feelings, she could not deny that Brook had always been honest with her and he had seemed genuinely enthralled by her last night. His kisses had been filled with a passion and longing she had never expected to feel, let alone be the recipient of. She had lain awake most of the night, feeling restless and aching to feel the touch of him once more.

But was that enough? It hadn't been a declaration of love.

Far from it, she had listed their agreement right before. She had clearly said what they both wanted from the arrangement and there had been no mention of true love or a happy marriage.

A pretend engagement that would benefit them both. What had happened after was—a mistake—on both their parts. They had allowed too much alcohol and emotion to get the better of them.

Thankfully, she'd had more sense than to lose all of her wits and let a man take advantage of her so thoroughly.

Did you? whispered the little devil inside of her. *Because if those mystery lovers hadn't entered the library, you might now already be ruined!*

The little devil spoke no lies and Marina sat down with a heavy thump at her dressing table while Betsy put her hair up into her usual chignon.

'Would you mind terribly?' asked her mother, removing the cloth once again, and propping herself up with pillows to see her better.

'Sorry, what did you say?'

'If we left now? I know we are meant to stay until after dinner. But honestly, I am desperate for my own bed and home comforts! I said my goodbyes to the Duchess last night and she confessed she probably won't be up until much later today, so she does not mind at all.

'In fact, she even offered us one of her carriages for the ride home! Isn't that kind of her? And, how handsome is the Duke? I bet you had a wonderful time dancing with him and twice no less! You looked absolutely *devine* waltzing with him, like a princess! I was so proud. Do you think he really will court you?'

'Who knows...?' Marina gave a wan smile to her mother through the mirror. Despite their private agreement, she was beginning to wonder if their engagement would actually happen. Perhaps it would be for the best if it didn't. At her mother's expectant expression, she added truthfully, 'It was magical to dance with him—and very kind of him to ask.'

She imagined a lot of people would dismiss it as that. Not a declaration, but a *kindness* shown to the daughter of a potential business associate. 'And, of course, I don't mind leaving now. I am eager to get home, too.'

Yes, let's go home and forget last night ever happened!

She could not face the Duke again so soon. If luck was on her side, she would not see him at all. Surely, he would remember his actions last night and be thoroughly ashamed of himself. The more she considered it, the more she doubted he would continue with their plan. He was probably embarrassed, and wondering what had possessed him to kiss her like that.

Brook rode his horse to the village and back. He needed to clear his head and leave his mother's house, which was still a battlefield of mess and nonsense. A couple of guests were still slumped over the card tables, their glasses in hand even as they snored. The stale smell of alcohol and sweat lingered in the air, despite the servants busy as bees trying to clean the mess and air the rooms.

Claret, cards and carnal pleasures!

That's what he'd told Marina he would fill his days with. Nothing seemed more pitiful to him now, or untrue.

He couldn't stand it, the waste and decadence. He longed for fresh horizons and meaningful experiences. He would not find it here, but then, could he trust his mother in his absence? Duty was like a tether around his neck, the dukedom had a stranglehold over him, from which there was no escape.

Although his mother's partying lifestyle disgusted him, he had to admit there was one aspect of last night's indulgence that had not been unwelcome.

Kissing Marina. He should never have done it, of course, but he could not regret his actions. She had melted against him, clung to him and responded eagerly to his touch. He had felt alive with her, accepted. Her excitement and pleasure had been like an aphrodisiac to him, pushing him to demand more from her with each heady moment that passed. If she wished it, he would gladly have pleasured her in every sensual way he knew and would have even hoped for more. He knew it would be good between them, hot and exciting—at least, it would be when she eventually accepted the eager responses of her body without embarrassment or shame.

He, for one, would never forget or regret what had happened between them. But he suspected by her hasty escape that she had felt differently and he would need to take his time to reassure and smooth things over with her. Explain to her that it could be a happy addition to their engagement if she wished and would definitely not affect their plans either way.

It could not affect their plans, he reminded himself. Indulging in mutual pleasure was one thing, but they both had to want the same thing. He just wasn't entirely sure what he wanted any more…

As he rode up the drive of his mother's house, he saw that one of his mother's carriages was already being boarded by Marina and her family, their luggage tightly strapped to the back. They were leaving early.

Brook urged his horse into a gallop, his heart matching the beat of his horse's hooves as he charged forward. As he drew close, he yanked on the reins to halt his horse and gravel sprayed a couple of feet as he jumped down from his saddle.

A footman who had been helping with the luggage rushed to his side to take his reins and with a distracted 'thank you' he strode towards the Fletchers, who were staring at him in disbelief, their jaws slack.

'Your Grace!' said Mr Fletcher, struggling to stand in the barouche so that he could give a polite bow.

'No need,' declared Brook, with a dismissive wave as he strode over to join them.

Mr Fletcher took an uneasy seat and exchanged a surprised look with his wife who sat opposite him. Marina sat beside her mother, closest to him with her maid on the seat opposite. He was breathless as he reached her, his hand grabbing the side of the carriage door as if he could somehow stop her from leaving.

'You are leaving?'

A blush stained her cheeks, and she gave a little nod.

Why did it hurt? Did she want to leave? Had he ruined things between them by kissing her?

He swallowed hard, aware her parents were less than a foot away and watching them curiously. Her father, in particular, was eagle-eyed about every moment.

'You left…' He reached into his jacket and pulled out the scarlet gloves she'd left behind last night. He could not admit to where he'd found them, or the fact that they had been alone together. 'You left these in the drawing room. I picked them up this morning. I thought I would return them to you after my ride.'

'Oh.' Marina stared at the gloves, then reached out to take them from him. Their fingers brushed against each other and it took a quick tug from her to release them.

He could not say what he wanted to. Society, convention

and their own devious plan forbade him from saying it. But he also couldn't let her go, in case she changed her mind, and for some reason he didn't want her to.

'Mr Fletcher.' He dragged his eyes away from Marina's blue pools to address her father. 'I wanted to formally invite you and your family to Stonecroft Manor—you will need to see it before you draw up any plans. I will call on you some time this week to make arrangements.'

'Yes, thank you, Your Grace,' replied an uncertain Mr Fletcher, who glanced at his daughter, immediately bringing Brook's attention back to her like a siren.

'You must bring some of your compositions with you, Miss Fletcher. I would very much like to hear them. Perhaps you will even play for me when I call on your family?'

Marina's mother gasped, but he couldn't take his eyes from Marina. It was an obvious request to begin a courtship and he waited impatiently for her answer. He searched her face, praying for no sign of rejection. Her eyes were wide, but as clear and steady as the morning sky that was—for once—not grey or full of rain.

Slowly, she nodded. 'Yes, Your Grace, if you wish. I would be glad to.' It was all he needed to reassure himself that all was not lost between them.

'You are to call me Brook, remember?'

She smiled in response, dazzling him with her quiet beauty.

'Good,' he declared and he smiled to her parents, who stared at him with open astonishment. Tapping the side of the barouche cheerfully, he said, 'Safe journey home!', then turned away to enter his mother's house, feeling a lot lighter in spirit now that he had seen her.

Chapter Twelve

A few days later, Brook arrived at the Fletchers' home in the heart of the city. Mr Fletcher had picked the placement of his home deliberately so that he was close to all the fashionable squares and theatres.

The outside of his home had an almost theatrical look to it, with its columns, arches and statutes looking down at him from the three floors above. It was also completely unique and like nothing else he had ever seen and, even though Marina had spoken proudly of her home, Brook had not appreciated its beauty until seeing it in person.

He climbed the steps to the front door and rang the bell. A maid promptly opened the door a few moments later. She stared at him in surprise, her eyes glancing to the ornate barouche behind him, and he was quick to reassure her.

'I am sorry, I don't have an appointment, but I was hoping the Fletchers were at home. If not, I can come back another day. I am the Duke of Framlingham.' He hated adding his title, but he knew it always opened doors.

Gulping with wide eyes, and a hurried curtsy, the maid welcomed him into the drawing room. 'I will let Mr Fletcher know you are here, My L—Your Grace.'

He gave her a bright smile to reassure her over the clumsy

address. 'Thank you.' With another awkward curtsy and hasty nod, she hurried from the room.

Brook glanced around the room and felt immediately comfortable. It was how Marina had described it, but now that he was here, he could appreciate the warmth of her home.

Beautiful bright furnishings that might have seemed vulgar in any other place seemed perfectly natural in this room, possibly because there was an artistic eye that ruled over every placement and colour. Not only Mr Fletcher's, he realised, but Marina and her mother's, too. The large marble fireplace dominated the room and the bookcases were stuffed with leather books, propped up with interesting little artefacts from all over the world.

He moved closer to inspect them. There were the usual fashionable trinkets and miniatures. He smiled at the family portrait above the fireplace, showing a young Marina and toddler Frederick, leaning impatiently beside their mother and father's chairs. Marina was holding a fiddle—even as a child, she had clearly adored music. Beneath the portrait was a beautiful oyster shell, the kind that could be picked up from any beach near Stonecroft, but it was placed among the unique pieces as if it were considered just as special.

He wondered if it had been picked up on one of her trips to the seaside. He picked it up to take a better look, the iridescent colours shinning in the daylight. Looking up, he searched for the mirrors that Marina had mentioned, chuckling to himself when he found them, discreet round mirrors in each corner of the room. Brook himself was very tall, yet only the top of his face was visible in its polished surface. Their purpose was obviously purely for increasing light, illuminating and bouncing it around the space. So simple and unassuming and yet wonderfully effective.

A pianoforte began to play in the room beyond and his heart quickened a beat as he realised how close he and Marina were. Only a couple of doors separated them.

He closed his eyes, imagining what she might look like playing. The music was soft, romantic and dreamlike. Would she also be closing her eyes? Her head dropped forward or back with pleasure?

He hoped her hair was loose, as it had been in the library, her fingers gentle as they danced across the keys. The memory of rain-soaked roses filtered through his mind, seductively reminding him of their passionate kiss on the veranda. He breathed it in deeply, as he had breathed in the perfume at the nape of her neck as he held her close.

'Your Grace, what a pleasant surprise!' said Mr Fletcher loudly from behind him.

The notes were abruptly silenced, as if the pianist had been struck down in their seat. He was certain Marina had just heard of his arrival. Brook might have laughed if he hadn't felt so awkward himself.

'Good morning, Mr Fletcher, I was just admiring one of your pieces.' He held up the shell, before placing it carefully back into position.

Marina's father smiled tenderly as he gazed at the shell. 'Marina found that on the beach as a child. She was very proud to be adding it to my collection of artefacts. We didn't have the heart to tell her it was only an ordinary shell. Now it is a sweet memento of a lovely day.'

'So not ordinary at all. Happy days are never ordinary,' Brook declared, thinking of his own time with Marina and how he could never describe her as anything less than magnificent.

Her father nodded thoughtfully before speaking. 'Indeed. Did you wish to discuss our upcoming visit to Stone-croft Manor?'

'Yes!' Brook reached into his pocket and drew out the invitation, handing it to Mr Fletcher. 'Here's the formal invitation from my mother and I. Remember how my mother spoke about another house party, near the end of the Season? Well, all the details are in there. We hope you can all join us. I believe Frederick will still be at school, unfortunately.'

'Thank you, Your Grace, and don't worry about Frederick, I am sure he will not mind.' Mr Fletcher took the invitation with a smile.

'Are your wife and daughter home?'

'Yes, come, I will take you through to them. Would you like to see more of my collections? Marina can walk you through them, if you wish?'

'I would like that very much, thank you.' He tried not to make his eagerness too obvious.

Mr Fletcher showed him through the formal drawing room and into the music room beyond. Marina and Mrs Fletcher rose from an embroidered love seat as they entered the room, Mrs Fletcher putting down her embroidery and Marina putting aside her pile of papers.

Curious, Brook glanced around the room where Marina spent most of her time. There was a pianoforte placed against the wall and scattered music sheets covered the hastily pushed back stool. A quill and ink pot sat on the top of the instrument, as if only recently discarded.

'Are you composing a new piece?' he asked.

'She was, but she is too much of a perfectionist! She stopped playing when she heard you were here.' Mrs Fletcher laughed, ignoring her daughter's scowl.

'But I would love to hear it.'

Marina glanced at the scattered music sheets and shrugged. 'It's nothing really, just something I was tinkering with.'

'I heard a little when I arrived. I have to say I am impressed! It was beautiful, powerful and—romantic—like Beethoven.'

A rosy blush stained her cheeks, but she gave an indifferent lift of her shoulders as if his compliment barely affected her. 'I doubt it is anywhere near as good as the Master, Beethoven, but you have my thanks regardless.'

'Marina, would you mind showing His Grace around my collection? You know it as well as I do and then I can prepare my portfolio to show His Grace afterwards. That way, I can get an idea about your taste and requirements before we go to Stonecroft Manor.'

'Of course, please follow me, Your Grace.'

'Brook,' he reminded her with a smile.

She nodded, a flush brightening her cheeks, before leading him down a book-lined corridor filled on both sides with leather-bound volumes from floor to ceiling.

When they were out of hearing of her parents, he asked, 'Are you still willing to go ahead with our plan?'

She didn't turn to look at him, but her shoulders stiffened slightly and her pace slowed. 'I am. But—how will it work?'

'After the ball, at my mother's next house party, I will ask for your hand in marriage. Our long engagement will begin and I can be away to Europe immediately.'

'Perfect,' she declared, her pace quickening slightly.

For some reason he longed for her to turn and look at him, to talk to him in an easy manner—had he spoiled it all by kissing her?

'I feel as if I have already been here,' he said softly, 'from how you described it. Except, I do not remember this...' He paused in the middle of the book-lined corridor and was rewarded when she turned to face him.

Between the rows of shelving was one large window that overlooked a small courtyard, with a large marble fountain in its centre, surrounded by a bench and several lush potted trees and plants. It looked like the perfect spot to read one of the many books in the Fletchers' sprawling library.

Brook glanced at the titles around them. There were works of fiction by authors he enjoyed like Jane Austen, Sir Walter Scott and Susan Ferrier, but also large tomes such as the recent publication of Malcolm's *History of Persia*, which came in two volumes.

'You are wrong, Marina. Your parents' library does rival my mother's.'

She laughed, the sound merry and light in the narrow space that smelled of musty paper, ink and rich leather, and he felt the easy manner between them return. 'Your mother probably has a thousand books. We have a lot, but not that many, and most are gifts from my mother's family and friends. They know how much she loves to read.'

'I suppose she read a lot, waiting all those years for her life to begin.'

Would Marina feel the same?

It was a worry that had been keeping him up at night.

Marina's head tilted and she gave him a curious look. 'What do you mean?'

'You said she spent years waiting for him.'

Marina rolled her eyes and took a step towards him, the smell of scarlet roses replacing that of dead books. 'I hope you are not pitying my mother.'

'I…'

He was, he realised.

'She must have missed out on a lot—socially.'

Her skin glowed like a pearl from the light of the courtyard and he wondered if another mirror was up in the corner of the hallway, illuminating her from above like an angel. She poked him in the chest with her index finger, and said firmly, '*Never* let my mother hear you say that! My father has always felt guilty over the sacrifices she made. But do you know what my mother says about those years?'

He shook his head, his breath held tight in his chest. 'Does she regret it?'

What he really wanted to ask Marina was *will you regret it?*

Marina's smile broadened and there was a wicked glint in her eye. 'She says…she was glad of the extra reading time.' Marina then shrugged lightly. 'There is no regret, when you choose with your heart.'

His whole body ached upon hearing her words, as if she had slain him.

How he longed to have such conviction and belief in those around him.

But in his experience, he had only been disappointed by those who professed to love him.

'Is that truly how you feel?'

She blushed. 'Within reason.'

'As you know, I have been disappointed by my heart in the past,' he spoke without thinking, captivated by her honesty, and for some reason hoping for more—with Marina he always wanted more.

'Yes, but you didn't say how,' she said gently, coaxing more out of him.

'I loved a woman once. I met her at one of my mother's parties, just after I finished my training and before I was sent to France. I thought she liked me. I even asked my brother for permission to ask for her hand.' She stepped

closer as he spoke, as if enthralled by him. He wished he had
such power over her, but he knew all too well that lust was
the only thing between them and that was a fleeting desire.

'What happened?'

'My brother did not approve of the match. He thought
her feelings for me were false and proved his point when
he showed interest in her and she dropped me like a hot
coal. Why have a second son, when you could win a duke?'

'I am sorry. That was wicked of her and unkind of your
brother, too. But—' she paused thoughtfully '—probably
for the best in a strange way. Like Mr Richards and I. I
mean—imagine if you were married to her now?' She vis-
ibly shuddered and he couldn't help but laugh.

'She would have both the face and the title that she
wanted! Lady Mary Kesgrave must be kicking herself now!
She could have had it all.'

Marina frowned. 'Lady Mary Kesgrave? Didn't she
marry some man twice her age?'

He nodded. 'She did. Lord Kesgrave is very wealthy, I
believe, but sadly not a duke.'

Marina shook her head with disbelief. 'Then she was a
woman who would never have followed her heart. You were
lucky to have escaped her. Perhaps your brother only hurt
you to avoid you having a miserable marriage?'

'Perhaps…' he agreed, although he had not believed it
at the time, and had viewed it as one of his brother's many
little cruelties. 'Now, lead the way before your parents find
us among the bookcases and demand I marry you straight
away.'

Marina rolled her eyes, but hurried forward, her hips
swaying delightfully as she walked. He had not thought
of Lady Mary in years—oddly the pain he had once felt
was long gone and the bitterness towards his brother with

it. He could even understand why his brother had done it. Brook was stubborn when his mind was set on something and he rarely backed down—had his brother known that?

In his odd way, had he tried to save him from himself? Or was it just to prove that he was always right in everything? Brook would never know.

Chapter Thirteen

Marina gave an apologetic smile as she showed Brook the Egyptian stone sarcophagus. 'I feel silly explaining these to you again,' she said, 'after practically giving you a guided tour of it before.'

Heat spread up her cheeks as she remembered their night together on the veranda of his mother's home. It felt like a lifetime ago—as if she'd been an entirely different person.

Brook smiled. 'It is impressive, better than I imagined.'

She gestured up at the ceiling. 'It looks good here, under the glass dome. Be sure to have some in your new house. They add such beautiful light to a home and when it rains it sounds wonderful against the glass.'

'I will be sure to add one, especially for you.'

Her chest tightened, and she tried to ignore the honey-like pleasure that pooled in her stomach at his romantic words, and they did sound romantic, even to her inexperienced ears.

'Is there anything else you would like to see?' she asked, taking a step away from him to try to regain her internal balance. The world felt as if it were constantly tilting when she was around him.

'Your Tower of Babel, I would like to see that,' he said, with a sly smile that caused her blush to deepen.

'Come this way then,' she said briskly, hurrying away from the stone tomb to the models at the back of the room.

She could feel the shadow of him pressing like a heavy weight behind her and she moved quickly, her silk slippers slapping gently against the wooden floor.

'Here it is!' she declared with a flourish of her hand.

Brook moved closer, the warmth of his body reminding her of how big he had felt under her palms, how broad and warm. 'It is magnificent.'

The tower was more like a large tiered hexagonal cake that had been cut into, the layers becoming smaller as they reached up into the heavens. The outer walls were removed in one section, so that you could see the tiny model people and structures within. Her father had built it like a beehive, with hexagonal rooms, and ladders between each level.

The very last layer was squished on one side, as if the hand of god had already begun its destruction. Brook reached out to touch the damage with an amused smile. 'Your work?' he asked.

She nodded. 'As you may remember. I was a little too forceful placing the final section. In my defence, I was very young.'

'It adds to the character of the piece,' said her father from behind them and they turned to see her parents were watching them curiously.

Mr Fletcher held up a large rolled-up blueprint. 'Would you like to see the sketches of the square we talked about, Your Grace? It will give you an idea of what I can accomplish as the manager of the project. I promise this building will not fall.'

Brook laughed at her father's terribly awkward joke. But her father's comment about managing the project was a timely reminder that Brook would still be leaving for Europe soon. Kissing Brook had been wonderful—but dangerous—not only to her reputation, but to her heart, which might never recover once he left. Look how shaken she had been after the incident with Mr Richards. And he wasn't even half the man that Brook was.

Brook and her father went to his study to look over the plans, then joined them for tea in the drawing room after. The conversation was polite and friendly, but in what felt like no time Brook had taken his leave with a polite bow.

Her family finally relaxed after their illustrious guest had left and they finished their tea and cake with more ease and enthusiasm, while Mrs Fletcher read the official invitation, with its details regarding the arrangements.

'Well, I wouldn't want to make any assumptions, but I believe the Duke is leaning more towards commissioning you than Mr Moorcroft. I guess after our visit to Stonecroft he will make his final decision.'

'It seems so. He'd like to see some sketches before the end of the visit. He's keen to finalise his plans before he leaves for the Continent.'

'Ah, yes! I do remember him mentioning that first night he wished to travel. Well, the swiftness of all this makes sense. Although I was beginning to get high hopes for Marina after he danced with her twice! Oh, well, it looks like we won't be joining the aristocracy after all!' Kitty chuckled to herself, but stopped abruptly when she saw that Marina wasn't laughing with her and reached out to hold her hand. 'I was only teasing, my dear.'

Marina gave her a bright smile and forced a merry laugh. 'Indeed! Sorry, I was a little distracted!' Suddenly realising that she would soon be required to pretend an engagement with him, she added weakly, 'Although he is very kind and interesting.'

Her father glanced at Marina and then Kitty, but said nothing.

'I am beginning to think of him as a close friend,' Marina said, then busied herself with refilling everyone's cups.

Would she have to lie to her parents about her feelings? Pretend she was in love with him and happy to wait until he returned from the Continent to speak their vows? She had been so busy imagining the freedoms such a relationship would give her in society that she had not considered how her lies might affect her family.

Would her mother be disappointed when all of this was over? Would Marina?

'True, and I imagine he is lacking in friends, considering he left the army only recently. Still…it is making me wonder,' her mother said thoughtfully with a delighted chuckle.

Hoping to avoid further discussion of the matter, until she had a better idea of how to handle it, she changed the subject. 'Shame we have to spend more time with the Moorcrofts, though.'

Kitty frowned down at the invitation as if it were a death warrant. 'I suppose we will just have to bear with it as best we can—for your father.'

Colin gave a little chuckle of agreement, taking the note from her mother and inspecting it thoughtfully. 'So, who is coming? There are the Moorcrofts obviously…'

'Delightful,' groaned Kitty, as she leaned forward to cut herself another slice of plum cake.

'Lord and Lady Redgrave, and their daughter Sophia.'

'Marvellous!' sighed her mother, plopping the cake on to her plate and then sinking back into her chair with a loud huff of displeasure. She had confessed to Marina that she found them dull company.

Marina peeked over her father's shoulder curiously. 'Also, Lord Clifton and Miss Grace Clifton, too. Pretty much the same gathering as before. Oh, she mentions that the Duke has sent Freddie a leather-bound sketch book as a gift and that Aunt Emma and her family are invited to the ball on the final evening.'

Her mother brightened considerably. 'Oh, how lovely! Isn't that kind, Colin?'

Her father nodded, as he sipped his tea and cut himself a huge portion of the plum cake. 'Indeed, that is very kind. I really do hope he is settling in well now. Perhaps we should write to him, check all is well?'

Marina knew her father still felt uncomfortable about Freddie running away from Knights Court. 'Let's write something now and pop it in the evening post.'

Her mother nodded eagerly. 'Oh, and we should make some appointment to go to Mrs Gill's modiste. We will need to buy a few new dresses and a new ball gown—to look our best. We can't possibly wear what we wore before!' declared Kitty, giving a horrified shudder.

Her father smiled warmly, despite the pain to his purse. 'Whatever you wish, my dear.'

'Oh, and, Marina—' said her mother with a worrying amount of casual indifference as she pointed at the invitation deliberately '—the Duchess has specifically requested you bring your compositions with you so that she might hear you play them. She has even asked her musicians to help you play them as a special performance for the opening of her ball.'

The plum cake turned to sand in Marina's mouth and she choked out a cough. 'What?'

'Yes, she mentions having a *little* concert before the dancing. You should probably take some time to practise—in between gown fittings and packing—the party is less than a month away!'

'Oh, Lord!' gasped Marina, as all warmth drained from her face.

Her first concert and it would be in a den of vipers!

Why had she even mentioned her music at all? It seemed to cause one awful situation after another.

Was this what Brook had meant by helping her with her music? She had thought— Well, she wasn't sure what she had thought.

Only that by being associated with a duke she might be taken more seriously at theatres and concert halls? He had said he could open doors for her and she thought that meant a few names for her to write and submit her work to. But not this—not a *performance*!

She loved composing, but she never thought much beyond that. They were for her pleasure alone and now she would have to offer them up to a group of people who cared nothing for her! She might as well strip naked and run through Stonecroft screaming obscenities, the humiliation was the same.

'I like that dreamy one you play...' Her mother began to badly hum one of her melodies, and her stomach flipped.

'Oh, Lord!' she cried and ran from the drawing room, intent on searching her scribblings to find something acceptable for this horrendous *little* concert.

Her mother's words just reached her ears as she fled towards the music room. 'I thought that was a decent rendition!'

Chapter Fourteen

Less than a month later, Marina and her family arrived at the Tudor gatehouse that dominated the house of Stonecroft Manor. Grey stone and hexagonal turrets looked down on them from a great height.

She had seen Brook a few times since he had visited their home. All at very dignified outings, fully chaperoned by her parents. Afternoon teas, soirées, it hadn't been deliberate on her part. But Brook always seemed to appear at all the social engagements her family attended and she was beginning to realise that *was* deliberate. The *ton* would have seen them in the same social circles and therefore would be less shocked by the eventual announcement. They had not spoken much, pleasantries and small talk only, but she supposed it would be enough to justify their relationship later.

A wicked part of her was looking forward to this house party, because she knew there would be more opportunity to find themselves alone together. But she reminded herself it was because she needed to speak privately enough to discuss their future plans—and, most definitely *not* because she longed to feel his lips against hers, his hands on her thighs, his—

'It looks like a castle!' exclaimed Kitty, distracting Marina from her increasingly wanton thoughts. She peered out of the carriage to better see the front of the brick and beamed Tudor building. It had felt like it had taken forever to travel here, out of the city, through the farms and fields of Essex to the low flatlands of Suffolk. Even when they had arrived at the Duke's estate it had taken nearly a quarter of an hour to make it up the long drive which was sheltered on both sides by rows of sycamores and oaks.

'I had heard there is a beautiful courtyard within...' said her father, excited as he helped them out of the carriage. 'But this building is truly magnificent! Now that I have seen it with my own eyes, I will have to insist that the Duke consider my suggestion of a fresh plot entirely. It would be a great shame to lose such a excellent example of Tudor architecture.' The historian within him was ruling his head for a change.

'I am sure he will take your advice, and building another house will be no hardship for such a wealthy duke, will it? He will probably be glad of the excuse!' Kitty laughed, taking his arm with a broad smile. 'Besides, I am sure there is plenty of land for them to build on.' Her hand swept out to the many fields and woodlands that surrounded them.

Footmen hurried their bags into the large open doorway and the butler showed them into the drawing room to greet their hostess.

'Welcome!' cried the Duchess as they entered. 'I'm so glad everyone has arrived safely!'

Marina curtsied and swept her gaze around the grand room. Miss Clifton and young Lord Clifton were absent, but the Moorcrofts were there, as were Lord and Lady Redgrave with their daughter, Sophia. It wasn't until she realised that the Duke wasn't there that she realised whom she had been searching for. The room was mostly furnished with heavy pieces of carved furniture that looked as if it had been here since the house was first built. Softening the dark oak chairs and tables were silk embroidered cushions, tablecloths and blankets in the Duke's colours of burgundy and gold. There was one mahogany sofa that looked a little more modern and that was upholstered in a pale ivory silk.

A small fire was crackling in the huge stone hearth and the wooden panelling of the walls shone in the glowing light, the beeswax used on them filling the room with a delicious scent.

'Thank you for inviting us and for the carriage—that was too kind!' said Kitty with a warm smile that the Duchess returned.

'Brook insisted you have his barouche. After all, he travelled with me and it seemed silly for you to have to hire a carriage when we had one spare! Besides, it will be good to have another anyway, for day trips. Now, you may wish to take the rest of the afternoon to unpack, rest and settle yourselves. I thought you all might be hungry after your journey here, so I have arranged for dinner to be served a little earlier at six. Stonecroft is an old building, so you may need time to get your bearings. Plenty of uneven floors, secret compartments and hidden corridors, I'm afraid!' She laughed.

'It's utterly charming!' said Marina's father.

'I quite agree,' replied the Duchess warmly. 'But it's not very big, unfortunately—which isn't great for entertaining. I worry it will not accommodate Brook when he decides to start a family.'

Marina almost laughed at the Duchess's lament—the house was twice the size of her parents' house—but when she saw the Duchess was watching her with interest, she felt a heavy lump of guilt fall to the pit of her stomach.

She looked away and the Duchess continued brightly,

'Perhaps I will live here when the time comes for Brook to settle down. At least then I won't be too far away if he should ever need me, while also not being a nuisance if he doesn't.'

'I am sure you could never be a nuisance!' exclaimed Kitty's mother.

Some more pleasantries were exchanged, then Marina and her parents were shown to their rooms. Betsy was almost finished unpacking her things, so she sent her to help her mother and father.

She walked over to the window, with its black wooden beams and lattice glass. Her room was south facing, which was just as well really considering the dull afternoon light—it had been unseasonably cold for months and she was desperate to feel some sunshine on her skin. She glanced at the stack of her music sheets she'd brought with her. Soon she would have to perform them—to at least a hundred people if the last ball was anything to go by. A suffocating heat clawed up her face and neck and she tried to fight the rising nerves.

'They won't expect anything tonight, try to not think about it!' she muttered to herself, trying her best to calm the panic already flooding her skin like pinpricks.

Leaning across the dressing table, she tried her best to open the window. It was a little stiff and needed some forceful pushing, but it eventually creaked open. Sucking in several deep breaths of fresh crisp air, she felt a little better.

The courtyard gardens below were beautiful, filled with roses and lavender as well as pretty climbers around the walls like honeysuckle and purple clematis. In the far distance she could see the slate-grey sea—it would probably take some time to reach it. But it had been many years since she'd gone to the seaside and she couldn't ignore the sudden urge to walk along a beach and carelessly throw stones into its hidden depths. To feel the brisk wind on her face and try—at least for a moment—to forget her nerves regarding the *little* concert.

'I'm going for a walk!' she called to her parents as she passed their room.

Her mother's voice called back, 'Make sure you leave plenty of time to ready yourself for dinner!' Followed by a grumbled, 'It looked like a diamond mine down there. I wish I'd bought my emeralds!'

Marina hurried down the stairs before her mother changed her mind and insisted on seeing every piece of jewellery she'd brought with her.

Brook relaxed on the large island rock that sat between the breaking waves of the cove and the open sea. He hadn't swum this far out since he was a boy.

The water was freezing and he'd had to stop to catch his breath more from the cold than the exertion. Truth be told, it wasn't his wisest decision that day, as it really wasn't warm enough to swim yet. But waiting for this trip had felt like an agony.

He had seen Marina a few times in the last month, but it had never been enough. Awkward and polite conversation as they sipped tea or fruit punch, an occasional country dance, where the hands only momentarily met—and were always covered by gloves.

Nothing like their early debauched intimacy, or the brutally honest conversations they'd had together. He longed to speak with her, almost as much as he yearned to taste her lips.

They would find some time alone together over the next

couple of days, he was certain of it—mainly because he was determined to steal them if necessary.

He'd been so full of restless energy, he'd had to do something to distract himself from her arrival, or go mad from the waiting. Still, he should go back soon, they were due to arrive any moment. Hopefully by the time he walked back they would be here.

His mother had laughed at him when he'd said he was going swimming.

Are you so anxious to see her that you cannot sit still? Young love, the sweetest of all obsessions!

He had almost shouted a denial, until he realised that was exactly how he was meant to be acting, like a man in love. It was all part of their performance, wasn't it?

However, it disarmed him that such a statement would be said about him when he'd not actually been acting. How could he be obsessed, when he wasn't even in love?

Surely it was just a combination of excitement and nerves. He was close to earning his freedom. After the engagement was announced, he could leave without any arguments from his mother. He would be settled in her mind and what happened in one or two years made no difference to him now.

Glancing back to the pebble shore, he realised he wasn't the only one who had decided to take some sea air. A lone woman was walking, trudging against the sharp wind that had suddenly whipped up. Her bonnet was pulled off her head by a sudden gust and went tumbling along the shingle, her hair flying out of whatever pins she had used to try to tame it, flowing backwards like a black sail. She ran after her bonnet, bending to catch it only for it to be tumbled further along the beach by another blow of the bad-tempered wind. He thought he heard her scream out in frustration and it made him smile.

It could only be Marina.

She has come to me.

He dived into the water, not caring that he only wore his buckskins and a white shirt. A wicked part of him wanted her to see him like this—maybe it would remind her of that night on the veranda and startle her just as much as her runaway garment.

She was so busy chasing her bonnet, she didn't see him approach until she had finally grasped it in her hands. As if suddenly noticing the pile of clothes he'd left on the beach beside her, she stared at them for a moment before she quickly stood up from her kneeling position and turned as if she were about to search the sea for any sight of him.

She almost knocked into him, her movement was so sudden, and she was still breathless from running after her bonnet.

'Brook!' she shouted, almost choking on the word, obviously shocked by his appearance and state of dress—or the lack of. Her eyes flew to the ground no sooner than they had taken in his wet body, but she must have seen enough, because her face flushed to the colour of a beet. Brook couldn't help but grin at her embarrassment—he found it adorable.

She had also called out his name, not *Your Grace*, or his title, but simply Brook—as if he were her friend—*or lover*. It warmed his chest despite the icy water still dripping from his skin.

She took a step back and then another. She was going to trip and fall over his pile of clothes if she continued to retreat. Instinctively, he grabbed her arm with one hand and swooped his other around her back to stop her from falling.

Marina gasped again as she dropped into his embrace. She stared up at him with wide eyes, her lips parted with shock. She only wore a short spencer jacket over her cream muslin gown and he wondered if it was the cold or his touch that caused her to shiver.

'I didn't want you to fall, my clothes are behind you,' he explained, but the space between them was so close that he could feel the light flutter of her breath against his chest as she struggled to catch her breath.

'Are you well?' he asked, amused by her continued gasping, as she now stared at his chest with utter shock.

'I… Yes, I am quite well!' she snapped, struggling to stand and shrug off his touch at the same time. Stepping to the side, she asked, 'Are you? You must be mad to go sea bathing on a day like this!'

Her eyes were staring out to sea now and he was a little disappointed not to have captured her attention a little longer. Bending down, he picked up the blanket he'd brought with him and roughly dried his hair and body with it, before shrugging on his long coat and shoving his bare feet into his boots, not bothering to put on his stockings, instead shoving them into his pocket with his cravat instead.

He laughed. 'I am perfectly sane. I wished to have some fresh air after a long and tiring journey. Much as you did, I imagine.'

Maybe it was the sea air, the biting cold or dullness of the day, but Marina's eyes seemed to have changed colour and he found them fascinating. They had darkened to a stormy greyish blue and she seemed anxious, over more than his appearance he now realised.

'Is something wrong? Are you not looking forward to the moment of triumph at the ball? It is only two days away.'

To his surprise, she groaned, 'Don't remind me!'

'I thought you would be looking forward to your moment of glory.'

She sighed, striding over to a nearby sand dune and sitting down on it with another loud sigh. 'Your mother is expecting a concert of my work—to *open* the ball!'

'Ah, yes, I do recall something about a performance.' He sat down beside her, using the dry side of the blanket to wrap around her shoulders and shelter her from the worst of the wind.

'Aren't you also cold?' she asked.

'I'm fine.'

Frowning, Marina threw half of the blanket around his shoulders. 'You have been in the sea, I have not. At least share it with me.'

He let her drape it over him, even though it was awkward for her to reach around his broad shoulders. It felt strangely nice to have someone fussing over him.

'Thank you. Are you really that nervous about it?'

She nodded grimly. 'Your mother wants the orchestra to play with me! A full band! I have always played my music to close friends and family—with one exception.'

A twinge of guilt plucked at his heart. 'I am sorry, it is my fault, I told my mother it was one of the things I admired about your character. I suppose she wishes to show off your talents now that we are likely to be engaged.' He didn't mention the other thing he had arranged for Marina, it would only add to her worries.

Marina swatted him playfully with mock ill humour, but then shrugged. 'If I am ever to take my music seriously, I must allow people to hear it, no matter how difficult I find it.'

He thought a moment before saying, 'I can understand how that unpleasant business with Mr Richards knocked your confidence, but one cruel man shouldn't dictate your future.'

How well did those same words apply to him?

'I know. And I didn't even like him.' She chuckled, although her laughter sounded dry and brittle. She began to play with the sand, pouring it between her fingers, then drew musical notes.

'Then there's no need to be afraid, is there? The opinions of people you don't like shouldn't matter.' Her fingers paused and he continued, 'I may not know much about music, but I heard a little of you playing before—that day when I came to your house. It sounded beautiful—I do not think you have anything to worry about.'

'You must think me such a coward.'

Her lack of self-belief astounded him. 'You are not a coward, Marina. I have seen you charge to your brother's defence, not caring what people may think of you. Which is why I am surprised you do not have the same conviction in yourself.'

She scrubbed away the markings in the sand with a sweep of her hand. 'I suppose—I am afraid to take a risk and fail. What if everyone hates it? I would be embarrassing my family—shaming them.'

'How could you *ever* shame them? I have never met a family closer or more supportive of one another than yours is. I doubt you could ever disappoint your family and they are the only people that truly matter. So, you have nothing to fear.'

Their eyes met for a moment and Marina smiled before looking away, squinting into the wind which was getting stronger by the moment, whipping up sand and throwing spiralling clouds of it along the shingle and sand beach. 'Thank you.'

'You are not a coward,' he repeated, suddenly conscious of her arm brushing against his beneath the cover of the blanket. He should move away, but he found himself lean-ing closer. 'And, if you wish to back out from all, or any of it, I will understand.'

Her face turned to his, the wind whipping her hair around her face. 'This is the second time you have asked me if I wish to back out of our plan. One might think it was *you* who wished to put an end to our arrangement and not I.'

He smiled at her accusation. 'Not at all, you have my word, I will not break our engagement.' But then another thought made his smile fall and his stomach twisted sourly. '*But* I have less to lose than you. When I leave for the Con-tinent, you will be left alone to face society as my fiancée. Won't that be difficult for you? Am I being selfish to ex-pect it of you? Perhaps we *should* marry, you could come with me then...'

'Oh, Lord, no!' She laughed and he tried not to flinch. Instead, he gave a dry chuckle of agreement.

'You're right, it could never work between us.'

'No, never,' she agreed, but there was a sadness to her expression that strangely comforted him, probably because it flattered his pride.

No man likes to think of himself as a bad choice...even if he is.

A long and heavy silence stretched between them and they both stared out at the crashing waves and blustery ho-rizon with grim expressions.

Marina was the first to speak, her voice brisk as she shook her head, sweeping back her hair bad-temperedly as it flew around her face like a whirlwind. 'Do not worry about me. I will have a very comfortable life while I *wait* for you. I will have independence and status. Then, when I *do* decide to break our engagement, I can begin the next chapter of my life, free from the burden of being a debutante.' She smiled hesitantly, using her hands like a shield to avoid the swirling tempest of her hair getting in her eyes, as she asked with a vulnerable expression, 'Will you write to me? I would like to hear about your adventures...' Then she chuckled drily, glancing away from him with a blush. 'Not the carnal ones, *obviously*, but everything else.'

'You will be the only one I write to,' he said, his heart tightening painfully at the confession. 'I never had anyone to write home to when I was in the army. My mother isn't very good at correspondence.'

Marina's hand reached for his beneath the blanket. 'Well, I am a devoted letter writer. You will be sick of hearing from me!'

'Will you truly not mind being left behind?'

'That was our agreement,' she said, her brow creased with confusion.

He struggled to find the words, probably because he wasn't even sure what he wanted to say.

Wait for me!

But he couldn't say that, it wasn't their plan—it wasn't *his* plan!

Pulling their entwined hands from the blanket, he stroked his calloused palm over the lilywhite softness of hers. 'I feel bad,' he eventually managed to say. 'To think of you wasting the best years of your youth on a man who can offer you nothing but loneliness in return.'

'That's a little dramatic!' She laughed, tugging her hand from his, a blush staining her cheeks, as she looked away from him, shuffling ever so slightly further away, as if suddenly aware of their close proximity to one another.

He looked out to sea, with its crashing waves thick with sediment, the sky overhead churning with equal ferocity. 'We should head back. I will take you to the garden, then walk around to the side of the house. It would not do for us to be seen together like this.'

Like this!

He almost laughed at the ridiculousness of his words, they had been in far worse situations than this—and neither of them had cared until they had almost been caught.

Standing up, he reached back to offer her his hand so that she could rise. Brushing her hands down her dress, she stumbled to her feet, avoiding his help. He smiled at her refusal and waited patiently for her, wrapping the blanket more tightly around her shoulders.

'No,' she snapped, dragging it off her shoulders and thrusting it towards him. 'You are wet and cold, you need it. Besides, people might question why I have it.'

He wrapped the blanket around his shoulders. 'True, and we must always do as society demands,' he said, but took no amusement in the statement, because if there were no rules, he would have laid her down on the blanket, and made love to her there and then, not caring about the weather, or society and especially about his own blasted plans.

Chapter Fifteen

At dinner that evening, Marina tried her best not to stare at Brook. He was wearing a peacock-green jacket, which brought out the lush colour of his eyes, and cream breeches with leather boots. As dashing as always, but somehow less wild than when she had seen him earlier.

A shiver of anticipation ran down her spine when she thought of how he had looked on the beach, all wet and muscular, looking down at her from his great height. His breath ragged from his swim, his hair falling into his eyes in the most charming of ways. He'd come from nowhere like a storm and thrown her heart into chaos.

He was every young woman's dream and he had crippled her with the sweetest of words.

Perhaps we should marry, you could come with me...

Her heart had stopped beating at those casual words and she had felt as if her soul had left her body. Then the crushing disappointment had come rushing in like a flood, causing all sensation to return to her, including her bitter wisdom. Head pounding, body aching, she had struggled to hide her breathlessness from him. As well as her fear and worst of all—her excitement.

If only he had meant it—which he hadn't.

Why else would he say such a rhetorical question and

ask it so lightly, too? As if he were pondering whether they should have fish or venison for dinner, rather than asking her to marry him and run away together.

He did not mean it—that was the only explanation.

Laughing it off as nothing serious had almost killed her. She had felt as if she were swallowing broken glass with every false word and chuckle.

Why would he say such a thing? Was he playing with her, tormenting her for his own amusement as Mr Richards had done? But those weren't the actions of the man she had come to know. Brook favoured the underdog, would never be unkind for the sake of it—he'd been thoughtless, that was what it was—he had not realised how it would affect her and, up until that moment, neither had she.

The excitement and disappointment had twisted in her belly like a knife, making her realise the awful truth. She wasn't sure *when* it had happened—whether on the veranda, or in the library, or in front the Tower of Babel—but she had allowed herself to fall in love with him.

She cursed her stupidity and the foolish vanity that had led her down this ridiculous path. They were friends, she had to remember that, he could not give her anything more and he had been honest and straightforward with her from the start.

She was the one to blame, for allowing her heart to get the better of her, not him.

What good was it to hope for more?

It was obvious he had not meant it. He wanted freedom, to travel, to experience all the joys and pleasures he had missed at war. And what could she offer him? Quiet nights in front of the fire, reading books he had no interest in and listening to her play music that she was too afraid to play in public.

A wallflower could never make a man as charming and as bold as Brook happy.

He was every young woman's dream, but she was not his.

'You seem distracted, Miss Fletcher. Are you well?' asked the Duchess and Marina's cutlery jumped in her hands.

'Oh! I am quite well, Your Grace. Just a little tired.'

'How was your walk? I am surprised you didn't see Brook—he went swimming, such a lunatic!' The Duchess laughed, but there was a twinkle in her eye as she sipped her wine. 'He never cared about the weather even when he was a boy. He used to dive straight in whenever he could.'

'I walked to the folly,' Marina explained quickly. Brook had carefully explained about it on their walk back, so that if asked, there would be no suspicion of their meeting one another.

'Ahh, the folly!' cried the Duchess, as if Marina had mentioned an old friend. 'A bit of a long walk, but it's worth it! Such a beautiful spot. Nestled just past the woods in a clearing overlooking the sea,' she explained, more for the benefit of the rest of her guests than Marina. 'My husband's father designed it to look like a Greek temple. Complete with tumbled-down ruins and a sacrificial altar! We used to spend days there, didn't we, Brook?'

Brook nodded, barely glancing up from his meal, and Marina saw the way his mother's eyes glistened with emotion, before she briskly looked around her and declared, 'Shall we go to the folly with a picnic tomorrow?'

Everyone eagerly gave murmurs of agreement at her suggestion.

'I would love to see it,' said Marina's father enthusiastically.

'As would I!' declared Lord Clifton. 'Follies are a personal favourite of mine!'

'Have you seen Broadway Tower, built to resemble a Saxon tower?'

'Yes! What did you think of it, Mr Fletcher?'

Marina smiled at the way Mr Moorcroft fairly bristled with displeasure at being left out of the architectural conversation.

'Something amusing, Miss Fletcher?' asked a deep voice from the side of her and she looked up to see Brook watching her with interest.

Everyone was distracted with talking about follies and the upcoming picnic. 'Nothing.'

'You seem happy.' There was a brightness in his eyes that made him look even more handsome than normal, which she might have thought was impossible until now.

'I am,' she whispered, as if she were confessing something truly wicked, such as how often she had dreamt of him, or the way she remembered over and over how it felt to be kissed by him. She suspected she would play this moment, too, again and again in her mind, a symphony of images. How the candlelight caught his eyes, the fabric of his cravat, cutting into the sharpness of his jaw as he turned to look at her with friendly affection.

Was this all part of his plan? One of the displays of the affection he was supposedly going to show during their stay to make their engagement more believable. How she wished she'd asked him more questions at the beach. She was so confused by her emotions and their lies that she wasn't sure what to think.

'You look lovely when you are happy. I think I will dream of your smile tonight,' he said it so casually, but his words stripped her bare.

It felt real and she basked in the light of his admiration.

Even knowing that it would one day end did not dim her pleasure.

'I am looking forward to your little concert, Miss Fletcher,' interrupted the unwelcome presence of Priscilla from the other side of him.

Marina tried not to groan at the reminder of the damn concert, or the disappointment in realising that they weren't actually alone.

'I suspect Marina's music will be the highlight of the ball. I can think of no better way to start the entertainments,' declared Brook as he eased back into his chair with a lazy expression that offered no opportunity for argument.

Priscilla did not seem to appreciate Brook's words and gave a tight-lipped sour smile in agreement. 'Yes, I am sure it will be most entertaining.'

'My mother has arranged for the musicians to meet with you on the afternoon of the ball in the music room, so that you can practise with them.'

Marina drank deeply from her glass, the tang of the wine rich and soothing on her tongue. 'Perfect!' she declared with more brightness than she felt.

Brook frowned at the obvious return of her nerves, but was kind enough to ignore it and instead began to question Priscilla about the latest plays she had seen. This seemed to distract her from Marina's discomfort and she was grateful Brook had turned the conversation away from her impending doom.

The next morning, Marina woke up to the light sound of raindrops on her windowpane.

Another rainy day.

As she dressed the rain began to fall with more force

and, by the time she went down to breakfast, the wind was howling against the manor walls.

'Well, that's certainly put a dampener on our plans!' said the Duchess with a pout. 'I was hoping we could all walk to the folly for our picnic.'

'I am sure it will clear up soon!' declared a cheerful Lord Clifton and the Duchess gave a pleased nod.

'Perhaps you are right. I shall ask the cook to still prepare the picnic.'

A window rattled and the whole group cast worried glances at each other.

'We could ride there,' suggested Priscilla. 'Then, if it does turn for the worse, it won't be a long journey home.'

Marina grimaced at the thought, but said nothing. She wasn't a good rider and was always a little nervous high up on a horse. She preferred to walk on her own two feet than trust the four hooves of a skittish animal.

Brook strode into the room, his hair wet and flopping in front of his face like ribbons of ink. 'Good morning!' he said cheerfully, grabbing a napkin from the table and using it to rub at his hair. His mother stared at him, appalled. 'Brook, what are you doing? Go to your room to dry off!'

'I was hungry,' he argued with a shrug, flopping down into the seat beside Marina's with a loud exhale. He smelled of fresh rain, leather and sea salt. 'Nice weather for ducklings. Not so good for me and my horse!'

'You have already been out riding?' Marina asked, surprised that he would be up and about so early.

'I like to rise early, especially after a restless night,' Brook said, but there was something a little wicked in his smile that made Marina pause, before returning to spread butter on her roll.

From the corner of her eye, she could see his mother's

glare intensifying. Thankfully the rest of the party seemed unaware of it.

'Waking early is a habit from his years in the military,' explained his mother. 'Discipline is very important.'

'As it should be!' said Mr Moorcroft. 'Look, the weather is already beginning to clear. I am sure we will still have a pleasant day!' A small ray of light flowed in through the small Tudor windows illuminating the breakfast table, cheering all those around it.

Chapter Sixteen

Brook looked around him at the gathered guests and noticed Marina was missing.

Was she not coming with them to the folly?

The guests were all gathered in the stable yard at the allotted time, preparing for their trip to the folly. The men and some of the women were climbing on to their horses.

They had two curricles—the large two-wheeled carriages were better on the country lanes. Each with a high seat to fit two people, they were light and fast, drawn by two horses. His mother and Mrs Fletcher were in one. Lord and Lady Redgrave were in the other. Everyone else had chosen to ride, with one exception.

He rode his horse over to his mother's carriage. She was busy adjusting the reins, while Mrs Fletcher looked uncomfortable beside her.

'Is Marina not joining us?' he asked casually, although he was already wondering how he could feign some problem with his horse. If Marina wasn't coming, he would much rather stay home, especially if it meant spending more time with her.

Mrs Fletcher shook her head. 'Not with the horses. She and her father set off on foot about an hour ago.' She eyed his mother's gloved hands nervously. 'Do you have much experience driving these types of carriages, Your Grace? They have always seemed a little precarious to me.' She glanced down at the considerable drop to the ground, the curricle's two large wheels rocking back and forth unsteadily.

'Of course! I used to race with Brook's father all the time—it was one of the few times I actually bested him in anything,' declared his mother, which only caused Mrs Fletcher to pale further. It was common knowledge that his father had died in a riding accident.

Seeking to reassure her, while completely misunderstanding the situation, his mother quickly added, 'Oh, don't worry! It was his son, Robert, who died in a carriage accident, not his father—and that wasn't even his fault, one of the stagecoaches ran him off the road.'

Mrs Fletcher gave a weak smile and then yelped as his mother cracked the reins and the two-wheeled carriage jerked forward.

'Race you there, Lord and Lady Redgrave!' called his mother merrily as she turned the carriage towards the gate. Mrs Fletcher was holding on to her bonnet, and the side of her seat with a white knuckled grip as his mother's carriage picked up speed and left the stable yard.

The Redgraves gave an awkward wave of agreement as they struggled to turn their own carriage around and Brook suspected the 'race'—if that was what you could call it— was already lost to them. He resigned himself to a slow ride beside the couple to ensure they didn't end up in a ditch.

'Did your mother request a race?' laughed George as he jumped on to his stallion.

'Of sorts,' Book replied with a frown. 'Everything is a game to her.'

To his surprise, George grinned in response. 'She's a remarkable woman, your mother!' But before Brook had a chance to comment on such a bizarre statement, George was already riding off, shouting, 'I'll make sure they arrive safely!'

'Thank you!' Brook called back, but George and his stallion were already galloping out of the yard, muddy clods flying from his horse's hooves. It really wasn't the best of conditions to go riding or walking in. The earth was waterlogged from all the rain and he could imagine one of the carriages getting stuck or damaged on the country lanes. Marina and her father should have gone on horseback like the rest of them. He dreaded to think of the state of them when they finally arrived at the folly, they would have mud up to their elbows. He glanced up at the sky—it did seem a little brighter, though. Perhaps he was being pessimistic.

Sophia, Priscilla and Grace trotted over to him, their spines straight in the saddle, their riding habits of the highest quality in jewel colours, as they lined up beside him.

'Lead the way, Your Grace,' said Priscilla, then she leaned forward a little with conspiratorial whisper, 'You don't want to be stuck behind Lord and Lady Redgrave. I suspect it will take them all day to reach the folly!'

Sophia blushed at Priscilla's statement and nodded sheepishly. 'I'm afraid my parents don't drive their own carriage very often.'

Brook, who had never really liked Priscilla in the first place, liked her even less now for making Sophia feel bad about her parents. 'You ladies go ahead. I will follow behind them and ensure they arrive safely.'

Grace sighed dramatically as if he had said something incredibly gallant, 'The strongest wolf always follows at the back of the pack. That way none are ever left behind. Very admirable, Your Grace!'

Brook raised an eyebrow at the strange comment and

waved his hand to usher them forward. 'Indeed, go ahead, ladies, I am sure we won't be far behind.'

They trotted off, their backs straight and their horses swishing proud tails as they rode out.

'Lord Redgrave!' he called, 'Pull to the left, to the left!'

There was a metallic rattle as an empty bucket was knocked over and spun across the yard by Lord Redgrave's curricle. A stable boy had to dive out of its way or risk being cracked in the shins by it. But at least Lord Redgrave managed to steer the carriage out of the open gate without any other mishaps.

Brook sighed. It was going to be a long day.

Marina and her father trudged through the woodland back up the same path they had walked less than half an hour ago.

'I thought you said you'd been this way before?' grumbled her father bad-temperedly.

Marina cringed internally, but plastered on a cheerful smile as she lied through her teeth. 'Only once and I wasn't paying much attention about the paths I took. I stumbled on the folly by accident, truth be told.'

'Well, I hope it was worth it! I've ruined my boots and I think I have a blister the size of my thumb on my heel.'

Marina hoped the folly was worth it, too. She had said as much, but as she'd never actually seen it, she feared her lies would all unravel if it proved less than stunning. 'I thought it nice...' she said weakly, then added, 'I am sorry, you should have gone in a curricle with Mother.'

Her father shook his head firmly. 'And leave you to walk alone? Never. I would rather have a thousand blisters...' He winced as his boot got stuck in the mud and he had to pull it out with a loud squelch. 'Which I might have by the time we return to Stonecroft.'

'I would have been perfectly fine on my own. We've seen nothing but squirrels and birds for the past hour.' She laughed, hopping over a large puddle to a grassy bank and then back on to the woodland path.

The Duchess had explained that walking by foot to the folly was much quicker, as the bridle path looped out and around from the opposite direction. So, rather than face clambering on to an animal three times her size, she had opted for the walk instead. After all, by the time everyone changed into their riding clothes and saddled up, she would be halfway there and probably still arrive before them, despite them riding at a faster pace.

'Ah, finally! I think I see it!' Marina said with barely concealed relief as she pointed through the trees to a meadow.

'Thank heavens!' said her father, striding up the grassy bank to avoid the large puddle with more purpose now that he realised the end was in sight.

'Careful of that—' cried Marina, but it was too late.

With a yell her father's foot slipped on a moss-covered log and his other ankle twisted beneath him as he struggled to regain his balance. Marina grabbed him before he slipped into the puddle and managed to brace him enough that he didn't completely fall.

'Ahh—' Her father hissed and wheezed obscenities under his breath as he tried to keep the weight off his bad foot and Marina helped him to sit on a tree stump a few feet away.

'Oh, Lord! It's not broken, is it?' she gasped, kneeling at her father's feet and gingerly lifting his boot.

'Don't take it off!' cried her father, his face twisted with pain. 'It's not broken... I didn't hear anything snap.'

Marina grimaced at the thought. 'You've twisted it badly, though. Should I go wait at the folly for the others, so that they can come help you?'

Her father shook his head, taking in some deep breaths as if to steady himself. 'No, I think I can walk. Just give me a moment to catch my breath.'

'I'll try to find you a stick…something to help you walk.' Marina clambered into the undergrowth, searching for a fallen branch that might be of use.

'Be careful! The last thing we need is both of us injured!' joked her father, but he looked a little flushed and still in pain.

A short time later, she had a big enough stick for her father to use as a crutch and had his other arm over her shoulders as they made their way up the path and out of the woods.

'Oh, it is pretty,' said her father with an admiring sigh, as they headed up the meadow to the Greek temple perched on the edge of a cliff overlooking the sea.

Marina tried her best to distract her father from the pain. 'Complete with its own deliberately broken pillars. It's a good ruin—it looks as if it's been here a thousand years.'

Her father laughed. 'More like forty. I do love a folly, though—such strange little buildings.'

'It seems the others beat us to it.'

'Not all of them and only just by the looks of it—they're still unloading.'

One curricle was parked a little away from the temple, the horses on a long rope free to graze. Lord Clifton was unloading the hamper from the back of the curricle, while everyone else was busy spreading blankets on the meadow in front of the temple.

Brook wasn't there. Just as she was beginning to wonder if he'd not come, she saw the Redgraves' carriage bouncing into the clearing from the opposite side of the field and behind them was a man on a giant chestnut stallion that could only be Brook.

The group at the temple waved to the carriage and lone rider. But Brook stopped his horse for a moment, then turned it sharply to gallop towards Marina and her father. She doubted the others would have even noticed them coming from the opposite direction if it hadn't been for Brook changing direction so suddenly.

As he neared them, he pulled on his reins to slow his horse and then jumped down from it in one smooth motion, which for some reason made Marina a little lightheaded to witness.

Possibly it had less to do with the cut of Brook's fine figure and more to do with the weight of her father pressing down on her neck. But she couldn't be sure either way.

'What happened?' asked Brook, rushing to help her father, while thrusting the reins into her hands.

She grimaced at the thought of leading such a huge animal, but had to admit that it was better than her trying to struggle with her father another step.

'I twisted my ankle a minute ago. I am sure it will be fine, if I rest it for a bit.'

Brook gave three short whistles and to everyone's astonishment the stallion's head dropped and it knelt in front of them.

'Marina, why don't you get on my horse and ride back up to ask the others for help—?'

Her father's laugh interrupted Brook. 'Your Grace, no matter how well trained your horse is, Marina would sooner walk through fire barefoot than climb on a horse and ride.'

Brook glanced at Marina in astonishment and she truly

felt like the worst of cowards. 'They make me nervous,' she said helplessly, the reins limp in her hand.

'Not to worry,' Brook said gently. 'It looks as if George has spotted us, anyway. Will you be all right holding the reins a moment? He won't move away, but it will reassure him until I can unsaddle him.'

She nodded, staring down at the giant beast that seemed as docile as any well-behaved dog. Brook whistled twice and the horse elegantly rose back to its feet.

'That is truly impressive, Your Grace!' said her father with a disbelieving shake of his head.

True to his word, Lord Clifton was jogging down the hillside towards them and beside him was her mother. Marina breathed a sigh of relief as she counted down the seconds until she would be able to step away from the horse.

In a flurry of questions, and sympathetic laments, Marina's father was helped up the hill by Lord Clifton and Brook, while her mother—knowing Marina's dislike of large animals—took the reins of Brook's horse and followed with her up to the folly.

A short time later, her father was settled with his back against a column. His foot was propped up on a cushion that was draped over a 'fallen' piece of temple and her mother had pressed a cup of fruit punch in his hand, for *medicinal* benefits, while she picked out food for him to eat as if he were a Roman emperor.

'I could become accustomed to this,' he joked, but winced when his wife scowled at him and thrust a plate of bread, cheese and pickles towards him.

'You gave me a fright!' she snapped, her voice lowering considerably as she added, 'And it's not my first one today either. Her Grace drives like a soul running from hell!'

Marina giggled at her mother's expression. 'Perhaps, you should walk back with me, then?'

Her mother nodded. 'That might be wise, although my poor dress will be ruined—look at yours!' She gestured at the bottom of Marina's dress that was thick with mud.

'That's why I wore one of my old ones today.'

Brook must have overheard them talking, because he said, 'I am sure we can sort something for the return journey. No need for anyone to walk back. Unless they wish it?'

Marina blushed at the implied question. 'I really do prefer to walk.'

He frowned, biting into a thick crust of bread topped with cheese. He chewed it thoughtfully, before swallowing. 'You could go in one of the carriages?'

Lord! He was going to make her confess it.

'I get nervous in gigs and curricles. They are…quite close to the horses. I prefer larger carriages, or walking.'

She expected him to laugh at her—it wouldn't be the first time. The landed gentry and aristocracy showed off their wealth by having the privilege to ride for leisure. Admitting that she was scared of horses was like admitting you were afraid of champagne.

'I see,' Brook said, his brow creased as if he were trying to solve a particularly difficult puzzle.

The picnic passed pleasantly enough, with a few word games and plenty of food and punch. But as the time passed, the wind began to pick up again and whip across their party. The ladies began to clutch their bonnets and shawls tighter around them, while the men tried to stop the umbrellas and the leftovers of their picnic from flying away.

'It's looking like it's going to rain again.' Priscilla sighed unhappily.

'So, how shall we work this?' asked Lord Clifton, looking deliberately at her father's ankle.

'We'll go the same way we came and someone can come back for Mr Fletcher and Miss Fletcher. They were the ones who chose to walk in this temperamental weather,' said Mr Moorcroft with only a slightly hostile laugh.

'Fine by me,' said her father good-naturedly.

Marina cringed. She didn't want to get on one of those precarious curricles especially one driven by the Duchess. 'I will wait with Father. It was my fault he came walking with me in the first place. But honestly, I'm happy to walk anyway.'

'Nonsense!' declared the Duchess. 'I can ride with one of the men. Lord Clifton or Brook's horse could easily take two riders. So...'

'No, Mother,' said Brook with a firmness that surprised everyone.

'Miss Fletcher can't ride,' said Priscilla with a sly smile. 'I heard she's terrified of horses. Is that true, Miss Fletcher?'

The Duchess, who was obviously a confident rider, looked horrified at the statement. 'Good God!'

'Really, Mother?' asked Brook impatiently. 'It is hardly a crime.'

'I wouldn't say terrified...' added Marina, although she doubted anyone cared about the distinction.

Her mother, God bless her, added helpfully, 'Just a little nervous, aren't you, my dear? I'm the same about frogs.'

'But surely you can ride, Mrs Fletcher? I heard your family collected racehorses,' said Mrs Moorcroft and the implication was not lost on her mother.

'Yes, I can ride.'

'Then, as Miss Fletcher has done the walk before, wouldn't it be fine for her to do so again?' asked Mrs Moorcroft lightly.

Marina was fed up and wanted a quick end to the conversation. 'Of course I am.'

'Marina—' her father said, but she shook her head.

'Honestly, let's not talk any more about it. Leave me with an umbrella and I will make the journey on foot. I'll be even quicker on the way back, now that I'm certain of the path.'

She ignored the frowns from her parents and Brook, her mind made up on the matter.

'It really is a disappointing day—weatherwise.' Lady Redgrave sighed, gesturing up at the grey sky. 'I'm grateful we bought so many blankets with us. There's quite a chill in the air!' She gathered her shawl closer around her and shivered as if she were in the Arctic circle.

'I used to practically live out here in the summer when I was a boy. Is there still firewood kept inside the temple, I could build us a little campfire if you wish?' asked Brook.

His mother nodded with a tender smile. 'Yes, I have always insisted on it being well stocked. And, I have heard it is sometimes used by locals, as a spot for *romantic* trysts!'

Lady Redgrave shook her head with a blushing laugh. 'Oh, I see… Well, I wouldn't go to the trouble of building a fire. But perhaps we shouldn't linger here too long?' She glanced meaningfully at the grey clouds building overhead. More than one person shivered and nodded in agreement.

Chapter Seventeen

The people who had come on horseback were the first to leave, although Brook and George stayed behind to ensure the curricles left safely. There really was only one change in the travel arrangements. Mr Fletcher would go in one of the curricles with his wife, while Brook's mother rode on his horse with him.

It took a little help from himself, Marina and George to get her father into the high curricle. Mr Fletcher's ankle had swelled disturbingly during the afternoon and he looked pale as he settled into his seat. It was clear that he would not have been able to walk back, or even ride on horseback. Marina's mother looked concerned and after a little tussle managed to take the reins off him. 'It might be best if I drive!' she said firmly.

'Are you going to be all right, Father?' Marina asked, her expression full of concern, as she covered his legs with a blanket.

Her father gave her a tight smile and swatted away her concerns like an annoying fly. 'I will be perfectly fine. A night of rest with my feet up and then I will be twirling you around the ballroom tomorrow, I promise. I am more worried about you walking back alone. Surely you can squeeze on here with us.'

'That might be for the best,' added Brook. It still vexed him that Marina was being so stubborn about walking back alone.

But Marina shook her head. 'You know how much I detest this style of carriage. Even stationary, they make me nervous.'

As if to prove her point, she very gingerly climbed down from the steps of the curricle and took several steps away from the horses as if they were wild beasts that might lash out at any moment and swallow her whole.

'Do hurry back, Marina,' implored her mother.

'I will. Look after Father.'

Brook turned to his mother and spoke quietly. 'I think it might be wise to call for the doctor.'

She nodded in agreement. 'I will get someone to fetch him as soon as we get back.'

'Are you sure you don't want to get into the carriage, Your Grace?' asked Mrs Fletcher, looking anxiously at his mother. She seemed constantly torn between seeing to her husband and worrying about her daughter. It was a testament to her character, that she had taken the time to worry about the Duchess giving up her seat at all.

'Honestly, I am perfectly fine, riding with my son. It's barely even a long ride, an hour at most,' his mother said cheerfully and she did seem more than happy to be perched in front of his saddle; nothing ever phased her.

They all set off, the Fletchers leading with their curricle, the Redgraves following close behind. They seemed to be more confident driving the carriage at a faster speed now that the dark clouds were gathering overhead.

Marina walked in the opposite direction with a cheerful goodbye, as everyone else rode out of the meadow and on to the bridal path.

As if to taunt him further, the heavens immediately opened, pouring a biblical amount of rain over the whole party. Unfortunately, the Redgraves hadn't managed to get very far ahead, their carriage wheels had become stuck in the mud, and they were failing to do anything more than rock back and forth an inch or two, which only served to wedge them further into the sticky earth.

Brook and George dismounted from their horses, and squelched towards the stuck carriage.

'Go ahead, Mother!' Brook said, handing her the reins.

His mother shifted into his saddle easily. She was a born rider and had been the one to teach him everything he knew about horses.

How had he forgotten those years?

'Are you sure?' asked his mother, trotting up alongside him, as he made his way to the side of the bridle path and began searching for branches to place in front of the wheels. George followed his example, while trying to calm the anxious Lady Redgrave with cheerful chatter.

Brook nodded. 'Someone needs to be there to help Mr Fletcher when they arrive. If it gets very bad, I will head back to the folly until it stops raining.'

Nodding, his mother began to shout instructions to the rest of the riders, showing them how to navigate around the stuck carriage, while he and George threw their shoulders into the back of the carriage as they tried to push it out and on to the branches in front of the wheels.

It only took a little while to get it moving, but eventually it was freed. The rain was falling so hard it stung his face and he was soaked through to the bone, despite his thick long coat. Mud was splattered up to his waist, but when George offered to take him on his horse he refused.

'Honestly, I'd be more comfortable at the temple than

riding through this and I fear we'd only lame your horse if we both burdened her in this weather.'

George frowned. 'Your mother will worry.'

Brook felt another tingle of awareness at his friend's words. 'Why are you so concerned about my mother, George?'

'No reason,' he replied sharply, before mounting his horse. 'Go back to the temple. Stay there and, if the weather remains bad, I'll bring your horse back for you.' His friend rode forward, following the slow bounce of the Redgraves' carriage. It almost got stuck for a second time as it turned the bend, but George managed to shout enough instructions to avoid the worst of the path.

Brook sighed, glad he had avoided following the Redgraves for a second time. Any trouble would be George's to deal with, but he suspected it would be a long time before George was able to return with a horse for him. He would have to hope the weather cleared first.

But as Brook trudged through the increasing rain, he became more worried about Marina. It was a shorter walk for her to reach Stonecroft, but the rain had started not long after she had left. She had one of the umbrellas, as well as a blanket, but only her spencer jacket for warmth and the muslin dresses were notoriously thin. He could well imagine she would still be frozen and soaked by the time she arrived back at the house.

She will be home soon, he reassured himself as he walked across the field and up to the temple.

However, as he approached, he noticed a whisper of smoke spiralling out of the temple's doorway and he quickened his pace, knowing instinctively who was inside. Because fate, whether it be Greek, Roman, or Christian, seemed to always be pulling them together.

'Marina?'

She looked up from the campfire, startled by his presence. 'Brook, what are you doing here?'

'What are *you* doing here?' he snapped angrily. 'You should be back home by now. What happened?'

Marina winced. 'A tree had fallen blocking the path, so I tried to go around it, but I got a little lost, and by the time I corrected myself it was pouring so hard I could hardly see my hand in front of my face. I thought it best to come back here, until it eased a little. But...'

'It's not easing,' he answered for her, glancing out of the temple's opening at the torrential downpour. A low rumble of thunder rattled overhead and both of them groaned at the sound.

'It's getting worse,' Marina added, 'but at least we have a fire to keep us warm!'

He looked at the circle of stones, and the huge pile of twigs, leaves and logs that were billowing smoke, a small tinder box open beside it. Walking forward, he bent to re-arrange the fuel. 'It will never catch with that much thrown on top of it. Have you never lit a fire before?'

'No, and as a first attempt I thought I was doing rather well,' Marina replied curtly and he laughed.

'Then I apologise. As a first attempt it's pretty good.'

She smiled at his praise before urging him with a flap of her hands. 'But obviously, go ahead, I'd be grateful for any help.'

Grinning he made quick work of improving the fire so that it blazed with enough heat to warm them, but didn't fill the temple full of smoke. Considering he was younger than nine when he'd last done this, it came surprisingly easy to him. He supposed the years in the army helped, too.

Marina sat down beside him and looked around the temple curiously. 'It is a strange little building.'

He smiled, seeing the familiar space through her eyes. The outside was built like a miniature temple of Artemis with rows of pillars holding up a triangular sculpted stone roof. But there were columns and statues dotted around the outside that were broken and shattered, as if the temple had defied the outside world by remaining intact when everything else crumbled around it. Everything, even the destruction, had been carefully designed and built—it was all an illusion.

The rectangular space inside lacked decoration, except for a carved altar at the back, and a small firepit, with a central smoke hole in its centre. Over time, people had left things in the chests at the sides of the room, Brook himself had been the main contributor as a child, filling the chests with blankets, firewood and toys. The tinderbox looked like the same one he'd used as a boy. In fact, it probably was the same tin with the contents updated and changed over time.

As if reading his mind, she said, 'Did you play here as a child? There are toys in some of the chests.'

'Yes, my father and I used to come here a lot. I'm surprised they haven't been taken by the local children.'

Marina grinned at him as she pulled a blanket around her shoulders. They sat on a pile of them, the stone floor cushioned beneath them, and a large blanket still available for each of them to wrap around their shoulders. 'I think someone must check on them regularly. Some have been repaired and there are even some new toys in there.'

'My mother probably... Frankly, I am surprised she would do something like that.'

'Why?'

Brook sighed, 'She isn't that maternal. She can be quite reckless and—selfish.'

Marina shook her head sadly. 'You are quite hard on her.'

The fact that she would defend his mother surprised him. 'I told you about her debts.'

'Yes, but she tries so hard to please you and always talks so fondly of when you were a child. And, I have not seen her gamble once, although she has been sorely tempted by others to do so. And—' Marina peeked up at him through dark winged eyelashes, as she seemed to consider her words carefully. 'How old is your mother? She must have been very young when she had you?'

Brook had never thought of that, she had always just been his mother. He had not considered her age once, except to pity her marrying his father. 'I suppose she is still young. She married my father when she was only sixteen, and had me not long after. My elder brother wasn't that different in age to her and was more of her companion than stepson.'

'It must have been hard for her then. Losing first her husband and then her stepson? I know they weren't kind to either of you—but it still must have been difficult.'

'I am sure it was,' said Brook, although the familiar ball of resentment still stuck in his throat.

It had been hard for him, too, and what had she done?

She had lost herself into partying, gambling and debt.

'Anyway,' Brook said, clapping his hands together as if he could strike the sorrow from his mind, 'George says he will return with a horse for me if the weather doesn't improve. As you will not have returned, I am sure he will come back straight away so that we can look for you together. Thankfully, he won't need to do that.'

'I really don't want to ride,' said Marina with a grimace and it provoked his temper enough for him to snap.

'You will ride, even if I have to throw you across my lap like a sack of potatoes!'

Marina glared at him. 'I suppose I will have to, then! But don't be surprised if I scream the whole way!'

'Scream away!' he replied tartly and after a moment of silence they smiled at one another. It was that secretively amused smile that he had seen her use with her mother the first night they had met. It humbled him that they were close enough with one another now to have a similarly shared understanding.

Feeling uncomfortable in his wet clothes, Brook began to shrug off his outer layers, draping them on a nearby pillar to dry off. When he returned to the light of the fire, he realised Marina was staring at him hungrily, as if she were consumed by desire.

Marina's mouth was dry as she stared at Brook's wide chest. His shirt clung to his muscular chest, the wet fabric moulding against his torso to show every dip and swell of his muscles, and the peaks of his nipples. Not to mention his arms! The fabric lovingly stretching as his thick biceps flexed.

She had not thought men particularly beautiful until she had met Brook. Now, she could not look away. He released a cascade of emotions within her, especially when he looked like this.

'This is the second time you have seen me wet,' he said, and the husky tone of his voice alarmed her in a way she didn't fully understand.

It made her wonder about things...

'You seem to like it,' he added and without thinking she started to nod, before she managed to regain her senses and look away. He laughed, the sound deep and rich and entirely masculine. 'I am sorry. I should not tease you.'

'You do not sound sorry,' she grumbled.

Brook shrugged. 'Honestly, it is a relief. I was half afraid that you hated me kissing you last time—that I had ruined things between us.'

'No!' she gasped and then blushed. 'I did not hate it.'

Brook crouched down on to his knees and then leaned closer with a sardonic smile. He reached across to lift her chin with one elegant finger. 'I am glad. I want to kiss you again. May I?'

Her breath felt painfully tight in her lungs and she sucked in a deep breath, trying to steady the chaos of her heart. 'I…would like that…'

His lips brushed against hers in the gentlest of caresses, causing her whole body to tingle with awareness. Brook moved back a breath, his eyes bright with firelight, and then when she thought that was all he was going to give her, he pressed forward. His arms circled her back and pulled her close, as his mouth pressed against her lips.

Knowing what he wanted from her this time, she opened for him and his tongue slid into her mouth to taste her. She welcomed his intrusion with a soft sigh, her hands reaching up to grip his biceps as her thighs clenched and damp heat pooled between her legs.

Her acceptance seemed only to entice him further. He pressed forward, pushing her down and on to her back as his kisses grew in urgency and longing. 'I want you, Marina,' he whispered against her lips. 'Every night I dream of touching you, making love to you. Kissing every inch of you.'

His lips moved to the side of her neck, and nibbled at the tender flesh beneath her ear. Her body ached for his touch and, when his hands roughly pulled up her skirts, she was grateful for it, moaning loudly with pleasure as he slipped one hand between her thighs to cup her. She had thought the pressure of his hand was sweet enough, but then his finger slipped down and then rolled over the bud of her most intimate flesh and she whimpered.

Brook pulled away from their kiss slightly, just enough to focus on her face as he growled with satisfaction, 'You're so wet.' He pressed another dizzyingly passionate kiss against her mouth.

The rolling of his finger built up a needy ache within her and she began to clench the fabric of his shirt, her entire body tensing in anticipation as he continued to command her body with a single stroke of his finger.

'Oh… Oh…' She began to whimper, her spine arching, and her toes pressing urgently against the blankets beneath them. He tugged at the shoulders and bodice of her muslin dress, finally releasing her breasts with another tug on her stays, and she was sure she heard something tear, but at that moment he could have ripped her dress in two and she would not have cared.

His mouth began to kiss and lick at her breasts, and her legs jerked a little at the unexpected sensation. Everything felt so bright and hot, and so incredibly dirty and yet, also right.

He was rubbing himself against her thigh, she could feel the stiffness of him against her, long and hard, and she wanted nothing more than to feel that strength inside her.

'Do you need to put it inside me?' she gasped. She was sure that's what happened between a man and a woman and if it gave her some relief from this spiralling aching pleasure than she wanted it, she wanted him.

'Brook?' she moaned.

He groaned against her nipple. The sensitive flesh was

already puckered and she bit her lip against the wave of sensation it wrung from her body. 'We shouldn't…' he whispered, but there was yearning and regret in his voice.

Shaking her head, she reached for the hardness beneath his waistband. 'I want to—more than anything.'

'Not like this…' To her frustration he shook his head, tugging her hand away and raising it up over her head. 'Come to me tonight. There is a passageway that leads directly from the bookcase in the music room up to my bedchamber. If you still want to, after you've had time to think… then…come to me.'

'But I want you now, Brook,' she groaned, helplessly lost in a relentless ache only he could control.

He kissed her deeply and then his fingers began to move in increasingly rapid circles. Her legs tightened and her spine arched and then, when she couldn't take it a moment longer, her body released into glorious spasms and she cried out his name, her nails digging into the wet fabric of his shirt and clawing marks down his back.

Chapter Eighteen

They lay together, holding each other tight, Brook carefully rearranging her clothing with tender kisses as he returned her back to some semblance of propriety. Once he was done, he began to turn away from her, to regain some foothold on his own composure—what was left of it.

'Please, don't regret this,' she implored, her small hand gripping his arm tightly as he brushed down the fabric of her skirts.

'I could never,' he murmured and brushed her lips with his. But already it felt like an apology. He had taken advantage of her lust and used it to slake his own. Worst of all, he had no plans to end it here. 'Will you come to me tonight?'

Her nod was immediate and his heart began to race. He was still painfully hard and aroused from their intimacy, but he knew that George could return at any moment. 'Do you remember where I said the passageway was?'

'Behind the bookcase in the music room. Is it an old priest's hole?' She sat up, gathering the blanket around her more closely, a rosy flush staining her cheeks.

To give himself time to cool off, he moved into a sitting position and stared into the fire while he tried to regain some of his control. 'Yes. The lady of Stonecroft Manor back in Elizabethan times was a Catholic.' He did not add that the priest's hole had also been used by lovers in his family for several generations since.

'It comes out in the corridor above, just outside my room. I will leave it open for you. But—' he paused, unable to look her in the eye '—I will understand if you change your mind...'

'Hello! Brook, are you in here?' bellowed an unwelcome voice from outside. It was George, cheerful as ever despite the rain dripping in a steady stream down his hat and coat. 'Miss Marina, what a relief to find you here! Your parents are sick with worry about you.'

Brook rose to stand. 'Did you bring my horse?'

George nodded. 'Yes, tied up outside. Although I have never seen a more obedient animal. Your mother just whistled and pointed at it to follow me. The tether rein seemed almost pointless.'

Brook turned back to Marina, who was grimacing and wringing her hands. 'You will ride with me, Marina.'

She opened her mouth as if to argue and he gave her a hard look. 'No argument, please. Your parents are worried and this is turning into one hell of a storm.'

George nodded. 'It is indeed. A couple of trees have been blown down, too. It would be dangerous to walk through the woods now.'

Marina rose to her feet with a resigned sigh. 'Fine, so be it.'

He extinguished the fire and put away the blankets for the next person, then, redressed into his still damp jacket and coat. Marina followed him outside, the blanket still wrapped around her, and over her head to keep off at least some of the rain. It was beginning to ease, but the wind was still ferocious and whipped at their clothing like a vengeful spirit.

They made for a miserable party, as they trudged out to the horses tied up against one of the pillars. George's mare seemed skittish and danced a little as another crack of thunder filled the air.

'Shall I help you, Miss Fletcher?'

'I have her,' said Brook, unsure of why he suddenly felt so possessive towards her. He mounted his horse and reached down for Marina, who still stood several feet away. Kicking his heels gently, he manoeuvred the horse to side-step towards her.

George laughed as he mounted his horse and wrestled with the reins to calm it. 'You Wyndhams really are exceptional horse trainers.'

Brook ignored him and focused solely on Marina as he whistled for his horse, Prancer, to lean down. 'Turn around and I will lift you on.'

Marina eyed both him and Prancer nervously, but did as he said. 'On three. One, two, three!' He pulled her up and in front of him, then whistled for the horse to stand.

Marina gave a loud shriek of fright and gripped his forearms tightly with clawlike fingers. He couldn't help but smile at her reaction, even though he knew it was unkind to laugh at her fear. Part of his amusement was due to his feeling the bite of her nails only moments before, but for an entirely different reason that made him harden just to think about.

George led the way, his horse skittish and jerking forward regularly at the sound of thunder. Brook, aware that Marina was in a more precarious position and a nervous passenger, took his time to navigate the meadow at a pace that would not make her any more nervous than she currently was.

She was practically sitting in his lap and it felt wonder-

ful. He tried to focus on the task ahead and not the softness of her bottom against his groin. But the memories of
her pleasurable cries, mixed up with her current sound of
fright, only tormented him further and, to his embarrassment, he grew stiff as a rod against her.

He tried to shift a little away from her, but it was almost impossible without risking her safety. Marina's hand
reached down and behind her to the falls of his breeches
and tentatively stroked over his hardness.

'What are you doing?' he asked, between clenched teeth,
the bite of lust a painful sensation.

'Distracting myself,' she whispered, her hand pressing
a little more against him, as they rocked together with the
motion of the horse.

He groaned against her, leaning into her neck to breathe
in her scent and kiss the spot beneath her ear, then grazed
his teeth across her pulse, a gentle warning that caused
her to shiver.

'Later…' he whispered and with a regretful sigh she removed her hand.

They arrived back at Stonecroft manner at dusk, although
it was difficult to be sure considering how dark and grey
the sky was. They trudged into the drawing room, where
the others were gathered.

Marina's mother gave a sob of joy when she saw her, running from her place by the fire and wrapping her in a tight
embrace. 'I was frightened to death when we came back
and you weren't here!'

'Sorry, but I thought it best to go back to the temple to
wait it out. Luckily the Duke felt the same and Lord Clifton came back to save us.'

'It sounds as if a lot of trouble might have been avoided

if you hadn't insisted on walking in the first place,' said Mr Moorcroft coldly and Mrs Moorcroft laughed in agreement as if he had made a good jest.

'How true!'

'How is Father?' Marina asked, ignoring Mr Moorcroft's comment.

Her mother gave her a reassuring smile. 'The doctor came and said nothing is broken, just a bad sprain. He's in bed resting.'

'Oh, he won't like that,' said Marina with a chuckle and her mother nodded.

'He's been restless since we got back. You should go and say hello to him, reassure him that you are well—and probably change—you look a bit of a fright, my dear,' she said more softly.

Marina cringed at the statement, but knew her mother was probably right. She had avoided looking in the mirror above the fire for that very reason.

'I am sure we all do,' declared Lord Clifton with a laugh and then he looked down guiltily at his boots on the plush carpet. 'I am afraid your housemaids will not be pleased with how much mud we've brought in!'

'Not to worry, at least everyone is safe and well. I will ring for a servant to come and clean them! But do take them off before you ruin my Persian rug forever!' said the Duchess with obvious amusement.

Many of the guests had to stifle their laughter as they watched Lord Clifton and the Duke hop awkwardly around as they pulled off their boots.

Marina had less trouble with hers and was able to unlace and slip them off with little notice. Placing them discreetly by the fire for the maid, she said, 'I will go and see Father and return for dinner.'

The Duchess nodded, her eyes still sparkling with humour. 'We won't be eating for another hour. Would any of you like a bath arranged for you?'

All three of them nodded eagerly and then Kitty said, 'I will come with you to see your father. Hopefully, he hasn't heard of your arrival—otherwise, knowing him, he will be trying to hop down the staircase!'

As they all left the drawing room and made their way up the stairs, they were greeted by the sight of Marina's father hopping down the hallway on a crutch, dressed in a nightgown and cap.

'What did I tell you?' Kitty said with a disapproving glare, but Marina's father ignored her.

'Marina, are you well? You look an absolute fright, my poor girl!'

She rushed to her father's side to help him bear his weight better. 'Never mind about me, I am perfectly fine. You should be more worried about yourself. Heavens! Look at your ankle—it's double the size!'

Brook joined her on her father's other side. 'Let me help you, Mr Fletcher.'

They turned and shuffled back up to her parents' bed chamber, waving absently to Lord Clifton as he made his way down the opposite wing of the house to his own room.

They quickly got her father back into bed, then her mother proceeded to reprimand her father in a most embarrassing manner.

'Marina and His Grace are soaked through to the bone and now they have had to delay getting washed and changed because of your impatience!'

'I am sorry, my dears,' he said, looking at both his wife and daughter miserably. 'But I was so worried and I was sure I heard the arrival of someone, so I had to come see for myself.'

'I understand, Father,' said Marina gently, kissing her father's cheek and then straightening. 'But I am perfectly well. Please do not worry yourself.'

'If she gets sick—' hissed her mother, but Marina interrupted quickly.

'I will go to my room now. I think I saw the servants carrying in a tub and hot water.'

Her father looked over at the Duke, his eyes full of emotion. 'Thank you, Your Grace, for bringing my daughter back safe and well.'

Brook looked uncomfortable at his words and gave a polite bow. 'There is no need to thank me. I will have a meal sent to your chamber, so that you may rest properly.'

'Thank you, Your Grace. I think I will stay with my husband tonight—ensure he doesn't get up to any more mischief!' Kitty gave a heavy look to her husband, who gave her a charming smile in response.

Marina and Brook said their farewells and left the chamber. Betsy was outside her door, waiting.

Brook turned to her, his expression mild, his words polite. 'I think I will also have a meal sent up to my room. After a warm bath, I imagine I will want to go straight to bed—early—perhaps you will want to do the same? I can have a meal ordered for you.'

'I… Yes, that would be wonderful, thank you,' she said, wondering if there were any hidden meaning to his words. Was he asking her not to come to his room tonight? Or was he giving her the opportunity to come as soon as possible?

'Goodnight, Marina. I will see you in the morning at breakfast. Unless, of course, your musicians arrive early and require immediate instruction?' he asked with a heavy expression, as if he were walking her down a path while she was blindfolded.

'I expect they will.' She glanced at Betsy, who was ushering in more maids with buckets of steaming water. She suspected that with so many baths being ordered they were rushing to fill them all.

'You know how to find the music room from here, do you not? You can avoid the main staircase entirely.'

She nodded, worried that perhaps he was being a bit too obvious about where he was leading her with his words. Thankfully, Betsy wouldn't know about the music room's secret passageway. 'Goodnight, Your Grace.'

He nodded, took a deep breath and gave a curt bow. 'Goodnight and good luck for tomorrow's performance. Know that I have the greatest faith in you.'

His words plucked at her heartstrings and she had to stamp down the overwhelming urge to reach up and kiss him. 'Thank you,' she said, and after a long soul-searching pause, they turned away from each other and went their separate ways.

Chapter Nineteen

Marina was still soaking in the warm water when the platter of food arrived. 'Leave it with me, Betsy. You should retire for the evening.'

'Are you sure, Miss? Your hair is still a little damp. I could help you dry it, put it in rags for tomorrow?' asked Betsy, although she could tell the maid was eager to leave and enjoy an early night.

'No, thank you. I think I will wear it up tomorrow anyway, the natural curl will be enough to work with. Please, go and enjoy the rest of your evening.'

Once Marina was alone, she climbed out of the bath, dried herself with a linen sheet and dressed in her night rail and dressing gown.

She brushed her hair in front of the fire until it was almost dry, then, because she felt a little vain, added some rouge to her lips and cheeks. The meal was far more than she needed, so she ate a little of it and then cleaned her teeth with a strip of linen.

Afterwards she sat and stared critically at herself in the looking glass.

Was she really going to do this? Creep to a gentleman's bedchamber in the middle of the night?

Never would she have imagined such a thing. It was far too brave and reckless for someone like her. Yet, she had touched him, kissed him, experienced such bliss beneath his touch that she was certain he had spoiled her for all others.

Why should she save herself for a man that might never exist when there was someone like Brook, who wanted her tonight? Frankly, she didn't care any more about the risk to her reputation. If anything, the idea of staying pure for the sake of a husband who was no more real or substantial than a ghost depressed her.

She wanted to be wicked—just once.

Tiptoeing to the doorway, she pressed her ear to the oak door of her chamber. It was silent outside—her parents would have gone to sleep by now, after all the excitement of the day. The others would be downstairs in the dining room, tucking into their second course. Leaving now would be the perfect time to go, no one would see her, she could be down to the music room in less than five minutes.

Her hand reached for the iron door latch and slowly gripped it. The lever clicked open with a sound that seemed deafening to Marina, but was probably as loud as a mouse squeak.

She sucked in a deep breath, wondering once more if she would be brave enough to go to him. To take the last step and become fully intimate with a man.

It could ruin you.

But then, so would a life alone, only in a very different way. She would become a spinster. Although there was freedom and happiness to be found in such a life, there was also a deep well of loneliness that awaited her.

She caught the scent of the rose perfume she had dabbed on her collarbone earlier. Roses had been blooming on the veranda where they kissed—she remembered their perfume fondly, a delicate and floral scent that somehow seemed wickedly wanton to her now. She had spent several days searching to find a perfume that reminded her of that night. She had thought that would be the only romantic experience she would have and she wished to remember it—to savour it.

For once, she didn't want to think about consequences, didn't want to fear the potential humiliation and scandal, and more than anything she wanted to fight for something that was purely for herself.

It could never work between them. He wanted a life of freedom and travel—all she wanted was a sweet love, as domestic and as simple as her parents had. Brook was passionate and bold. He was not *domestic*. He was built for battlefields, swimming in stormy seas and climbing Mount Olympus. He would eventually fall in love with someone equally brilliant and she would always be...his friend.

Even when he had suggested they marry on his return, it had only been for practical reasons, to save her embarrassment and to produce his heirs. No words of love had been spoken, no vows of devotion uttered. That proved more than anything where his heart lay, and it was not with her.

He might think her as a charming and convenient companion, might even desire her for a short time—although that still surprised her—but he would never love her, not in the way she wanted, and she would accept nothing less.

However, nothing was a heavy weight to bear for the rest of your life. The truth was, she might never experience true love. If that were the case, then she wanted to taste more of the pleasure Brook had given her. Even if it was only for one night.

She opened the door and stepped out into the silent hallway. Closing the door behind her, she scurried down the hall to the servants' stairs and rushed down them as quickly and as quietly as she could. She would say she was thirsty if anyone saw her, but thankfully no one did, as the staircase was empty.

The only time she became fearful was when she dashed across the open hall to the music room. She could hear conversation from the dining room and she thought she heard a door open and close in the distance.

With her heart hammering in her chest, she slipped into the music room and pressed her back against the wooden door. The room was dark, but the curtains were open, and a little moonlight showed the silhouettes of the musical instruments and furniture. She squinted through the darkness, searching for what might be a bookcase, and cursed her lack of forethought at not bringing a taper or lamp with her.

Still, someone might see a light from beneath the door and come to investigate, so maybe it was best she hadn't.

Think logically, Marina! The priest's hole won't be by the windows.

She glanced around her and noticed a bookcase to the far left of her. The sound of her bare feet padding across the room was the only sound she made and when she arrived at the bookcase she noticed it was very slightly ajar as if it were waiting for her—tempting her in.

As she eased it forward with her fingers, the entire bookcase opened like a very heavy door. Behind was a very narrow and steep ladder. She stepped into the space and strangled a yelp when she saw two very large feet braced on one of the steps above. Her back banged into the back of the door as she jumped back a step.

'It's me!' whispered a masculine voice from above. 'I was worried you would be frightened. So… I came to wait for you.'

'In the dark? How long have you been waiting—not since we parted earlier?' she asked, horrified at the prospect.

'No, only a short time, I promise,' he reassured her, dropping down into the space. His bare feet thudding between them, most of his tall body was in shadow and she could barely see his facial features. But she was sure she heard a little hissed groan as he emerged from the hole and straightened his spine. 'It's only a short climb to the top, but take care on the ladder, it's very old.'

'Lead the way,' she whispered, prodding at him to go back inside the chamber. She didn't like being out in the open like this, someone could walk into the music room at any moment. At least when she had been alone, she could have used some excuse as to why she was wandering around in the dark—being found with Brook would be an entirely different matter.

Brook ducked back into the hole and began to climb the ladder. She did the same, leaving the bookcase door a little open to let the moonlight in.

Brook was already several feet ahead and she quickly followed him, being careful not to get her feet entangled in the light cotton and lace of her night rail and dressing gown.

At the top, the hole that awaited them was a small square, no bigger than a barrel, and she wondered if she'd be able to squeeze through it. She was reassured a little when Brook managed to ease himself through, despite his wide shoulders, and so she wiggled through, her hips lightly scraping against the sides.

Brook helped her to her feet and she gave a disgruntled huff. 'Well, that was possibly the most undignified thing I have ever done.'

A rich chuckle answered her and then he bent to replace the wooden panelling that hid the doorway from view. His hand found hers in the darkness and he pulled her along with him down the pitch-black corridor, until they were safely behind his chamber door.

The light from the lamps and fire felt almost blinding after so much darkness and it took a moment for her eyes to adjust. Brook's hand remained wrapped around her own, big and warm, all-encompassing.

Bending towards her, he brushed a kiss against her lips. 'You came,' he said as if in awe of her. 'I was afraid you wouldn't, that you would change your mind. You still can, if you wish.'

Swallowing the ball of nerves at the back of her throat, she shook her head. 'I don't want to change my mind.'

He kissed beneath her ear, pressing her lightly against the back of the door. 'You smell wonderful, like the roses in the garden. Whenever I smell roses, I think of you.'

She shivered beneath his touch, her skin coming alive with sensation. 'That night on the veranda—I think about it a lot.'

He chuckled, the sound vibrating through her body as if she were a tuning fork. 'I think about every moment with you. When I saw you asleep on the wet grass, I wanted to undress you then, make love to you on the damp earth.' His hand tugged at the cord at her waist and her robe fell open. 'Would you have let me?'

She gasped, her hands reaching up to his arms, circling the muscles as best she could and gripping on to him for balance, even as her mind raced with a thousand images of him raising her skirts as he had done in front of the fire earlier, of his hands cupping her bottom like they had the night of the ball. 'Yes…'

'And when we rode in the carriage together. Could I have kissed you then…touched you?'

'Yes…' She sighed, whimpering as she closed her eyes

and imagined his fingers sliding between her legs and rocking against her in motion with the carriage. She leaned her back against the door, bracing her legs a little wider instinctively. 'You can do anything you want to me.'

He groaned, his head falling forward to nestle in the nape of her neck, his breathing ragged as he drowned in the scent of her. 'I want you in every possible way that a man can have a woman. But—' She tensed in his arms, as if waking suddenly from a pleasant dream, and he leaned away to see her expression better.

'Please don't tell me you have changed your mind, not after I clambered up that ladder to be with you,' she said lightly, although he could see the fear in her eyes.

She thought he might reject her. It would be easier if he did.

'Are you sure you want to do this? It could—'

To his surprise she interrupted him, placing a finger against his lips. 'I know what it could mean. But I would rather begin my life alone, having experienced at least one night of how it *could* be.' She took a deep breath and reached for the buttons of his shirt, slowly undoing them. 'There is no need to complicate any of this with...feelings. I know there is no love between us, and I do not expect anything more from you.'

Why did that hurt so much?

It was everything a seducer wished to hear. That she viewed this as a sensual awakening and not a declaration of love. They could not love one another, he wanted to leave England. He wanted to travel and discover who he was— beyond his life as the Spare Heir Duke, beyond the broken boy rejected by his family.

He could not do that with a new duchess in tow, with a wife, it was too much. The responsibility, the duty and the fear was overwhelming to him—he couldn't face it, couldn't stay. Brook didn't know how to love—his parents had been a vicious disaster and his brother had shown him how fickle the heart could be. He could not bear it, to be vulnerable and broken once again. It made him want to run and hide as he had always done as a child, to seek adventure and distraction instead of torment and pain.

True love was rare. Marina had said that and she at least could recognise it, he could not. Perhaps this lust would fade after tonight and they could remain friends.

Damn it! That was what he wanted more than anything—to never lose her as a friend.

That was why he was afraid to take this next step with her, that was the reason it hurt to hear her say she did not love him: he was afraid of losing her as a friend—one of his only true friends, and he did not have many. No one else knew as much about him as she did—and for some reason she still liked him in spite of it.

At least, Marina did not love him romantically, *could* not love him.

How could she love him when she didn't even know him—when he didn't even know himself?

And he could not tell her his own feelings, because he did not trust them, did not trust himself.

'Brook,' she summoned him back to her, her face uncertain, her fingers slipping into the opening of his shirt to feel the heated skin beneath.

He gripped her face, tilting it so that she would look him in the eye. 'I care for you…' he whispered, the emotion raw in his throat. 'You are my dearest friend.'

Tears gathered in her eyes and she smiled. 'As you are mine.'

Reaching up, she placed a tender kiss against the pulse

at his throat. It sent a bolt of lightning to his heart and all of his fears and doubts were forgotten in a heartbeat.

He pulled off his shirt and then parted her robe, letting the delicate fabric slip down her shoulders and fall into a puddle at her feet. The nightgown she wore was frothy with lace and ribbons, not what he might have expected her to wear, but then the real Marina was nothing like anyone would expect.

Pulling at the ribbon ties gently, he watched the collar loosen slowly around her décolletage. Her hand had left his body when he removed his shirt and he lifted one hand gently, placing it against his chest. He undid the silly little ribbon that held her wrist captive, pushing the cloth up to her elbow, he raised her wrist to his lips and gently kissed her pulse.

He could feel her heartbeat, the rapid beat of her excitement, and he smiled to reassure her, but could not say another word. What he wanted to say gathered in his chest with no hope of escape like a thousand needles pinned to his heart.

He raised her other hand and did the same, untying her ribbons and replacing them with kisses. His hand moved to her hips. Crushing the soft cloth in his hands, he pulled it up and over her head.

She stared at him, her mouth slightly parted, her cheeks and eyes bright with anticipation and nerves. Her hands were back at her sides, creeping anxiously towards her middle to cover herself.

Gathering her in his arms, he carried her to the bed, as if she were his bride. If she wanted to know how it *could* be, then he would gladly show her.

Marina's back sank into the feather mattress, her hands gripped the embroidered linen beneath, unsure what to do with them. Brook was playing with her, teasing her with promises of the pleasure to come. He had undressed her, and carried her to bed tenderly, placing her gently down with a care that made her feel precious in his arms.

But now he was looking down at her with a hungry and dark gaze that promised much more. It promised thunder and lightning, and an experience as all-consuming as the storm they had weathered earlier. He did not take care with his own clothing, he yanked at the fastening of his breeches with hard swift movements, removing the last of his garments swiftly and casting aside the ball of fabric as if it irritated him.

Marina swallowed nervously as she allowed her gaze to take in the full length and breadth of him.

Thankfully, before her fears could solidify, Brook eased down to lie beside her. Cupping her face, he began to kiss her, softly at first and, as their passion built, the kiss deepened. Her nerves melted away like mist, leaving only warmth and desire behind.

He began to stroke and touch her body, as he had done before, and she found herself opening her legs wantonly for him and arching her spine to press against his body. Touching him eased the ache inside her and she greedily ran her hands all over him, marvelling at the differences between them.

How can two souls, so different from one another, fit so well?

But they did fit and although this would be the only time they gave into the demands of their desires, she knew she would not regret it; this was what she wanted, what she had been too scared to accept until now. Finally, she was brave and free.

They became entangled in each other's limbs, pushing and pressing against each other for more, their hot pants filling the air between them as they clung together. Brook positioned himself at her entrance and eased forward into her wet heat.

There was a stretching, a slight sharp pain that was gone as quickly as it had come. She had tensed a little at the discomfort and Brook had murmured a heartfelt apology that she answered with a deep and searing kiss.

He rocked inside her, their bodies wrapped tightly in each other's embrace, their lovemaking slow and gentle at first, as they adjusted to the feel of one another. He moaned against her ear and lifted her hips up a little to adjust the angle, moving her as he wished. She obeyed his silent commands willingly, confident that whatever he did would only increase her pleasure.

She trusted Brook, more than herself, she realised.

When his pace increased, he gathered her close, their sweat and moans filled the space between them. She cried out as her orgasm hit her in a wave of blissful release and Brook's mouth smothered hers, groaning his own release, which soon dampened her thigh. They lay together, exhausted and spent.

After a while, Marina's old anxiousness raised its ugly head and she squirmed a little beneath him. 'I suppose I should go back to my room…'

Brook's arms tightened around her and he raised his head. 'Not yet,' he murmured, gently stroking the hair away from her face and pressing a kiss against her neck. 'I still have so much to show you.'

It wasn't difficult for him to persuade her to stay.

Chapter Twenty

When dawn began to creep out from the foot of the curtains, they had to concede it was finally time for her to return to her room.

In the doorway of Brook's room, they kissed one last time. But as Marina turned to leave, the priest's hole's panel creaked and then shifted slightly. She didn't even have time to fully comprehend what was happening before—with one quick tug—Brook pulled her back into his room, leaving only a crack of his door open, so that he could peer through at whoever else was using the priest's hole at this time.

Marina covered her mouth with her hands, terrified that she might inadvertently make a sound. She stared at Brook. His eyes were sharp as they peeked out of the doorway, then with a scowl he pressed lightly against the wood to close it.

Marina felt like a frightened rabbit caught in a trap. Footsteps passed by the door and she gripped Brook's arm to steady herself. He looked down at her and, at her frightened look, his expression softened into a reassuring smile and he kissed the top of her head.

A door at the very end of the corridor clicked closed and Marina breathed a heavy sigh of relief. 'I thought I was going to faint for a moment there!' She gasped, tugging a little on the ribbons at her neck.

'It was George, he wouldn't say anything, even if he did see you,' he said, although his mouth was twisted bitterly.

'Still, I am glad he didn't see us. He didn't, did he?'

'No.'

Another thought suddenly occurred to her. 'Why was he coming out of the priest's hole? Do you think he had a liaison with someone?'

'I imagine he did.'

Marina gave a baffled laugh. 'Who? Priscilla or Sophia? Surely not, they're both so prim and perfect—'

'I think I know who it is,' he replied and his jaw flexed.

'Who?' she asked gently, realising how deeply shocked he was by his friend's behaviour.

'My mother.'

Marina didn't mean to gasp quite so loudly, and immediately felt guilty for doing so. 'Sorry! I was just a little surprised, that's all...'

Brook sighed and rocked back against the door, banging his head lightly against the wood. 'I wish I was—surprised, that is. I have suspected something between them for a while now. I think that's why she's always inviting him to her house parties. It's not for my benefit, or even his. As usual she is being self-centred and deceitful! Doing exactly whatever she wants and forgetting how it may hurt other people. I will have to insist that George end it—whatever *it* is!' He cursed under his breath and stared up at the ceiling as if it might offer him guidance, or at least crash on his head and offer him mercy from having to have such an awkward conversation with one of his supposed friends.

Marina stared up at him for a moment before answering. 'I am not arguing with you...' she said slowly and he had the distinct feeling he wasn't going to like her next words, 'but I think you need to speak to your mother about it first, privately. I think there is a lot still unsaid between you, not just about how she has been behaving recently, but regarding the past. So much might be improved between you, if you were only honest about what has driven you apart. You might find that some of her behaviour is connected with your own struggles.'

'I doubt it! My mother quickly forgot me, when the entertainments of high society beckoned to her. She lives only for the moment and enjoys gambling and risk-taking—both at the card tables and in her bed, it seems.'

Marina gave him a hard and disapproving look, then poked him in the chest. 'You are quick to judge her. I would remind you that the main reason you wish to go travelling across the Continent is because you wish to taste freedom and a life without the control and expectations of your father and brother. How is she any different?' Her eyes softened and she cupped his face with a gentle caress. 'Speak with her. If nothing else, you will understand her better—for good or bad.'

Brook closed his eyes, hoping to blind himself to Marina's words. He knew she was right, but he wasn't sure if he could speak with his mother, so much had always gone unsaid. Even through the terrible years with his father, they had lived in make-believe.

When he opened his eyes again, he said, 'Let's get you back to your room. I will worry about my mother later. People will be up and about soon.'

They hurried out of the room and in no time at all, he was closing the bookcase door after her. He stood in the darkness for a while, wondering if there were some secrets that should never see the light of day, or if, by burying them in the dark they only grew more terrible, like the monsters under a child's bed.

* * *

'Marina, you still look exhausted. Are you sure you haven't caught a chill?' asked Kitty with a worried frown.

Marina tried and failed to smother another jaw-cracking yawn and ended up covering her mouth with her napkin in an attempt to hide it. She had slept only a couple of hours before Betsy had come to wake her for breakfast.

She wished she wasn't so tired. Today was her big performance, after all, but then she wouldn't have given up her night with Brook for anything, so it was a moot point.

He wasn't down at breakfast when she arrived and she wondered if he were sleeping in or if he'd gone riding as he usually did first thing.

'Should I cancel your meeting with the musicians, my dear?' asked the Duchess with her usual bubbly cheerfulness.

Marina found it hard to believe that Brook's mother had probably not slept any more than she had. But, unlike Marina, she looked none the worse for it.

Perhaps Brook was mistaken?

'I didn't sleep very well. But—' she took a deep breath, steeling herself against her fears '—I still want to meet with the musicians. I will have a nap this afternoon. I am sure that will improve me greatly and I will be well enough for the ball later.'

'Wonderful!' declared the Duchess, returning to her jam and bread.

Brook strode into the breakfast room and took the only empty seat which was beside Marina and sat down. He smelled lightly of horse, hay and morning dew and she had to force herself from breathing him in deeply and sighing with pleasure.

'How was your ride, dearest?' asked the Duchess, smiling warmly at her son.

Brook stiffened and avoided her gaze, reaching for the coffee pot and pouring himself a large cup. 'Good. It's amazing what you see when you rise at dawn,' he said curtly and Marina nearly choked on her bread. She had to force herself to swallow a badly chewed lump, so as not to begin a horrible coughing fit there and then.

As if completely oblivious, his mother asked, 'What did you see?'

Brook turned to look at his mother. 'I think I have decided on the right spot to build the new house.'

'Really?' interrupted Marina's father eagerly. 'Perhaps you could take me there before we leave?'

Brook nodded. 'We can go there after breakfast, by carriage. If you are well enough?'

Marina and her mother exchanged worried glances and her father pointedly ignored them. 'The swelling has gone down considerably and I can bring my stick!' He lifted up the walking stick he'd used as an aid this morning. 'All I need is to see the lay of the land—where the light rises and falls.'

'Whereabouts is it?' asked his mother curiously.

Brook glanced up at his mother. 'Near Chorlton fishing village.'

'Oh, that is a lovely spot. Perhaps we can all go and enjoy the village after. There is no chance of sea bathing in this temperamental weather.'

Several enthusiastic murmurs of agreement rippled around the room.

Marina decided to speak up before she got carried along on this trip. 'When are the musicians arriving? I would like to give them some instruction, perhaps even practise with them?'

As if remembering something, the Duchess nodded enthusiastically, 'Of course, my dear, they are all waiting for you in the music room. I said you would probably want to see them long before the performance, so asked for them to come before noon. But they arrived early. They usually play at the Hanover Square Rooms and are very eager to meet you. Brook mentioned in his letter to them what a bright young talent you were.'

She had felt brave earlier, when the ball still felt as though it was on the distant horizon and the afterglow of her night with Brook still burned bright in her memory. But now the casual mention that these musicians were some of the best in the country had her mind spiralling into a pit of despair.

'They are already here...waiting?'

'Yes, in the music room, as I said, but do not worry, they will happily wait for you.'

Marina's hand was trembling as she set down her cup and she quickly slipped it into her lap to hide her nervousness. It would be her first ever grand performance—not a soirée, or a concert in front of her family, but a display of her talent—or lack of—in front of hundreds of illustrious people. It could make or break her.

Brook was staring at her, but she didn't dare look at him. The panic was swirling around her mind like a swarm of bees, stinging her with all the possibilities for disaster.

What if I make a mistake?

What if they hate it?

What if they think it's so bad they refuse to play it?

Or, worse, what if they play it begrudgingly, all while laughing at my impertinence the whole time?

What if it is worse than the Haxbys' soirée? And I shame not only myself, but Brook and his mother, too?

From beneath the table warm fingers wrapped around

her hand and she jumped at the unexpected contact. The hand clasped her firmly, pressing down against her muslin-covered thigh.

'Breathe,' said Brook quietly, his eyes fixed on the windows opposite as he raised his cup to his lips with his free hand and took a sip. Anyone looking would not realise they were connected beneath the table and she sucked in a deep breath, followed by another.

Not quite sure if Brook's touch was helping or making her more nervous, as her heart was still leaping in her chest, but more from excitement than fear. Either way it seemed to shake her out of her panic and his hand gave one light squeeze before slipping away like a thief in the night.

Thankfully, she had eaten most of her breakfast, so she quickly wished everyone a pleasant day and hurried to her room to gather her music sheets and her courage.

Chapter Twenty-One

B rook walked through the familiar hallway of his ancestral home and smiled at the latest arrivals as they came in from the rain and handed their umbrellas, overcoats and bonnets to his staff.

Despite the continuing bad weather, many people had still dressed up in their finery and come to his mother's end-of-Season ball. Most were the local landed gentry, but there were also important figures who had travelled in from London. Not only his mother's partying friends, but politicians and heads of industry. Stonecroft would be full to the rafters tonight and most of the surrounding inns too, as most of Bloomsbury and Mayfair had made the trip.

If the Queen's Ball introduced the debutantes to the Season, his mother's ball was what closed it and often her ball was the last chance for unlucky debutantes to secure a match. It warmed his chest to think that Marina wouldn't suffer the wallflower's fate tonight as she would become his official fiancée before the end of the evening.

Everything had to be perfect and he had instructed his staff accordingly.

The manor's many chandeliers were all lit and the old Tudor house seemed both magnificent and comfortingly familiar in its glory. Dark timber and white plaster shining in the candlelight.

The history of the building was present in every shining suit of armour and intricate tapestry on display. The portraits of his ancestors looking down on him included the beautiful Lady Agnes—the secret Catholic, her bejewelled hand covering her chest demurely. His mother had once told him that her hand was placed there deliberately, to cover the rosary beads she wore beneath her clothes, a signal of her enduring faith. Pure fancy, some might say, but he gave Lady Agnes a respectful nod as he passed her. She had kept her secrets to the grave. You had to admire that strength of will.

Oddly, he had never hated this house, despite the dark memories he had had here, possibly because he hadn't been alone. Unlike at Knights Court, his mother had been with him. She had made it bearable.

He still hadn't faced the George issue with his mother and, as more time passed with further distractions, he wondered if it might be better to just let sleeping dogs lie.

Servants were carrying around sparkling glasses of champagne as well as fruit punch and he took one from a tray as he passed. As he took a deep gulp his eyes roamed the guests in search of Marina. He had not seen her since breakfast and it irritated him that he had even suggested parting from her. But then he knew she would appreciate time alone to prepare for the performance, and getting everyone out of the house for the day had seemed the perfect opportunity to do so.

He passed the dining room, but couldn't see her among the crowd. The cooks had outdone themselves, several tables groaning with exotic and delicious dishes. A pineapple from the hothouse stood in pride of place, among a wide display of strawberries, pears and even a few peaches.

A member of the House of Lords spotted him and Brook ducked out of the dining room before the man could apprehend him. He couldn't remember his name, but he always remembered a face and that one evoked memories of a very dull hour.

Perhaps Marina is already preparing for the performance?

Brook strode towards the ballroom. His mother had said that's where her pieces would be performed, right before the ball officially began. Not everyone was here yet, but he imagined it wouldn't be long. They were waiting for one very important guest to arrive. Mr William Dance, one of the founders of the recently created Philharmonic Society, and a respected teacher and musician in his own right.

As Brook walked into the room, he immediately spotted Marina, a brilliant ruby in a sea of pastel. Her back was turned to him, her hair high on her head, showing off the elegant neck he so loved to kiss. A scarlet feather plume topped her hair and diamonds dangled from her ears like a cascade of starlight. He longed to see her face, and hoped she wore the same rouge on her lips as she had last night.

She was talking with her parents and his mother, so he made his way over to them. He wasn't the only one joining them, however. The Moorcrofts slid in beside his mother when he was only a few feet away.

Priscilla spoke loudly, no doubt for his and every person within hearing's benefit. 'Is that not the dress you wore at the last ball?'

He couldn't see Marina's expression, but he saw the flash of irritation on her mother's, before she smiled cheerfully and answered, 'Marina insisted on wearing it again, for luck!'

Priscilla laughed merrily. 'How delightfully superstitious

of you, Marina. I always thought you quite level-headed—it surprises me to hear such a thing. However, if it gives you comfort, who are we to judge you for it?'

Marina thought her scarlet dress was lucky?

It was the dress she had worn when he had kissed her on the veranda. He swore his heart trebled in size at the realisation that she now considered it her good luck charm.

'You look beautiful, Marina,' he said softly and there was an audible gasp from more than one lady. Marina looked up at him and he was delighted to see her lips were as red as a berry.

His mother scowled at him as if he had just slung mud at her, but was quickly distracted by someone over his shoulder. 'Ah, look! Mr Dance is here! I will ask the servants to gather everyone for your performance, Miss Fletcher.'

'Oh…' gasped Marina and she paled significantly.

The people began to stream into the room and Marina stared at them with owlish eyes as she gathered her papers and gave final instructions to her musicians. She sat at the pianoforte and desperately shuffled with the papers for some time, appearing to do nothing more than check them over repeatedly. Eventually, she gave them a couple of firm taps to straighten them out, before placing them on the stand in front of her.

'Would you like me to help you turn the pages?' asked Brook, 'I am useless at reading music, but if you nod your head, I will move it to the next sheet.'

Marina nodded, her feather quivering. 'Yes, please, thank you,' she said, her voice high and slightly breathless, her face flushed. She turned to the waiting audience, who were gathered and talking loudly among themselves.

Eventually, an expectant hush descended over the crowd. Marina spoke, her voice trembling a little as she raised it enough to be heard over the murmuring conversations. 'I will start off with some of my early work, then finish with something I have been working on recently. It may seem a little bold, but, ah, well, we shall see what you think.' Clearing her throat, she turned back to her papers.

Mr Moorcroft laughed. 'It really is a concert, then? I was thinking it would only be a couple of merry ditties.'

Brook gave the man a hard stare that immediately stifled his sniggering.

'Good luck, dear!' called Kitty and Marina sucked in a deep breath, her hands raised above the keys as she took a moment to compose herself. Then with a brisk confidence that pleased him greatly, she dipped her head respectfully towards the conductor. 'I am ready, sir.'

At the wave of his baton the musicians began to play. Marina joined them, her fingers flying across the keys with impressive precision and speed.

Brook had to concentrate on watching her closely to ensure he turned the pages at the right moment, but even he—with his lack of artistic talents— could appreciate the beauty of her music and he was swept away with the swirling melody that filled the room.

At the end of the first song, she waited through only a couple of moments of applause, before ploughing straight into another piece.

Brook smiled, realising that Marina was more concerned with the next song rather than enjoying her well-deserved praise. When she reached the final sheets of music, he realised how 'recent' the composition was—it still had scratched out changes and smudges on the paper. Unlike the others that had been carefully reproduced from early drafts, this one was still fresh.

Marina turned a little in her seat and said, 'My final piece.'

She glanced up at him as she turned back and then stroked the sheet as if straightening it, but then he noticed she was pointing out the title to him: 'Roses in the Rain'.

His heart hammered in his chest as Marina dipped her head gracefully and began to play her final piece. She threw herself into the music. The melody began soft and dream-like, gradually building into a crescendo that was dramatic and powerful, yet wildly beautiful. Her body jerked, a tendril of her hair falling from her elegant chignon, as she struck the keys with passionate abandon, and he was reminded of the woman who had crushed her body to his with glorious intensity.

At that moment, no woman on earth was more beautiful to him than Marina.

The final note reverberated around the room and the musicians, who had never before charged through a concert *quite* so quickly, gulped in deep breaths with rosy cheeks and enthusiastic smiles.

Stunned silence filled the room.

Marina turned to the shocked faces of her audience and that's when he saw her fragile confidence begin to shatter. Cruel agony captured in a single moment, like a butterfly pinned to a board.

Her breathing slowed and he saw Marina's heart slowly begin to break. She looked for her parents and their eyes were glistening with unshed tears. Her head lowered and her shoulders drooped, the hands—her wonderful, clever hands—lay limp in her lap.

But…then something wonderful happened.

Something that surprised only Marina.

The crowd roared with applause. His own shout of

'Bravo!' was drowned out by the sheer flood of others'. People were whooping, clapping and stamping their feet in appreciation. Her parents both sobbed and squabbled with each other as they struggled to find a handkerchief to wipe their eyes with.

Brook clapped his own hands so hard his palms stung and then it was as if the pin had been removed from the butterfly's back, because Marina slowly rose from her seat. Her face flushed with the happiest and widest of smiles, confidence and joy straightening her spine and making her appear at least a foot taller. Fanning out her scarlet skirt like wings, she curtsied to her adoring crowd, dipping her head in elegant gratitude. The chignon gave up trying to contain her hair and it tumbled forward in soft bouncing curls.

When she rose up her eyes were bright and clear, as if she finally believed the truth: that she deserved it.

Chapter Twenty-Two

The crowd surged forward and Marina took a nervous step back. People were praising her left and right, she could barely say thank you before another came to replace them.

The only dampener on her joy was when she overheard a man congratulating her parents on having such a talented daughter and he wondered if her father had *helped* with the compositions.

The rudeness of the questions might have upset her before, but she decided she no longer cared what anyone thought. This praise, so different from the awkward silence and nasty comments of the Haxbys' soirée only proved one thing—art and music were subjective.

Besides, such a dismissive comment about her talent was to be expected—unfortunately, because women, and especially young women, were not thought of as capable, let alone gifted. Her father grinned broadly in reply and declared that the only help he had given her was to buy every instrument that she asked for. Marina caught his eye and he gave her a wink, his chest puffed up with fatherly pride.

Mr William Dance came to stand in front of her and Brook quickly introduced them to each other, although Mr Dance needed no introduction to Marina, who had attended many performances organised by him. He seemed a kindly sort of man, if a little sombre. 'Some lovely work. A little rough in parts, but it could easily be polished. I particularly enjoyed the last composition—what was it called?'

'"Roses in the Rain",' she squeaked, losing all confidence under his piercing gaze.

Mr Dance glanced towards Marina's father. 'If it not too impertinent, I would love to ask your daughter to play at our next meeting.'

Marina's father gave a nod of immediate agreement, already knowing her thoughts on the matter by her eager expression.

Mr Dance then began speaking to Brook about potentially supporting the Philharmonic Society by becoming a patron, which to Marina's surprise he readily agreed to.

Taking the opportunity to slip away from the conversation and take a moment to gather herself, she went to retrieve her music sheets from the conductor, a man in his late fifties called Mr Jonas Short.

Jonas wore an old-fashioned grey wig, black breeches, with white stockings up to the knees, a black jacket and waistcoat with a billowing lace cravat. After the exertion of their performance, he took a moment to mop at his brow with a lace handkerchief, before handing her music sheets back to her.

'If it is not too much trouble, Miss Fletcher, I have written down the details of the playhouse I work at. If you ever wish to produce music for one of the performances, please do write to me. We would welcome your talent. It may not be as grand as what Mr Dance can offer, but we would welcome you all the same.'

'That is very kind of you,' said Marina warmly. 'I would welcome all work, particularly from a playhouse. I do love the theatre, almost as much as I love music.'

The conductor returned her smile warmly and pressed the papers into her hand. 'You are exceptional, Miss Fletcher, *exceptional*.'

Marina hurried up to her room to deposit her music sheets before returning to the party. She hoped Brook would dance with her again—it was the only thing that could improve such a wonderful night.

She was elated by the reaction to her performance, and slightly horrified that she'd had the confidence to put her art out into the world and lay herself bare. Never before would she have dared to play such a personal piece as 'Roses in the Rain'. It was the music of her heart and soul—it was *Brook*.

She had written the composition after they had made love and had barely finished it in time. But the performance wouldn't have been complete without it—it was the culmination of years of questions.

Would she ever know true love or pleasure?

She had answered the question with 'Roses in the Rain'. Yes. And it was both wonderful and tragic, as fleeting and as magical as a passionate kiss in the rain.

She sank on to her bed and flopped back against the coverlet, taking a moment to let the bittersweet joy wash over her.

'Marina?' came her mother's soft voice from the doorway. She raised herself back into a sitting position, as her mother came into the room.

'That was magnificent!' Kitty declared, sitting next to her daughter and giving her a quick hug. It was probably the third or fourth time she had said it, but it still made Marina grin.

'Thank you!'

Her mother pulled away and looked at her shrewdly. 'Has something happened...between you and the Duke?'

Marina felt a blush creep up her neck.

She cannot possibly know, she reminded herself firmly, trying and failing to regulate her skittish heart.

'What do you mean? I like him...he is a good friend.'

Her mother frowned, tucking her loose hair behind her ear.

Laughing self-consciously, Marina said, 'I will have to ask Betsy to help me put it back up.'

'Leave it down. It suits you better.' Her mother then grabbed a brush from the dressing table and knelt behind her on the bed to begin brushing it. As she did all this, she spoke with a gentle firmness that surprised Marina with its uncharacteristic solemness. 'He may ask you to call him by his Christian name—after all, the aristocracy are allowed their eccentricities. But remember—to us, he is still a duke.'

'I know that!' Marina winced as her mother's brush snagged on a knot. 'Ouch!'

Her mother ignored her whining as always. '*And*,' she warned firmly, 'a duke can do as he pleases. He has taken to spending a lot of time with you, some of which was alone...'

'That was unavoidable. It was a storm!'

'I know, but—' her mother sighed helplessly '—I don't want you to be disappointed.'

Silence stretched between them and then, because she realised, she had been a coward in not telling her parents sooner, Marina turned to her mother and looked her straight in the eyes.

'It is not like before, I promise. I will not be disappointed. Brook and I are getting engaged. It will be a long engagement. He plans to travel and in the meantime I will work on my music. The arrangement suits us both. So, try not to be too shocked when it is announced later. I would appreciate it if you could tell Father, too.'

The brush dropped limply into her mother's lap as Kitty digested her words. 'You speak as if it is already done.'

'It is.' She shrugged.

Her mother's face flushed with anger. 'Do we have no say in the matter, then?'

'What argument could you possibly have? You said your-self—he is a duke! I thought you would be pleased. I suspect the Duke will also ask Father to manage the construction for his house, too, although that business is a separate matter. So, do not worry that he is trying to drive down Father's price. I had heard that was a concern. Come, Mother! Be happy! We will have triumphed over the Moorcrofts once and for all! And, as an engaged woman, I can now be free to do as I please. No more being a wallflower at silly debutante balls, I can concentrate on my music.'

But Brook will leave.

The realisation stung and her previous joy bled from her like an unchecked wound, the optimistic words dying in her throat.

Her mother's eyes widened in horror and it seemed to take her several moments to gather her words. 'Marina, is this what you want? I mean, I know I have not always be-haved *maturely* regarding the Moorcrofts, but I don't re-ally mean it. You and your brother's happiness will always come first in my mind. Please tell me this arrangement is for the *right* reasons. So far, I have heard nothing that comforts me—it sounds more like a business arrangement than a marriage.'

'Most marriages are, Mother.'

Her mother's face became pained and tears glistened in her eyes. 'But not for you. I wanted *better* for you.'

'What could be better than a duke?'

'Love?' her mother asked softly and Marina's throat tightened painfully and she looked away. She suspected her mother would think that gesture was a denial of feeling, but nothing could be further from the truth.

She did love him, but he did not love her.

My dearest friend.

His words had cut through her like a knife, but she had gone to him anyway, because she loved him and there was no other option but to fall.

'You waited for Father,' she eventually answered.

'Because there was love between us. But if your Duke is going on a grand tour, he could be gone for years. What if he—?'

'Forgets about me?' Marina laughed bitterly, knowing this would be her parents' greatest objection to the match. It was why she hadn't mentioned it sooner. 'Perhaps he will! Does that mean I cannot enjoy what I have now?'

Her mother's brow creased with worry. 'What *do* you have now?'

Marina feared she had made a mistake, and she sidestepped the question, 'Tonight! The performance—the pride of becoming engaged to a duke! So, what if it does not last? I have never hoped for marriage. I have always known I can never hope to have what you and Father have.'

'Why not?'

Marina gave her mother a firm look. 'You are the only happy marriage I know of.'

Her mother's jaw tightened. 'If there is no affection between you, then you should refuse him. Whether he be a duke or not! I waited for your father because we loved one another and because he could not marry me until he had risen in social standing with his business. You have no such circumstances holding you back. You can wait for a man whom you truly love and who loves you back.'

Marina was dumbfounded. 'I should reject a duke? Mother, have you hit your head?'

Her mother glared at her. 'Are we poor?'

Marina shook her head numbly, unsure of what to say.

'Are we not respectable?'

Again, Marina shook her head.

'Then we do not need a duke to raise us up, or to sell our precious daughter to a man who will soon leave her! *And, most of all*, I refuse to give you up to a man who does not adore you as much we do. I would never forgive myself and neither would your father.'

She stared at her mother, tears spilling down both of their faces. 'Mama...' she whispered.

How could she explain her feelings?

Brook was the source of her courage and the cause of her downfall. She would never experience a happy loving marriage after this—how could she, when he was the only man she could ever see herself making love to? 'You are right,' she whispered, choking on the truth.

What had she once said? That she would accept nothing less than true love? Yes, she had found it, but it was a one-sided love and that was still heartbreakingly nothing.

Her mother took a steadying breath and wiped away her own tears. Then she cupped Marina's cheeks and wiped away the moisture with the pads of her thumbs. 'Then you will refuse him?'

Marina nodded, her head low with the weight of her decision. 'Yes, because I *do* deserve better, even if it is unlikely.'

Chapter Twenty-Three

Brook glanced towards the ballroom's entrance doors and was disappointed for the hundredth time when he couldn't see Marina's scarlet gown.

His mother came to stand beside him. 'Will you dance with me?' she asked lightly and, still feeling jubilant from Marina's success, he gave a deep bow and offered her his arm.

'Gladly—shall we take to the floor?'

They began to dance and he made himself swear not to look towards the ballroom doors until the song had at least ended.

'I think I saw Mrs Fletcher go up after her.'

He frowned at his mother, knowing full well whom she meant, but feeling compelled to deny it anyway. 'Who?'

His mother just rolled her eyes.

They began to dance, the complicated steps familiar despite the years spent since he'd last had need of them.

'Do you remember me teaching you this dance?' she asked with a whimsical smile.

'Yes.' It was one of the few times after he had begun school that they had spent together, one of the short visits at her house in Twickenham. He must have been thirteen or fourteen at the time, an awkward and lanky youth, clumsy with his feet. It was the few times after his father's death they had laughed together.

'It is still one of my happiest memories of you as a young man.'

Unable to bite his tongue any further, he replied, 'I suppose you don't have many to choose from.'

She stiffened as if he had slapped her across the face and he immediately regretted his harsh words. But then she nodded with acceptance. 'That is fair. At least you had school and all your lovely friends from there. George is—'

No, he couldn't listen to her praise his friend, when all along she had been sleeping with him. 'I know about George.'

She paled and it was her turn to pretend ignorance. 'Know what?'

Gritting his teeth, he stepped towards her as part of the dance and whispered in her ear, 'I know you have been *sleeping* together.'

When he pulled away her eyes glistened with unshed tears, but she quickly blinked them away and lifted her chin as she followed the music, without missing a step. Always poised and elegant despite the chaos that followed silently in her wake.

When the music brought them together again, he could tell she had composed herself. 'It is already over,' she said.

'Good, that saves me from an embarrassing conversation with Clifton.'

Her eyes narrowed. 'There is no need for you to be so sanctimonious. *Especially* when you have been *deceitful* with that poor Miss Fletcher!'

'Deceitful?' He bristled at the implication. Nothing was more honest than what he had with Marina.

'Do you think I am blind to the heated looks that have

passed between you? How you stare at her with longing, while also buying your passage for the Continent...*to travel next week!* I saw the papers on your desk! You have no intention of marrying her, do you?' She paused, studying his face, and then with a disgusted snort she continued, 'I can see by your lack of argument that I am correct in the matter. To say I am disappointed is an understatement. I had hoped you would settle down.'

He sighed. 'Tonight, we will announce our engagement.'

'How can you become engaged when you are leaving?'

'Marina and I have an agreement.'

His mother almost choked on her bitter laugh. 'An agreement? And what does she gain from this but future misery and humiliation?'

'She wants to focus on her music and a long engagement will suit both of us.'

'So, you will marry her when you return?' Her perceptive gaze missed nothing and she looked at him as if he were mad. 'You will not. What a farce!'

'We are aware—'

His mother's waspish tone interrupted him. 'Do not dare to make excuses! If you took even a moment to consider it properly, you would see it for what it is! A cruel farce!'

The knowledge struck home like a bolt of lightning. He was being cruel and selfish, and a hundred other wicked things. He had taken her virginity, played on her dreams and desires, all so that he could have everything he wanted, without any consequence to himself. So that he could run away and leave her behind as a shield.

The dance drew to an end and Brook was unsure of what to say. Eventually he said, 'I will speak with Marina.'

However, his mother was not done in her torrent of criticism. 'Good, because frankly, I have come to admire the

Fletcher family and I do not wish to see them upset or humiliated in any way by this. So, you must sort it out and quickly—which shouldn't be too troubling for you, as you are constantly throwing yourself into my affairs.' Then, as if she could not contain her anger a moment longer, she hissed, 'And you *dare* to censure me over *my* behaviour? The only person I have ever hurt is myself and if you are using her, I will never forgive you. Marina does not deserve *you*!'

She strode away from him then and he winced as he realised some heads had turned, their eyes filled with curiosity.

When Marina re-entered the ballroom with her mother at her side, Brook was nowhere to be seen.

'You must be thirsty, come let's have some punch!' Her mother pulled her along to the huge silver punch bowl on a table at the back of the room. As they were pouring themselves a cup, the voice of an old crone, from the other side of the ornate dish, carried over to them.

'Her family may be rich, but there isn't a drop of noble blood in them!' declared Lady Donnelly nastily. Even with her back towards them, Marina recognised her from the London Assembly rooms.

Most people avoided her. She was filled with her own self-importance and found fault with everything and everyone. She always wore elaborate court dress that looked slightly ridiculous on her withered frame, as if the clothes and its wearer had known a more glorious time and was still stuck in that golden age.

'Oh… Well…' replied the cheerful lady beside her, one of the members of the local gentry, who'd had the misfortune to find herself trapped and unable to free herself from Lady Donnelly's company. 'A person cannot be blamed for her lack of birth. I thought her music quite lovely. It has certainly got me in the mood to dance.' The poor woman looked weary and desperate to leave.

But Lady Donnelly was oblivious as always. 'I do not care for this music, or for the amateurish drivel that girl produced. So self-indulgent, obviously the whims of a rich girl who has been overly pandered to all her life.'

Her mother took a step forward as if to confront the woman. Marina gripped her arm to stop her and shook her head. 'It is only Lady Donnelly,' she whispered, and her mother gave a sniff of disgruntled agreement. For all her venom, most people ignored the ramblings of the most bitter and spiteful lady in London.

Lady Donnelly's companion's patience appeared to be wearing thin as well. She answered coldly, 'Mr Dance appeared to think her talented. He even congratulated her at the end of her performance. Surely that is high praise indeed from such a famous musician, respected teacher and one of the founders of the Philharmonic Society?'

Lady Donnelly had a response for everything, even when it contradicted her own words and diverted from the original topic of conversation. 'She is a tolerably talented musician and composer. But the Duchess does not approve of a match between Miss Fletcher and her son and who could blame her? I have even heard she will never forgive him if he goes ahead with the engagement.'

'Did she really say that?' gasped the lady. 'I thought—'

Lady Donnelly interrupted imperiously, 'I heard it from a close friend.'

'The Duke does not stand for idle rumour, especially regarding his family. Some of the local shopkeepers were disgruntled over the Duchess's late payments—they feared the estate was heading to ruin. Completely unfounded, of course, and the Duke credited each account immediately. But he did threaten to withdraw all his business in future if they did not come to him first about such grievances. So, respectfully, I would caution against listening to rumours, Lady Donnelly. They do not end well for anyone.'

This statement seemed to anger Lady Donnelly further, because she snapped back, '*Respectfully*, I would caution you to remember *whom* you are speaking to. I heard it from a trusted friend and therefore it is not a mere rumour, but fact.'

Kitty's mouth dropped open in astonished disbelief over what she had heard and normally Marina would have agreed with her. She might have even tried to laugh off Lady Donnelly's ludicrous words, pointing out that most people who demanded respect and recognition did not usually deserve either. But Marina noticed other people were giving her fleeting glances from around the room and it was not with admiration.

'What on earth has happened since we went upstairs?' snapped Marina's mother.

'I have no idea,' whispered Marina, feeling as if she could no longer breathe in the stifling heat of the ballroom. She drained her cup of punch in one swallow, desperate for any excuse to leave the room. 'Where is Father?'

'Resting his foot in the drawing room, I believe.' Her mother grabbed her hand. 'I will find out the meaning of all this. Look! There is my cousin, she will know what has happened.'

'I cannot bear it in here. I will go find Father.'

Her mother gave her a sympathetic look and patted her hand. 'Go, I will come to you when I have news.'

Marina tried to leave with as much dignity as she could muster, forcing her feet not to run from the room with its suffocating judgement and criticism.

As she stepped out into the busy hall, which was bustling with servants going back and forth between rooms, as well as several groups of guests talking cheerfully among themselves, one figure seemed out of place.

A short man, in a soaking wet riding coat, stood talking with a servant by the front door. He was wet through, rain still dripping from his hat and riding crop.

'Reverend Peasbody!' called Marina and she made her way swiftly through the crowd to join him. 'How lovely to see you again. I didn't realise you were coming tonight.'

The servant darted off towards the ballroom and Reverend Peasbody raised his head to stare up at her grimly. There were lines of worry and shadows beneath his eyes.

'Miss Fletcher, I wish I were here under better circumstances. Are your parents nearby? I must speak with them urgently.'

Dread pooled like molten lead in her stomach, hardening to rock, and a cold shiver ran down her spine. 'What has happened? Is Frederick all right?'

'There was…an incident. He is alive, but I have come to fetch your parents—he needs them.'

'Alive?' she gasped. 'Why would you say it like that? What has happened to him?' Horror and fear crashed together and she fought to control her emotions, as Reverend Peasbody gave her a pained look.

'It would be best if we made haste and I explained it to all of you together.'

Marina shook her head to steady herself, and forced herself to think practically. If the servant had gone to the ballroom, then they would be the ones to fetch her mother.

'I will get my father!' she declared and rushed towards the drawing room.

She quickly returned with her father limping beside

her, his hand braced on her shoulder. The Duchess and her mother were also rushing from the ballroom, their skirts rippling behind them as they hurried to the manor's entrance.

'What happened?' asked her father.

'How is he?' demanded her mother.

The Reverend gave them the unpleasant news as quickly and as succinctly as possible. 'Frederick was involved in an incident yesterday morning. He was at the back of the schoolhouse, climbing several crates to reach the roof. I believe he was trying to retrieve his leather-bound sketch book—the one you gifted to him—someone had thrown it up there. Then a brick was thrown at him, it hit the side of his head and he fell. I thought it best to fetch you immediately. I rode the entire way here, only stopping to change my horse. I am sorry, but when I left, he had not woken since the incident.'

Kitty began to cry and her father wrapped his free arm around her to pull her close. Marina's face felt numb and she suddenly no longer cared if people hated or loved her music, or thought poorly of her for whatever reason. She only wished her brother was safe and well.

Chapter Twenty-Four

The Duchess's calm and reassuring voice was the first to speak after the Reverend had shared his awful news. It was a welcome comfort from someone who they all knew had suffered her own personal tragedies.

'I will give instruction for your clothing to be packed on to one of our carriages immediately. I assure you we will have you on your way as soon as possible. But first, come, let us take some tea in the Duke's study. This must be a terrible shock for you.'

They were ushered from the hall, curious eyes following them from a distance as they made their way down the east wing to the Duke's study. To everyone's surprise, it was already occupied by the Duke himself, who sat alone at the card table in the centre of the room with a bottle of whisky and several papers laid out on the table in front of him.

He rose as they entered and stared in horror as Marina's weeping mother was ushered to one of the chairs at the table by Marina and her father. 'What has happened?'

Marina shook her head, unable to control her own emotions, and barely able to croak out the words, 'Frederick has been hurt…badly.'

Reverend Peasbody and the Duchess followed quickly into the room and Brook went to speak with them quietly in the corner, as they filled him in on the circumstances. Marina glanced at the papers that lay on the table: there was a map of the Continent, a sheet of paper with a complete travel itinerary and a ship's passage ticket in front of him. The date of departure was within a week.

Marina swallowed the bile in her throat and deliberately looked away from them.

She had to focus on her family.

Brook re-joined them. 'My mother has ordered some tea to be brought in, but would anyone prefer a whisky?'

'Yes…yes, please,' gasped her mother.

'And I,' said her father.

Brook nodded and picked up his glass from the table and gestured with it towards one of the servants who waited by the doorway expectantly. 'More glasses, please.' When he turned back to them, he seemed to realise what he had left on the table and hurriedly snatched up the pieces of paper and took them over to his desk.

The servant returned almost immediately with a tray of crystal glasses and placed them down. 'Thank you,' said Brook. Not bothering to wait for the servant, he began to pour the whisky in generous uneven measures and handed them out, pressing one into Marina's hands his fingers cupping around hers and gave them a light squeeze before moving on.

They were all gathered around the table now.

Her parents' hands were interlocked, as if they had been cast adrift by the news and were each other's only tether. 'Tell me everything again, every detail,' said her father.

The Reverend Peasbody nodded. 'Frederick moved boarding house and seemed to be getting on well with some new friends. I had thought the issue was resolved. But it appears some of the boys believed Frederick was receiving special treatment and became resentful. They began stealing and hiding his books from him. Unfortunately, it escalated to the point where they stole his sketchbook, to goad him into climbing up for it.'

'They threw a *brick* at him?' Kitty asked, her tears drying on her face, the redness of her eyes turning quickly from sorrow to a mother's rage. 'Where is that boy now? Please tell me he is nowhere near my son! I swear, if it was Herbert Moorcroft I will—'

'It was not Herbert who threw the brick. The boy who did it has been sent to his boarding house to await punishment. Frederick is with the school nurse in my chambers. He is perfectly safe and the boy who threw the brick was immediately sorry for his crime and came to fetch me, while the other boys ran away. But believe me, *all* the boys will be dealt with regarding this matter.'

'Let's focus on Freddie's recovery first,' said Colin gently and his wife nodded, leaning into his embrace.

'By the time you left him, how long had he already been unconscious, Reverend?' asked Marina.

'About an hour. I left not long after the doctor had seen him. I thought it best with such a serious injury to come to you immediately. Trust me, he is in good hands with the nurse and the doctor hopes he will wake soon.'

'He *hopes*...' Kitty said miserably, and the word hung in the air like a gloomy spectre, the merriment of the ball outside mocking the misery within.

They had all heard tales of people never waking from a head injury, of people wasting away in their unnatural sleep. Those that did wake found their memories or senses stolen from them and were never the same after.

'I fell off my horse as a child. Knocked myself out for a couple of hours. I woke up a little confused and with a pounding head, but was otherwise fine. Let us pray Frederick will fair just as well,' said the Duchess and Kitty gave her a weak smile.

It wasn't long until Betsy arrived to tell them the carriage was ready to depart and they left quickly, ignoring the surprised looks of the other guests.

Marina's parents hurried to the carriage, turning to give Brook and the Duchess rushed apologies for leaving the party early.

'Think nothing of it!' said the Duchess, waving them towards the carriage. 'I completely understand and will pray for Frederick's good health. Do let us know when he wakes.'

'Thank you,' Colin said, his face sickly pale, 'and thanks again for the carriage.'

Brook shook his head. 'Keep it for as long as you need it and use it to bring Frederick home.'

'Thank you!' Kitty said tearfully, as she turned back to help her husband into the carriage.

Reverend Peasbody climbed into the carriage with them, leaning out of the carriage to speak with Brook. Marina, who was opposite him, heard every word.

'Edward, send a messenger as soon as there is any change in Frederick's condition. I will reimburse you the cost. In fact, send me one as soon as you arrive.' Brook glanced at Marina. 'May I write to you as well?'

Marina strengthened her resolve. The answer was laid out with those papers she had seen on the table.

'Marina?' he repeated, his green eyes pleading with her to respond, his fingers gripping the open window of the carriage tightly.

'It will be lovely to hear about your travels from time to time, and I will let you know about Frederick. But...there is no need to contact me otherwise, I think, perhaps, it is for the best that we missed tonight's announcement. In fact, I think we should forget about it entirely. I wish you well, Your Grace.'

Brook stiffened, but he nodded, a sad smile on his resigned face. 'You are a wise lady, Miss Fletcher.'

See, he agrees, thought Marina, pushing down the crushing disappointment until she could deal with it at a less fraught time.

Brook stepped back and the carriage rolled forward.

It took most of the night to drive back to London, where they changed horses and then headed straight on from there down to Knights Court. It was a long journey, but everyone was in silent agreement to waste no time in stopping unless completely necessary.

As the wheels of the carriage crunched to a standstill outside the school, dusk was slowly setting across the dreary sky.

The playing fields were eerily silent, except for the occasional squawk of a crow. As they stiffly climbed out of the carriage a woman came out to greet them with a warm smile. She was no taller than the Reverend and gave him a beaming smile as she approached.

'Reverend! Frederick is awake, he awoke not long after you left!'

Her parents released a collective sigh of relief and Marina sank against the wood of the carriage. 'Thank god!' she whispered.

'Excellent news, Nurse Dorothy. Lead the way and let us know if the doctor had anything more to say.'

Dorothy did as he asked and they were swept into the school and taken to the headmaster's private rooms. 'The doctor said he should recover quickly with plenty of rest, but that we should keep an eye on the swelling. He couldn't eat at first, but managed some water. He's been in and out of sleep since. But I did manage to get some broth into him this afternoon.'

Frederick lay in bed, the curtains closed and with an oil lamp burning on a table by the door. He looked pale and so small in the large bed. A white bandage was wrapped around his head, his face swollen and bruised on one side, distorting his face in a way that seemed inhuman and completely unlike the boy she'd seen only a few weeks ago.

Kitty rushed to his side, kissed and petted his hand, trying to rouse him from his sleep. 'I am sorry, my darling, but just wake up for a moment so that I can see you,' she whispered, and when he was able to crack open his good eye, she smiled. 'I just wanted you to know that we are here.'

'Mama?' Frederick's voice was as dry and brittle as winter leaves.

'Yes, my darling!' she cried, tears pouring down her cheeks, as Marina and her father also gathered around the bed. 'Look, we are all here! We have come to take you home when you are well enough, that is, no rush.'

Frederick's bottom lip was quivering, but he surprised them all with his answer. 'I am not the one who should leave.'

'We will talk about it when you're feeling better,' urged his father, tapping his leg lightly in a soothing gesture.

'Rest, Freddie.' Marina reached across and patted her brother's shoulder. They all wanted to touch him, to reassure Frederick and themselves that he was alive.

Frederick's swollen gaze fell on the Reverend. 'Sir, please don't blame Peter. Herbert put him up to it. He said they would leave him alone if he threw it and he's such a bad throw—I doubt he imagined it would even hit me. It was such bad luck.' Exhausted and relieved to get out the words,

Frederick sank back into the mattress with a weary sigh. 'My head hurts. Can I go back to sleep?'

'Of course, my darling,' sobbed her mother, stroking a hand down his good side and planting a quick kiss.

Marina looked at the Reverend firmly. 'Freddie's right. He shouldn't be the one to leave.'

Chapter Twenty-Five

Brook hadn't slept for two nights. He waited in his study, ignoring his guests and occasionally leaving his room to see if a messenger had come from Edward.

Nothing came and so he returned to his study. The whisky was gone and he'd fallen asleep slumped over his papers when there was a tentative knock on the door.

'Come in!' he shouted, startled awake by the sound, but desperate for news.

The butler came in, a letter on a silver tray. Brook strode forward to meet him and snatched the letter. 'Tell the messenger to wait for my response, I will pay triple.'

Nodding, the butler hurried from the room as Brook read. It was from Edward, which was to be expected, but it still somehow disappointed him.

He sank on to his desk with a sigh of relief when he read the words *Frederick has woken...*

Then he took a moment to savour it, before reading more.

...and he appears to have all his faculties and is recovering well. We have decided that he should remain here with his family for the next couple of days, before being transported home. Both I and your driver have assured Mr Fletcher that they have the use of your carriage for the foreseeable future. But

he wishes me to tell you that he will reimburse you for the inconvenience, and will shortly be purchasing his own carriage, so as not to burden you in the future.

Brook shook his head. He would gladly buy Mr Fletcher fifty carriages if it helped Marina in anyway. He could well imagine her now, flitting between helping her father with his injured ankle and soothing her worried mother. The Fletchers were wonderful people, but difficult times could bring out the worst and best in people.

He read the rest of the letter, unsurprised by the details regarding Herbert's involvement, then quickly wrote a reply of his own. Asking Edward to again reassure Mr Fletcher that he could have the carriage for the 'rest of his life', if he so wished it, and that it was no inconvenience for him to be without it. He also warned Edward to expect the imminent arrival of his personal London physician, Dr Havering, whom he had sent instruction to not long after they had left.

Staring at the scratches of his pen, he wondered whether to write anything for Marina's benefit, but what could he possibly say?

That he wished her well? Hoped she would progress with the Philharmonic Society under Mr Dance's advice?

It all seemed so remote and cold. He glanced at the papers of his grand tour beside him. The arrangements were booked, he would leave and not return for at least a year.

There was so much he was going to see…and so much he would miss.

Marina most of all.

Pushing aside pointless thoughts, he left the study and gave the letter to his butler. His mother's commanding voice carrying to him from across the hall. 'Brook, you're…

awake,' she said, looking meaningfully at his crumpled evening wear. He still hadn't changed out of since the ball.

'I was about to go and change.'

'But was that news from the Fletchers?'

'He is awake.'

'Thank heavens!' She gestured into the breakfast room, 'Come and have something to eat and drink, before you go upstairs. You will feel much better for it.'

His stomach gave a groan and he realised he was hungry so he joined her, halting at the doorway when he saw the Moorcrofts were also sat at the breakfast table.

'Will I?' he grumbled under his breath, and his mother gave him a look of warning before gesturing him to the seat beside hers.

It was a very late breakfast, as everything was still in disarray since the ball and the guests wouldn't be leaving for another day or two. He wasn't sure what they had done yesterday—probably slept most of the day, he presumed.

The servants had provided a buffet of both hot and cold dishes that morning and Brook served himself some bread and jam, which he then forced himself to eat.

'Tea?' asked his mother.

He nodded and she poured it for him. 'No sugar. See, I remembered,' she said, pouring in a splash of milk and then serving it to him.

'Thank you,' he said, giving her a grateful smile that she returned warmly.

'Did something happen to the Fletchers, is that why they left so early yesterday?' asked a sleepy Miss Clifton.

His mother explained, 'Their son was hurt in an accident. He hit his head badly, but has thankfully regained consciousness.'

'Gracious! There were rumours flying around that they

had offended you in some way.' Miss Clifton laughed, oblivious to the weight of her words.

'Offended us? Who said that?' growled Brook, slamming his teacup down into its saucer and spilling a splash of hot liquid on to his fingers. He ignored the pain. 'Their son was badly hurt. How *dare* someone lie about such awful circumstances!'

'I really don't see what all the fuss is about,' declared Mr Moorcroft. 'Boys get into scrapes all the time and it sounds like a silly prank gone wrong. I am sure he will be fine after a day or two in bed. Honestly, *that* family. They pamper and coddle their children beyond all reason. I am sure the boy is perfectly fine!'

Brook's fists clenched on the table.

His mother noticed and gave a cheerfully forced smile. 'Let us hope that is the case. But you can understand why they would be worried.'

Mr Moorcroft laughed. 'That boy has always been an odd and sensitive child, prone to hysteria. I know you find Miss Fletcher charming, but frankly, I would avoid any connection with such a fam—' Mrs Moorcroft nudged her husband sharply in the ribs, cutting him off and begging him with her eyes to stop speaking. It was at that moment he glanced towards Brook and realised his grave mistake.

Dark rage pounded in Brook's veins, causing his tired eyes to blur, but he refused to look away from the focus of his displeasure. 'My mother is not *you,* but the Duchess. We are not on close terms, Mr Moorcroft, or even friends from this moment onwards and I will have you refer to us by our titles or *Your Grace.*'

Mr Moorcroft's face paled and then moments later flushed to the colour of a beet. 'Yes… Your Grace, I…meant nothing by it… Forgive me.'

'Furthermore,' he shouted, causing everyone in the room to jump nervously in their seats, 'I suggest you go. I will not be using your firm in future and you may wish to collect your own son from Knights Court. I believe he has a lot of explaining to do regarding this incident. You may leave immediately, as you have your own carriage, I am sure that will not be problem.' He glanced at Miss Clifton who gulped nervously. 'If anyone should ask, the Fletchers are considered close friends to our family and have our full support at this difficult time. And—' he paused '—they always will.'

He rose from his seat, threw down his napkin and strode from the room.

Brook washed and changed into fresh clothes. Deciding he wouldn't be able to sleep in his current state, *a ride might help with his melancholy.*

As he descended the staircase, he noticed one of the servants had rushed into the drawing room at the sight of him and was unsurprised when his mother came out shortly after.

'We need to talk,' she said with surprising firmness.

'I am going riding now, we will speak after,' he replied. He was in no mood to be lectured about the rules of propriety and politeness, especially by his free-spirited mother.

'It won't take long,' she said sharply and marched towards his study.

Sighing, he followed.

The inside of his study looked a little better since the last time he had been in it. The servants had pulled open the curtains and cracked open a window. The used glasses and whisky had been put away, the cushions plumped and placed back in their correct position. The only thing not dealt with were the piles of papers on his desk that seemed to taunt him from afar.

As if to mock him further, his mother walked up to the desk and leaned against it, her fingers resting an inch from them.

Taking charge of the argument, he said, 'I will not apologise to Mr Moorcroft. I want him and his family out of my sight, regardless of how long they have left of their stay.'

'They are already gone.'

That surprised him. He would have thought his mother would have argued it. She was the party queen of London, known for her hospitality, she would hate for *that* reputation to be tarnished.

'Good.'

'It was actually quite easy to get rid of them. I think your mention of Herbert spooked them. Did he throw the brick?'

'He incited the person who did. It appears Frederick isn't his only victim.'

'Oh, how awful! I am so glad you never suffered—'

'I did.' The words were out before he had a chance to stop them, perhaps he was tired of pretending. His mother stared at him for a long moment, blinking slowly as if replaying those two words over and over in her head and still not quite comprehending them.

'You did?' she finally whispered, and then with a gasp she took a step forward. 'But you always said—'

'I was never happy there. It was why I joined the army so young.'

'But—' Horror dawned across her face and she shook her head. 'Your father and brother loved it there. Robert insisted you go—that I would only make things worse for you by keeping you at home.'

So, Robert had broken them apart in more ways than one.

'I am sure they did love it there. They were different people.'
They were also bullies.

There was no need to say it—his mother knew it all too well.

Her pained eyes met his. 'Yes, I suppose you're right. Why didn't you ever tell me you were unhappy? You always wrote in your letters to Robert that you were happy.'

'I am surprised you read them,' he answered bitterly, before adding, 'I didn't want you to worry. You seemed to be finally happy. I didn't want to take that from you.'

'Robert was worse than your father,' she said softly. 'He didn't hit me, but he kept me from you. Your father for all his faults never did that. Robert forbade me seeing you too often. He said our relationship was unnaturally close. That I was—' her voice cracked '—*weakening* you, making it more difficult for you to become a man later on, and I was afraid he was right. You had been the only thing keeping me sane for all those years with your father. I feared I relied on your presence too much, that I was stifling you. Stopping you from being a *normal* child.'

Her confession shocked him—he had always thought she had more freedom under Robert. 'Why would he do that?'

Her eyes met his and she sucked in a deep breath before speaking. 'Robert considered me a bad influence. He blamed me for your father's death. Punished me in every way that he could. I thought that at least if you were happy at school, it would make our separation more bearable and he wouldn't be able to use you to punish me, like he did that first Christmas. When he locked me away.'

Brook stared at her in shock. 'He said you didn't want to see me, that you were tired.'

His mother smiled sadly. 'I am sure he did, but it wasn't true, and I wasn't allowed to write to you either. He only let me read your letters if I'd behaved, sometimes months after you had written them. Over the years, you seemed so happy, you did so well at school and you were eager to begin a career in the army. I thought perhaps he was right. That I had relied on you too much to support my own happiness. That my loneliness had made me selfish and that I shouldn't have kept you with me...' Tears began to fall down her cheeks and she swiped them away angrily. 'I should never have believed him!'

Brook's throat tightened as he realised that she was still lonely and so was he.

'How could he blame you for Father's death? It was an accident.'

His mother shrugged. 'I went riding with him that day. The conditions were bad, but your father wouldn't listen. He insisted on jumping a fence and I let him. Robert thought I'd pushed him to do it, that I wanted him dead—which sometimes, I confess—I did.'

'It wasn't your fault. There was no stopping him when his mind was set,' he reassured her.

'I know,' she said, nodding her head. 'What about you? Is your mind set?' She stabbed the papers on his desk with her finger. 'Are you still leaving?'

'I always said—'

'Yes, yes! I know what you said!' snapped his mother and he was surprised by the anger in her tone. 'You want to travel and to see the world.'

He nodded.

'And you can't do that with a wife?'

'A grand tour is for young bachelors, not married men.'

'Convention be damned!'

Rolling his eyes, he said, 'Of course, *you* would say that!'

'I know what you think of me! That I am reckless and

selfish. Maybe I am! I know I have made mistakes. But I fear I will go mad if I am forced to watch you make the biggest mistake of your life!' She gestured around her. 'I don't belong here, I never did! This is your chance to do what we never could, to make it a *proper* home for a family and for a duke! I couldn't, but I think you could—with Marina. You could be happy!'

'I do not want a wife.'

'Things change, Brook! *People* change! And do not deny that you have developed feelings for her, it is obvious for all to see! When she enters a room your eyes search for her. When she laughs or smiles, you breathe more easily. When she was playing her music, you looked at her with adoration and pride. You admire and worship her, Brook. You *love* her. Why would you give her up?'

Brook walked around his desk and slumped into his chair. 'She does not love me and that is her only stipulation for marriage.'

'I do not believe that for one moment!' she snapped, as if his words were the ramblings of a mad man. She gave him a shrewd look. 'Perhaps she is only saying that because you have been so adamant about leaving? What woman would confess her love to a man with one foot out of the door!'

Doubt began to break through his misery like light through moth-eaten curtains. Why would she have gone to his room and risked her reputation if she did not care? Why would she have written that beautiful 'Roses in the Rain', if he meant nothing to her?

But he was still too afraid to tear down the rotten curtains completely, afraid—not of what he would see—but what he would reveal about himself. 'No, she told me more than once that she did not want me. Remember the last time I thought myself perfectly matched? It did not end well...'

'Lady Mary? I remember that hideous woman and, for once, I was relieved when your brother intervened. He did it cruelly, there is no denying that. But as I said at the time, she was not right for you. And it is clear that Marina is!'

'But I am not perfect for her! You said it yourself: *I don't deserve her!* Besides, Marina's music is in the early stages of beginning to flourish. Why would I uproot her? Take her from her family, especially after what Frederick has been through.' Even as he made the argument, he realised he was making excuses.

I am afraid that she will reject me!

And how cowardly was that? He had faced death in war, torment at school and in his own family. But he was more afraid that Marina would tell him she did not love him, could not love him, because that was what he believed his mother had done. By remaining silent for all these years, they had only made matters worse between them. He could not make that same mistake again!

His mother seemed to agree, as she fixed him with her sharp emerald eyes and declared, 'Then you must decide what is more important to you. What will ultimately make you happy? You don't need to travel the world to find that, it's here for the taking! Believe me, I know! I have searched for happiness in all the wrong places, with gambling and parties and men like George. I just wanted to *feel* something: joy, passion, despair, it did not matter what it was, only that it could temporarily fill the emptiness of a life unlived and soothe the pain of giving up my child. But I can tell you, without a single doubt, that the only time I was truly happy was when I was with you! No matter how far you sail, or how many wonders you see, they will be nothing in comparison to what you could have had with Marina. What you *still* could have! It is time we both put the past aside and make things right for our future. Personally, I think you are more than capable. So, I suggest you stop dithering and just get on with it!'

Brook stared at his breathless and imperious mother with admiration, respect and love. She had always tried to protect him, even when she'd been misguided in her actions. 'Thank you, Mother, for everything,' he said and tears gathered in her eyes, but she gave a little nod of acknowledgement.

She was right. It was time for him to take a risk, to finally confess his feelings to Marina, and let the cards fall where they may. Even if Marina did not love him, he had to know the truth and running away would not help.

Then he glanced down at the papers—they had once symbolised his freedom, but now seemed more like a chain around his neck. Picking them up, he handed them to his confused mother. 'Perhaps you should be the one to go and live a little? It sounds as if that's what you really need.'

His mother stared down at the papers and, after a moment of hesitation, she shook her head and said, 'I want to see you married first.'

Chapter Twenty-Six

The Duke's carriage rolled into the drive of Knights Court the following day, heavily burdened with cases and two very impatient passengers.

They were already out of their seats and walking to the entrance, when Reverend Peasbody stepped out to welcome them.

'Your Grace, what a pleasant surprise!' He glanced at the heavily loaded carriage. 'You must be on your way to Falmouth?'

'Yes,' declared his mother cheerfully. Brook was only surprised she wasn't feeling nauseous after excitedly reading the itinerary over and over. He had managed to talk her down from waiting to see him married, to seeing him confess his love to Marina. But she still wasn't entirely happy with the compromise, even though he could tell she was thrilled about the upcoming trip.

'Hello, Edward! How is the patient?'

Edward's smile broadened. 'Much better. Would you like to see him?'

'Yes, please!' said Brook and they followed the Reverend through the corridors of the school. The sounds of children reciting Latin and Greek coming from numerous rooms was familiar. But Brook was also delighted when he passed one class that had several young boys busy painting at easels and another where the sounds of a strangled violin could be heard from within.

'It is certainly different from my day,' said Brook, trying to hide his wince when the violin screeched in distress at a poorly executed note. 'I cannot imagine old Master Thornton is very approving of the new curriculum.'

Edward answered smugly, 'He left. He said he no longer recognises the place.'

Brook laughed. 'I should take that as a compliment if I were you.'

'Oh, I do.'

They walked into the bedroom Frederick was resting in, and was delighted to see the boy sitting up in bed, a sketchbook spread out in front of him. His face was a little puffy on one side and covered in a hideous purple bruise, but he was surprisingly cheerful in spite of it.

The large bay window was open, letting in plenty of light and fresh air into the room. People had begun complaining in the press that this was the worst year of weather ever recorded. But as the light streamed in, lighting up Marina's face as she sat on the deep window ledge. Brook couldn't imagine a more perfect year.

The bad weather had brought them together more than once and now sunlight bathed her in pearlescent beauty.

Marina looked towards the door as it creaked open. She had heard a carriage arrive, but hadn't realised who it was until Brook and his mother walked into the room. As they entered, she jumped to her feet, stumbling into a clumsy curtsy as she tried her best to hide her shock. Her parents did the same, rising from their two armchairs beside the bed.

'Look who stopped by on their way to Falmouth!' declared a cheerful Reverend Peasbody and Marina's stomach dropped with disappointment.

He had come to say goodbye...he was still leaving.

She'd always been certain of it, but somehow it still hurt seeing it happen before her eyes.

Her father limped over to Brook and shook his hand firmly. 'I cannot thank you enough, Your Grace. Doctor Havering was an excellent physician and helped Frederick's recovery greatly! He even took a look at my ankle, and prescribed some exercises to help heal it. I will design your new home free of charge!'

Brook smiled. 'Thank you, Mr Fletcher. But you do not need to do that.'

'I *insist*, Your Grace,' said her father grimly and with a severity that surprised all of them. 'Even if you do nothing with the designs until after your return. They will be waiting for you.'

'Oh, Brook's not going anywhere,' declared the Duchess with delight, her eyes focusing on Marina meaningfully. 'I am.'

'What?' Marina gulped a knot in her throat, as she realised she'd fairly screeched the question.

Heat clawed up her neck, and her father gave her a horrified look that seemed to ask *What is wrong with you?*

Her mother came to her side and discreetly draped an arm around her waist, as if to catch her in case she fell.

However, there was no way she would have fallen. Brook's green eyes pinned her to the spot. When he spoke, she felt as if she were dreaming, the words made no sense to her and yet they were everything she had hoped for and more.

'I am not leaving, but my mother is. We stopped by to see you and Frederick before she left.' He turned to her brother. 'How are you feeling, Freddie?'

'Good. My head's stopped aching since Dr Havering gave me that tonic. He reckons I will be up and out of bed by tomorrow.'

'Only for a little while!' barked Kitty, 'Then we will head home early for the summer, where you will rest some more!'

Freddie gave a grumbling sigh and Brook glanced down at the sketch he'd been drawing. 'It's your sister—you captured her well—she is always composing even when she is away from her music,' said Brook, looking down at the image. 'May I have the final artwork? Honestly, that would be thanks enough.'

Marina glanced down curiously at her brother's sketchpad. She hadn't realised he'd been drawing her. She was turned away, looking out the window, her knees drawn up, her fingers poised as if she were playing the pianoforte. She'd been composing a piece in her mind at the time, but she hadn't realised she played the notes with her fingers.

'Sure,' said Frederick with a shrug, probably wondering why anyone would want a picture of his sister.

'My legs are very stiff from the long journey, Brook barely let us stop,' complained Brook's mother, with a theatrical groan. 'Shall we go for a walk around the grounds? Then return for some tea? I have to say, I am famished and I doubt I will eat again until my next stop for the night.'

The Reverend jumped into action at her words, 'Yes, of course! I will get something arranged for you in my drawing room. Why don't we all head out for a walk to the orchard and back? That's always a pleasant stroll.'

Everyone nodded, except Frederick who grumbled about being left out of the excursion, but was eventually silenced by one heavy look from their mother.

'I could stay with him?' Marina offered.

'I shall remain with Frederick. Doctor Havering did

warn me not to overdo it,' said her father, pointing down at his bandaged ankle.

'May I walk with you, Miss Fletcher? I wish to speak with you. If you will allow it?' asked Brook, with a politeness that seemed unsettling in its uncharacteristic nature.

'As you wish, Your Grace,' she replied with equal courtesy.

Was he going to tell her that she shouldn't read too much into his staying in England? That he did not and could not love her as she wished?

Well, she already knew that and did not need another reminder. However, the conventions of society dictated that she should accept.

The party all moved outside and headed towards the orchard.

Marina's mother fell into step beside the Duchess who loudly complained of stiff joints and stopped regularly because of them. In the end she waved them ahead. 'Do carry on, we'll be right behind you!' she eventually declared and Marina was certain she caught her winking at her son, whose jaw tightened in irritation before he gestured at Marina to continue.

'Will your brother return here in the autumn?'

Marina nodded. 'Yes, he has insisted on it. Which has been the biggest surprise of all. My mother, in particular, is not happy about it.'

'I can understand that,' said Brook thoughtfully. 'But it does seem a lot better now. Before, the school only focused on and helped a few students, now it appears broader in its curriculum.'

'That's what Frederick says, apparently there's a famous artist coming to give lectures in the autumn and he refuses to miss it.'

'What of Herbert?' asked Brook.

'He has been excluded. Although, for the benefit of all involved the official reason is that the Moorcrofts have decided to place him elsewhere next year of their own accord and that he is too ill to finish this term.'

'Good. However, you may wish to prepare yourself for some vicious rumours. They do not seem the type of people to go quietly without a fight.'

Marina nodded. 'I am sure they will claim they are the victims in all of this. But who cares? At least Freddie is safe and happy, that's all that matters… The opinions of people who are not our friends and family do not matter.' She looked up at him and gave him a shy smile. '*You* taught me that.'

'A wise decision. People will see through the Moorcrofts soon enough, especially when your family remain so quietly dignified on the matter.'

Marina laughed. 'If I had been at the Manor when we heard of Herbert's true involvement, believe me, my mother and I would *not* have been dignified!'

Brook laughed, throwing his head back in that way she so rarely saw from him, with pure relaxed joy. She stared up at him, committing it to memory, delighted to be the cause.

He stopped walking and turned to face her. They were in the shadow of the trees now and Marina glanced back, surprised that her mother and the Duchess were so far behind.

Strangely, she was relieved to have such a gap between them and in a moment of madness she grabbed Brook's hand and pulled him around the trunk of a nearby oak.

'Why are you not leaving?' she demanded and was a little shocked at herself when she realised, she'd pushed him up against the tree!

Brook smiled. 'Well, that's given me hope.'

'Hope? For what?' She took a step back.

'Would you consider me, Marina? To be your husband? Not in a year, but now?'

'Now?' They stared at one another, each searching for an answer the other was too afraid to speak.

'I no longer want the three Cs in my life,' he said quietly, his eyes becoming hooded as he looked down at her face. 'I want only one thing. *You.* I love you, Marina. Will you have me?'

'You love me?' she whispered, unsure if she were dreaming, then realising by the arrogant smile blooming across his face that it was definitely real.

'Yes. But will you have me?'

Her throat closed around the ball of emotions stuck in her throat. Eventually, she gave a little nod in reply.

He kissed her tenderly, and then deeply, and she clung to him, wrapping her arms around his neck and clinging on to him for dear life.

'Our mothers are coming!' gasped Marina, pushing at him a little breathlessly. Brook peeked around the tree and grinned.

'My mother appears to be showing your mother a very interesting gooseberry bush. They appear to be fascinated by it.'

Marina laughed, and then pressed another kiss to his lips, dragging his attention away from their poor chaperons. They indulged themselves in each other for a moment and then a breathless Brook pulled himself away.

'So, you will marry me, even though we both know I do not deserve you.'

Marina shook her head, causing his heart to flutter with panic, then she smiled tenderly. 'Why do you say that? You are the kindest, nicest, most supportive and generous man I have ever met. I would be mad not to say yes.'

He grinned. 'So, it's a yes?'

'Yes.'

She laughed as he swept her up in his arms with a cheer.

'But…just so you know, my mother wants to see me settled first before her grand tour. So we need to marry now.'

Marina laughed. 'How could we possibly manage that?'

'Well, I am close friends with a reverend.'

She laughed and pressed her lips against his, unable to resist. 'It's a deal!'

* * * * *

If you enjoyed this story, be sure to read
Lucy Morris's previous Historical romances

Her Bought Viking Husband
Snowed in with the Viking
The Viking She Loves to Hate
Beguiling Her Enemy Warrior
Tempted by Her Outcast Viking